CW00863015

PATRICK

LEAH MACMOIRE

ISBN: 978-1-4834-2618-1 (sc)
ISBN: 978-1-4834-2617-4 (e)

Lulu Publishing Services rev. date: 03/31/2015

For Vicki Tubridy, Gerard Brady, and to the memory of Ann.

Co talla forum, ré n-dul it láma,
mo chuit, mo chotlud, ar méit do gráda.

CONTENTS

Chapter One

The dead man wouldn't lie down.

Patrick was flattened by the press of the other prisoners, his wounded back squeezed against the flood cold wood. Directly facing him was his old teacher, the dead man. They had both fought hard, and been beaten and flayed for their pains. Unlike his young charge he had been an elderly man, and took his beating badly. Now he sat in effigy, a parody of his living self. Beside him his childhood nurse, wept quietly, as the ship groaned and lurched through the Irish sea.

The boy sat as dully as his dead teacher. Although he did not move, he talked, the rambling disjointed comments of the very ill, or the insane. He was not the only prisoner so affected. From the gloom below deck could be heard much moaning, and weeping, and gnashing of teeth.

When the ship put into port the dead were cut loose from their chains, and the survivors linked up by the neck. As Patrick stumbled into place he was greeted by water, wind, and nausea. The wind whipped salt water from the sea, burning the scars on his back. Rain bled through his hair, down his face, his back, his front. Every single part of him was wet. His breath came in shuddering sobs as the slaves were dragged from the stinking hold. Thrust down the gangplank his legs felt weak as the water all around him. He was drowning. The rain chilled right through to his bones, fluxed in his cramping gut. It kept his wounds wet and aching. If not for the pain he would have imagined himself already dead, descended into Dis... not the hell of fire that his grandfather spoke of, but the chill dead country that the slaves spoke of, the land of grey exile between one life and the next. He couldn't remember now whether it was the Irish or the Greeks who talked of the country under wave. They warned that some people never emerged from the drowned land of the recently dead. Perhaps he was there already. Perhaps the ship had gone down while he lay beneath decks raving, and he had already died.

He retched, and brought up bitter water, as though he had truly drowned and swallowed the sea. It burnt his throat and mouth, was filthy on his tongue. He was not dead. The dead surely did not ache so. His head throbbed at the base, where the skull curved over the spine, and he could feel the cap of blood crusted to his hair and scalp.

His fine clothes had been stripped from him at some point, and he stood nearly naked in the foreign rain, clothed only with an oblong of cloth around his waist, for modesty's sake. One of the other captives in the hold, a kind but rough spoken man who had known him from his infancy, had offered it to him. Patrick had accepted it numbly, not considering that in doing so the man was depriving himself of some comfort. Now Patrick looked for him, a familiar face, but could not see him. His eyes could not yet focus correctly. He saw the world through light that pulsed uncomfortably from grey to white in time with the pounding in his head. He knew that they had done him an injury, but he couldn't remember exactly how.

This was his own fault. He had argued with his family, rebelled, and run. The old teacher, Simon, a freed Greek, had been sent to reason with him, and had been remonstrating with him at the very moment that the raiders came over the horizon.

Old Simon fought, unarmed as he was. A philosopher – what could *he* know of the arts of war? Yet, for all his frailties Simon fought to protect his errant student. He fought; he died for it. Patrick felt as though the old man had died at his hand.

Now he stood with the survivors from his father's farm, all of them chained together, bound with iron links like beads on a Giant's necklace. The woman chained in front of him was a weight, hanging loose from her neck brace and...

Time fractured for a moment. The barbarians shouted, and everyone was made to move. Something happened – Patrick stepped over a dead body – then time was moving again, and he couldn't remember what he had seen. They were being counted. Most of those he stood with had been slaves of his family, a few freemen who worked for pay. Free no more.

The man who had given him his garment had been a blacksmith, that he did remember, a skilled slave who, like Simon, had earned his freedom, and that of his wife and children. Patrick's grandfather Potitus had conducted the wedding. Like many such unions the man and woman had been together for years. The church blessed a done deal, and the man's daughters wove floral chains for their mother to wear to the little church.

The man's daughters.

Patrick's memory twisted away from a horror, and he allowed himself to be propelled, lurching up the beach, while the crew of the ship sorted out the rest of their haul. Under the weight of the stumbling cargo the stones ground against each other with a noise like teeth. On either side of the slaves were pigs, sheep and horses, shaken and distraught by their journey over sea. The pirates were cursing as they drove them up the crunching slope. Some of the slaves had already been forced to carry goods. Wine and oil and clothing, stolen from his father's vaults. Patrick carried nothing. He had become nothing, one link in a chain. Not even that.

It began to distress him that he couldn't see the blacksmith. He couldn't make sense of anything, couldn't work out where he was or where he was going. Worse than that, his mind kept returning to the fact that he could no longer remember the man's name. It was like a splinter turning yellow under the skin, he couldn't get it out of his mind. *The blacksmith… what is his name?* Patrick had known him all his life. Sometimes the man would sing to Patrick while he worked, the hammer striking metal like a strange kind of drum. Enchanted, Patrick would watch from a safe distance as the sparks flew, and the man would laugh in his deep baritone and sing louder. When Patrick had been a very little boy the man had given him apples, and swung him up in the air so high and fast that he thought he was flying. Patrick was troubled that he couldn't remember his name.

All around him were slaves, many of them completely naked. It hardly seemed to matter anymore. Now they were off the shingle, and trudging along a broad path, churned by constant traffic. The whole world was made of mud, and stink, and sky. The earth was black mud, the sky was steel grey, and the slaves were ghosts walking through Tartarus. The only colour left that mattered was red. He could see it behind his eyes, at the back of his head, always. Even with his eyes closed he could see the blood.

Screaming. He heard again the children screaming as the pirates hacked at them. Brigitta carved in his memory, standing over her dead child with her left arm curled over her head, fingers pointing like the cruel beak of a crow, calling down the Morrigan on the murderers, before they silenced her by splitting her open, chest to groin, her guts spilling out over the ground.

Patrick stumbled at the memory, and the man in front cursed as the chain connecting them neck to neck caused him to stagger backward. One of the pirates stepped in smartly and struck Patrick with a wooden switch across the open wounds on his back. He straightened and carried on walking.

Behind him Fionula whispered something. He distantly understood that she was speaking to him in his own tongue, and supposed they were words of comfort, but they might as well have been in the harsh barbaric jargon of her own people. He felt detached, despite the pain and nausea, as though he was watching the whole scene from a distance. For a while it seemed that he was walking next to his own body, keeping it company while it moved at another's command. He looked at the waxen ghost, with its torn back and empty eyes, and pitied it, forgetting it was himself he was staring at. For an instant he floated above the scene and saw the whole long snake of human misery as it progressed across the black scar of the road, but the horror of the sight brought him crashing back into the wretchedness of his own skin, and he closed his eyes in despair.

They had finally arrived in something that looked like a market, only much larger than any he had ever seen before. All around him the din of the Irish savages jangled, streams of speech he couldn't understand. Interspersed in this babble were snatches of the common Greek spoken by the traders, and even Latin, but they washed over him; empty noise, void of meaning. There were hundreds of slaves being lined up now, not just the survivors of his father's farm, but captives from other raids, other ships. He could hear some of them moaning in their own tongues, praying to foreign gods. One man, with the beard and long curls of a Jew was weeping silently as his wife was led away. Patrick did not understand her language, but he could see from her face that she did not expect to live. Yet, she was almost singing, though tears ran down her face: "'Shema Yisrael....'" A British voice cried out suddenly, and Patrick looked to see the blacksmith. "Mudebroth," the man cried out again, and Patrick's heart lurched with horror. The first words he understood on this foreign soil seared into his brain.

"Wrath of God."

The whole world had fractured around that one knock on the door.

Everything before that early morning summons was life, and the busyness of it, the scurrying and bustle of the day to day workings of the farm. Little joys, little woes... even Patrick's misdemeanours were only boyhood pranks, things that a father could smile about.

There had been no premonition of the coming disaster, though Conchessa was already beginning to rewrite her memories of the last week. Soon she would be blaming herself for not having listened to hunches or presentiments that were so vague as to be useless, if they were ever there at all.

It was true that the boy's behaviour had darkened recently. He had become openly rebellious against Potitus, refusing to enter the church, jeering at his mother in order to make her cry. Her husband Calpornius was always forgiving about it... because what boy didn't rebel against his family? Surely he would grow out of it, as his father had done. Yet now Conchessa was beside herself, convinced that Patrick was being punished by God for his boyhood indiscretions. She was more than half mad with the fear that her only child had died at the hands of the pirates, and was in hell.

Calpornius sat beside his wife, chafing her hand between his, while she continued with her wailing and her grief. He was dumb. He felt like he'd been stabbed in the chest. It hurt to breathe.

That hammering on the door, the urgent frightened face of the slave who brought the news... The whole shape of life was destroyed by the sound of a fist pounding on a door. Everything after that knock was shattered pieces of broken clay.

Calpornius was stunned past the telling of it.

Chapter Two

"I can't say I'm impressed," Gill remarked, looking scornfully up and down the long line of merchandise. "Where did you get this sorry lot?"

"Oh, they're a useful bunch. Most of them don't need to be broken in, we took them from a farm. They're already familiar with hard labour."

"Hrumph," Gill shrugged, carefully maintaining his air of detachment. "Perhaps they're already worn out. My master has had bad luck with field hands… they don't tend to last many years. Last one we got from you barely lasted ten months."

"From what I hear that was pure accident, the wolves got him."

Gill curled his lip, sourly. He wasn't aware that story had spread so far. He really was out of favour if the gossip had run ahead of him to this extent. Affecting an air of disregard he said, "What use is a shepherd who can't defend himself and the flock from a few wolves? We didn't just lose the boy; we lost several sheep as well. It was an expensive mistake."

The merchant rolled his eyes. He knew as well as Gill that a sheep boy was pretty much expendable, particularly in wolf country. The sheep were worth considerably more than the slave. He also knew that the man was so far out of favour with his master that he'd been sent on a fourteen league journey across the country with no defence. In other words, Gill's posturing was sheer bluff… the man was simply following well the established traditions of the market place and trying to knock down the price. No doubt he thought if he haggled enough he might win both a bargain and his master's forgiveness.

"It was your own fault the boy died," the merchant pointed out. "He was too young for the job. If I'd known you were planning on using him as a sheep boy I'd have told you to send someone out with him, at least for the first year. You need someone older. How about this one?"

They paused in front of a large, well muscled man, bearded, balding, with angry blue eyes and clenched, square hands.

"He looks strong and able to look after himself, but he's too old. A sheep slave needs to be old enough to work hard, but young enough to be trainable. This man doesn't look particularly trainable. See? He resents us, just look at his face. He wouldn't make a shepherd." Gill took the man's face, and turned the head from side to side. He snorted, and turned back to the merchant. "See? Fleck burns on his face and hands, he's worked with fire. A blacksmith perhaps. Useful to someone perhaps, but not us... we have a blacksmith. We don't need him. Something younger."

"Well, how about this one?"

They paused in front of a tall youngster, with dark red curls cut short in the Roman fashion, and no facial hair. He stood awkwardly with his hands in front of his groin, looking at the ground. His skin was very pale, other than the bruises which purpled his abdomen and the right side of his chest. *Some things never change,* thought Gill. *They kick them when they're down.*

"He's not a eunuch is he?"

"No, he's not a eunuch."

"Well, why's he covering himself like that then? What's he got to hide?"

Gill stood forward, snatched at the cloth that surrounded the young man's waist, and pulled. The youth gasped, and tried to step back. The merchant grasped the slave's hands at the wrists and raised them so that the customer could inspect the merchandise. So, good. The merchant hadn't lied. The slave was not a eunuch at least. Gill prodded the boy's chest speculatively. "Ribs are broken," he suggested, knowing it wasn't true, but hoping the seller wouldn't spot the lie.

"No they aren't. Maybe cracked, a little, but he's strong boned, like a horse. See the thickness of the wrist?" The merchant demonstrated, by encircling it with his hand. The fingers and thumb didn't meet.

"You have small hands," Gill pointed out.

"Not that small," the man replied, scornfully. "It would take more than a bit of a kicking to break those bones. And his chest is clear, no rattling."

Gill snorted. It had been worth a try.

"Well, at least he's not a eunuch," he conceded. "He's not a man though. How old is he?"

"He's probably thirteen, fourteen."

"Tall for his age," Gill scratched his beard. The merchant was probably lying – younger boys fetched higher prices. This one looked nearer sixteen than fourteen. Even so, Gill knew from experience that a youth of this build had more growth in him if his voice had not yet broken. This particular boy was large skulled and broad in the shoulder. He was probably an orphan, Gill decided; many women died giving birth to whelps like these. Gill tipped his head and sucked his tongue between his teeth as he speculated the odds of the boy surviving the first few years and growing in value as he put on muscle and girth. There was breeding potential in this one, if they could find a strong enough woman. The boy might turn out to be a sound investment for future generations. He could sire strong stock and make a good return for them. Some farms made a decent income with this sort of thing, hiring the men out as stud.

"Has his voice broken?"

"I don't know."

"What do you mean you don't know?"

"He hasn't spoken since we took him."

"Well then, make him talk."

The merchant turned and looked at the boy, and spoke to him in British. The boy said nothing. The merchant raised his voice, pushing his face right up into the slave's. The boy stared at him unblinking, with strange grey eyes.

"Great, just what we want, a broken child. What did you do to him?" Gill laughed – he had some knowledge of what the pirates got up to when they brought in pretty people, of either gender. He'd been pretty himself once, when he was first taken.

"Nothing like that," the merchant said. "There wasn't time. And apparently this one fought."

"Did he now?" Gill stared at the boy's damaged knuckles. From the looks of them – split, swollen and crusted with blood – he'd got some good blows in himself before he was incapacitated. *Huh.* Gill was impressed, but lifted a shoulder and huffed through his nose to convey scorn. "I can't imagine that he put up much of a fight. See? He has soft hands." He turned them over to hide the knuckles from the merchant's attention, and revealed pale, uncallused palms. Ah – he was wrong. One tell-tale bump, a rough knob of skin on the first joint of his middle finger. This boy used a stylus often enough to have developed a callus from writing. Gill examined the hands further – they told him nothing else – then let go of them dismissively. "So, maybe he fought. He didn't win, so he didn't fight well enough. And he's not done much in the way of work. Some Roman scholar, or simpleton."

"He fought hard enough. They had to brain him..." The merchant stopped, and silently cursed himself. The price had just gone down.

"So he is damaged then."

"Nothing a little time won't cure, look at that skull, and those bones. There's a lot of strength to develop in there."

Gill pursed his lips, and walked around the slave.

"Strength, but not much muscle. And he's taken quite a beating to his back." This was beginning to look good for Gill; since the slave had automatically depreciated in value he might get a good deal here.

"He refused to walk. But as you can see the fight is gone from him, and that's to your benefit. He's already mainly tamed. But the fact that he's naturally strong and isn't scared to fight does mean he might fare better against wolves than your last purchase."

"I don't know..." Gill pursed his lips. "It's hard to train someone whose mind has gone. He could just be dead weight."

"He'll pull his weight."

"Really?" Gill grabbed the matted clump of the boy's hair, at the back, where it had scabbed, and sniffed it. "That was quite a blow to his skull. You haven't even cleaned him up." His lip curled. "I mean – look at all that blood."

"Blood is blood. You know scalp wounds bleed more than others. They're never as bad as they look."

This one looked as though it would heal to Gill's practised eye, despite the size of the swelling, but he still affected an air of mistrust. "I really don't know. Maybe his brain's been scrambled." He pinched the boy's arm and twisted. "See, he doesn't respond. He's gone with the dead. What you have there is an empty shell, as useful as a stone boat."

"You know as well as I do that shock does strange things to a man. When we took him he was fighting to defend the little children. He fought like a wolf. I'm telling you, he's good stock."

"Were they his family, do you think?"

"It's hard to tell. The woman he was with was a witch apparently. She was struck down mid curse over the body of her young. Perhaps he is grieving his mother."

Gill barked out a laugh and stood backward, as though he'd lost interest in the product. "So you want to sell me the red headed son of a witch? Not only that, but one whose spirit has gone ahead of him with the dead and left him empty? Do you have any idea how much trouble such a purchase would be?"

The merchant looked sly, and pointed out, "If he is a witch's son, who better to fight off wolves?"

Suddenly the boy spoke. "Mudebroth," he said, looking straight at Gill. The man felt his flesh crawling. The slave's eyes had the look of a familiar landscape made strange by winter, and they were fastened right on him, as though he could see through him. "What does the boy say?" The merchant paused for a moment, looking uneasy, then said, "I don't recognise that expression." Gill knew instantly that the man was lying, and almost accused him to his face. Then he realised. The boy's voice was a clear treble. It had not broken. There was growth and strength in him yet. And the fact that the boy had spoken and looked at him, no matter how odd the gaze, was also a very good sign.

"Alright," he said, as though doing the merchant a favour, "how much do you want for him?"

The haggling began. Eventually a price was agreed that suited Gill well, and the merchant less so. There was even money left over to purchase a woman for the house. He might yet redeem himself from the recent...

misfortunes. To return with a sheep boy and a woman for the price of one slave should do a good deal to bring him back into favour.

The woman proved to be an easier choice than the boy. Gill knew his master's tastes, and picked a country woman, though from another tribe, and reasonably pretty. It was obvious from her figure that she had born babies, but her beauty was not gone. In particular her long black hair and vivid green eyes were pleasing. Since she was fertile she would almost certainly enrich the master by bearing stock for him... or maybe even an heir if she particularly pleased him. Gill smiled to himself. That would show the Lady of the house. He wasn't the only one who could fall in and out of favour.

An added advantage to this purchase was that the woman was compliant, spoke when spoken to, kept her head down... in all things a mannerly, well-trained slave. She admitted to being a slave, and added that she spoke the boy's language, and would translate until he had learned to speak. She also reassured him that the boy was intelligent enough, and would speak in time. Yes, she had known him since his youth. He was strong, and healthy, just shocked. All things considered Gill imagined his master would be pleased with this double bounty. He might even agree to give Gill the woman for a while. Although Gill was a slave himself, he did occasionally get these little perks, when he was in favour.

The boy and woman happened to be standing next to each other, and were already chained to each other from the neck. However, for safety's sake Gill decided to put leg irons and hand cuffs on the boy, in order that he not suddenly put up a fight again. You could never be quite sure with males of that age. They were volatile. He hoped this one didn't have a temper, it would be a shame to have to geld him. Amongst other things, it would serve to prevent his body from strengthening... assuming the boy survived such a procedure in the first place. At his age it was particularly tricky. However, with good management, it shouldn't be necessary.

The woman he expected no trouble from. The fact she had been a slave before, and Irish to boot, meant that she knew that running would do her no good here. She also seemed to care for the boy. That might ease the transition until the boy spoke in a sensible tongue. He had returned to his dumb show, but Gill imagined the woman wouldn't waste time talking to him if he was nothing but an animal.

"Well, I've paid for them now, it will have to do," he muttered.

His business concluded he turned and whistled to his purchases to follow him. The woman complied readily, and the boy stumbled after her. It was already time to start the long, and potentially dangerous, journey home.

"He will come home," stubbornly Conchessa rolled on her sick bed, and turned her face away from her husband. "He's not dead, he's coming home."

Calpornius sighed, and looked pleadingly at Potitus. "Father... please, can you talk to her?"

"What can I say?" the old man replied. He put one heavy hand on his son's shoulder and squeezed. "It's grief, we all have to bear it. We wear it differently, that's all."

Calpornius looked at his father, and was suddenly struck by how much he had aged in the last few days. His jowls hung slack beneath the unfashionable beard, and his face looked grey. Pity overwhelmed him, as he realised that the loss of Patrick was not just the end of his own line, but also of his father's. Already neighbours and well-wishers had assured him that he could have other sons. But even if Conchessa had been strong enough to bear another child, he couldn't imagine any child replacing Patrick.

His son.

His eyes flooded with tears again, and he blinked them away to avoid humiliation. He smiled at his father, painfully. "Please", he whispered, "she's become unreasonable. She can't accept that he's gone."

"Neither can I," the old man replied. "For all we know, she's right, and he did survive."

"But for how long? They were Irish raiders. If he's been taken to that barbarous land, how likely is he to survive hard labour?"

"We can't..." the old man shook his head, and winced. "We can't speculate. I don't know why this has happened, and God alone knows how it breaks my heart. If the boy is dead, he is lost indeed. But perhaps your wife speaks truth. A mother often knows more than a father does."

"That's womanly softness," Calpornius declared, startled by his father's words. "Superstition – how could she know he's alive, or that he's coming home?"

"We don't. And we don't know that he's dead. Perhaps Patrick is coming home, but not to our home. Perhaps God will draw him to Himself in that foreign land. All we can do is pray."

Calpornius dropped his gaze, ashamed. His wife's unreasoning fear of her son's death and damnation had now turned to an equally stubborn insistence that all would yet be well. He had not expected his father to be swept up in this tide of emotionalism.

Yet, he knew the old man prayed, he always had done. Now, when the very worst had come, Calpornius realised he couldn't pray. How could he pray to a God Who let such dreadful things happen? He felt impoverished. He had only become a deacon in the first place because of the tax breaks... and now God had taxed him his only son. Perhaps it was not, as his wife thought, Patrick being punished, but him.

He shook his head. This was fanciful, false. There was no punishment, no reason for what had happened. It just happened. Trying to put a pattern to life was unreasonable, and though all else failed him, Calpornius still had his reason.

Conchessa was crying again, and Potitus knelt by the bed and started to pray. The woman's sobs gentled, as she joined him. "'Pater Noster,'" her voice strengthened, "qui es in caelis, sanctificetur nomen tuum.'"

Calpornius put his hands together, but said nothing. Their voices droned on: "'Adveniat regnum tuum. Fiat voluntas tua, sicut in caelo....'" Let them pray. Guilt spiked in his chest again, maybe fear. What if he was wrong? What if he had offended the most High God?

Patrick was gone. There was no God. Or if there was, He was a monster. Calpornius looked at his wife, then to his father, kneeling quietly at the head of the bed, and his eyes stung; pity or shame, he didn't know. Grief.

Whether God was a monster or not, Calpornius would not be. Although every part of him wanted to rail at the barren heavens, he knew he could not. Not now. Not in front of his family.

Wearily, he got to his knees. He bent his head on the mattress, so nobody would see his tears. If prayer comforted his father, if prayer comforted his wife, who was he to voice his doubts to them?

CHAPTER THREE

"You need to eat."

Patrick blinked, and woke. He remembered again what had happened. He groaned, and shut his eyes, but the voice returned insistent. "Wake up. You need to eat." Fionula. He opened his eyes, and sat up.

There were new colours in the world. They were surrounded by a vast expanse of green, dotted with flowers. Patrick blinked, again, surprised. He had heard some of the Irish slaves say that the grass was greener in their country. It seemed that they were telling the truth. The fact of it shocked him, assaulting his eyes. More than any other thing, this vibrancy told him he was in a new land. He looked around, and saw that they were sitting on a wooden road, chained to each other and a wheeled cart. Also tied to the cart stood a horse, patiently eating from a nose bag. The horse lifted his head out, dropping meal onto the floor, gave Patrick a dismissive look, huffed, flicked his tail and went back to eating.

This was undeniably real. Patrick was undeniably here. He swallowed, looking at the planks of the road. Nothing like a Roman road, of course. For a moment he creased his forehead, not understanding – then he remembered his history. This wooden path, constructed similarly to a rope bridge, was one of the floating roads that crisscrossed the treacherous bog lands of this strange country. Several generations ago there had been roads similar to this across Britain and Gaul. Then the Romans came, and bound the land in stone; their roads running straight and true, no matter the geography. Nature conceded to Rome, never the other way round. And Roman roads endured. They would endure long after these slender wooden roads. Long after the slats, and pegs, and rope fell into disuse. Patrick could see it now. The very path on which he sat drifting to the bottom of the bogs; the whole Celtic network vanished out of sight, forgotten by all but whatever ghosts walked them.

What was he thinking? His mind was dizzy and confused. He felt as though he'd been wrenched out of the natural progression of the days and flung backward to a time when his own ancestors had been savages such as these.

Fionula sat next to him, staring intently at his face. He turned away from her gaze, suddenly ashamed. Fionula had been given a garment, something like a sack with holes cut into it for her head and arms to go through. It was tied by a rope at the waist, and descended to just above her knees. As a slave to his family she had been dressed in dyed linens, with woollens in winter. He looked down at himself and flinched. Except for the chains, he was naked.

"Good, you're with us." Fionula took his chin in her hands, turning his head back to her as she continued her close perusal of his face. "Look at me, can you see me?"

"I can see you," he replied, flushing at her unwanted touch. He knew she was examining him as a doctor might, but he was humiliated. He drew his legs up to cover himself, and turned his head abruptly from her hands. The movement made his skull ache, though it was less painful than it had before. He was aware now of thirst, and his scalp itching – both maddening sensations. He concentrated on the itch, to distract from the greater craving for water. His injured head felt as though ants were devouring it. He tried to put his hands to the back of his head. But of course he couldn't move his hands freely, and the itch went untended to. Why couldn't he remember the other chains being put on him? Why couldn't he remember losing his loin cloth?

He curled his body up as tightly as he could, hunkering so that his chin rested over his knees, and tried not to be ashamed.

"Well, at least you're talking sensibly now," Fionula said, with obvious relief. "Do you remember what happened?"

Patrick shut his eyes again. He didn't want to concentrate too much on remembering.

Fionula persisted. "What do you remember?" He sighed, realising that she wasn't going to let up until he answered.

"We were taken," he bit out. "By pirates."

"We were taken," she affirmed, "Do you remember what happened next?"

"We were in a ship," he closed his eyes to remember. At the time he had believed he was in the belly of a big fish, that he'd been swallowed alive. "There were many people in there, we were chained."

"We were so. And do you remember what happened next?"

He remembered arrival, the grinding of a giantess's teeth, a black snake swallowing them whole, the blacksmith in the rain pronouncing God's judgement, and a woman who fell before him as the world went away. But he was sure this was not what Fionula wanted to hear. His memory was awry. He shook his head.

"We've been bought by a farmer's man, and we're being taken to his place, Foclut, on the other side of Ireland."

"I'm sorry I brought this on you."

"What did you say?" Fionula looked at him with surprise. "What did you bring on me?"

"The Wrath of God."

"This has nothing to do with your god, what are you talking about?"

"I did something, I…"

He stopped, and looked away.

"I sinned," he said. "I mocked God, and He saw me like a thrush sees a snail. He brought a rock down on me."

"Patrick," the woman looked at him with a sympathetic condescension. "You've never believed in the god of your father before now. You know as well as I do that the god of your people is not a god of these islands. He came in with the Romans, and foreign slaves. Whoever heard of a god that left his shores? Even if they do, they're weak as water, and need constant sacrifice to have any power at all. Your god doesn't even accept sacrifice, so what power can he have? This is not a punishment from your god."

"Grandfather says that He is the living God of the whole of heaven and earth, that all things are under Him, and there is no other God but Him. He is everywhere."

"Well, child, he's not here. Potitus hasn't been everywhere in the world, so how can he know that this god of his is everywhere? Can you see his god? Can you hear him? Of course you can't. Whoever heard of an invisible god?" She laughed dismissively, and patted his knee. "Besides, your Grandfather also says that his invisible god is a god of love. Why would such a god bring punishment on you for laughing at him? Why would he punish me along with you?"

Patrick shook his head. She didn't understand what he was talking about. How could she? Even a week ago he himself had laughed at God, thought Him nothing more than the fancy of weak women and old men. His father was a deacon of the church, but not truly devout. Calpornius had simply followed in his father's line of work, mainly for the tax breaks. Patrick had felt contempt for his father's utilitarianism, but equally despised his mother's earnest devotions, and laughed at his grandfather's unshakable loyalty to a crucified God.

His mockery had been growing in recent months, and finally he had made his mother cry, telling her to her face that he would never pray to a naked Jewish carpenter nailed to a cross. Grandfather had warned him then, reminding him of the first and the fifth of the Ten. "You not only sin against God, Patrick, you sin against your mother. You will break her heart."

Patrick laughed scorn in the old man's face.

"Be careful, boy," Potitus warned him sternly. "The day will come when every knee will bow to Him, and every tongue confess. Will you kneel with joy, and willingly, or will He have to break your legs?"

God of love, indeed.

And here Patrick was now, naked under a foreign sky. He was beginning to realise his situation. God was watching him. God would have His revenge.

"I don't understand," he looked up at the sky, still grey and silver with clouds. "I can understand why You punish me, but why punish Fionula, and Simon, and the blacksmith, and Brigitta, and the... and the..." He broke off and moaned, from his belly, trying to push the memory away. *Oh, God.* He rocked over his knees, and with his two hands clenched struck himself on the forehead. Fionula's eyes widened in concerned. He was still not right.

"Children," he whispered, and stopped rocking, opening his eyes suddenly. She flinched at their fierce and frightened intensity. "Did you see what they did to the children?"

"I saw," she answered. "Don't think about it. There's nothing to be done. You must still eat."

He looked away, then turned his face back to her. "Where are we now?"

"You've been walking in a trance for hours," she said. "I was beginning to think you were never coming back. Where was your soul walking?"

"I don't know," he said. He remembered the broad path churned black, the snake, and the grinding teeth. "I think I was in hell."

She flinched at that, and moved back as far as her chain would let her. "Well then, eat. You don't want to go back there." This she knew was good advice. Those who walked with the dead needed the bread of the living, before they ate dust in the deadlands and never returned.

Patrick looked at the lump of bread she offered him. He hadn't eaten since the raid. How long ago was that? Two, three nights ago? More than hunger though, he felt thirst.

"Is there water?" he asked.

"Thank Brigid for that, we have water." She pointed the horse's bucket to him, and he crawled toward it. She painfully followed him, also on all fours, the neck chain still binding them together.

"Don't drink too fast, or you'll be sick."

He obeyed her advice, and instead of immersing his head into the water and gulping it, as he longed to, he drank in sips from his hands. 'Thank Brigid,' she had said, and he shuddered, aware that he had thanked nobody. He looked up beyond the sky again, past the large body of the dun horse. The sky looked bound with metal, but he knew God was behind it. God terrified him, but there was no hiding from Him. He had to be acknowledged.

"Thank you God for the water," he whispered, and slaked his thirst. His grandfather spoke in his memory. "'I am the living water. He who drinks of Me will never be thirsty again.'" Patrick shook. He had spurned the living water, and now he knew thirst hurt.

After a while he felt better, and looked to Fionula again. She seemed far more comfortable with the situation than he did. It dawned on him that though he had known her all his life he knew nothing of her background, other than that she was Irish. She had never seemed so fierce and foreign as the stories warned of these wild people, but in this strange land she seemed strange herself. It felt as though he had never looked at her before.

"Why haven't I died yet?"

"Because I've been getting some water down you," she laughed. "I've minded you from a baby, you can be glad I know how to deal with fussy children."

"Did I fuss?" he tilted his head, seeking memory. Nothing.

She sighed. "Not really, it was I who fussed. I worried about you, I thought you would die."

"Perhaps it would be better if I had."

Her eyes flared with sudden fury, and astonishingly she smacked him, as she had not done since he had been a dimple kneed toddler staggering into danger. He flinched with shock at the sudden shift in their status. "Silly boy," she snapped. "What, because you are a slave you think you want to die? I've been a slave since I was twelve years old, you don't see me complaining."

"Sorry," automatically Patrick deferred to her, as he had done as a child. Then it hit him.

"Fionula?"

"What?"

"When you were taken as a slave, were we as cruel to you?"

"Cruel?" Her voice trailed off and she looked away. "Why do you ask?"

"I never thought before, what it might be like... to be a slave I mean."

"Why would you?" she sneered, bitterness in her voice. She shook her head, and when she spoke again she simply sounded weary. "It depends on the master."

"Were we cruel?"

"Your family sold my children. What do you think?"

Patrick sat back, and took a shaken breath. He had never thought of Fionula's children. They were there for one brief span of time in his childhood, tumbling companions to his infant adventures, then they were gone. It was just what happened to slaves. He blinked; tears spilled unnoticed down his cheeks. "Fionula," he whispered, and had no words. He knelt then and pressed his head to the road in front of her.

"What are you doing now?" She looked at him askance, obviously discomfited by his strange behaviour.

"Begging your forgiveness," he whispered.

"Get up," she hissed. "When the man comes back he'll flog you if he thinks you're mad."

Patrick scrabbled back to a sitting position.

"I'm sorry. For what my family did to you, to your children. I'm sorry."

For some obscure reason Fionula was angry. She had buried this grief, years ago, and now the young master had resurrected it. His apology seemed to her an insult... he only cared when he himself was a slave? What sort of an apology was that? He wasn't sorry for her, he was sorry for himself. She turned away, fists tight, and vowed to stop talking to him. He had gone mad with it. That was all it was, madness. What was the point of talking to a madman?

Then she remembered how she had loved him as a child, how he had wept when her own children were sold, and wrapped chubby arms around her knees to comfort her. So, he had forgotten her children in the years since, but he was still the only child she had ever been allowed to keep. Her heart softened a little. After all, his family had not been deliberately cruel, not like previous masters. None of them had ever raped her, she had hardly ever been beaten, and only then by the overseer, never by any of Patrick's family. She wasn't even sure if they knew when a slave was beaten. What was it to them, in their world?

No wonder the boy was shocked, to have fallen down so far.

She glanced at him, her heart a painful mixture of compassion and resentment. He was still her responsibility. She still hated that. She still loved him.

She picked up the bread and threw it at him.

"Take, eat," she said curtly, and turned away.

Behind her, Patrick shifted, and the chains clanked. Then she heard him chewing the stale crust. He was whispering. *Talking to his god again,* she realised, sadly. *The poor boy's broken. He'll never be right again.*

Chapter Four

Gill was getting frustrated by the tedious journey. Having examined his options he chose the longer, somewhat exposed route home, rather than risking the woods. Although the trees provided more places for them to hide, they also provided shelter for bandits and war parties. Taking all things into consideration, Gill decided that going across the long bog lands was safer.

His decision made, he stuck to it grimly. Despite his bravado, the longer he remained on the road the more anxious he felt, and the more keenly he was aware of his loss of status. Imagine sending him all this way without any guards to protect him and the merchandise! Nothing but a war hound. The big grey dog was useful as a watcher during the night, and made a noise so like that of a wolf that the few war parties that passed their way moved on. The gods must have been smiling on him, for the only warriors to pass had done so at night, when the sound of a wolf was more likely to strike terror into even a brave man. Gill should be grateful for the dog. Even so... he resented the solitude. He should have been given more protection. One dog, a shield and a sword. He knew that he was being tested, and it irked him. It was almost as if the master wanted him to be captured by another tribe. Gill was a strong man, trained in war, and armed, but still, these were dangerous paths. It hadn't been his fault that the last shepherd got himself eaten by a wolf. No matter what the house slaves said.

He was beginning to think that the gods were indeed smiling on his journey, and that there would be no trouble with war parties, when, on a clear bright day with nowhere to hide, trouble came.

He heard them before he saw them, the tramp of horses causing the road to rock and sway like the rope bridge which, technically, it was. Then he heard the clangour of swords, the lowing of cattle, and the laughter of men. This was not another innocent party on their way home from market, with warriors for their protection. This was a taraigeacht, a war party, returning successfully from a raid on a rival tribe's cattle. Gill recognised the victory in their voices. Their hot blood had not cooled, from the sound of it; they might yet be spoiling for a fight. He knew well the signs, the songs and laughter.

He threw his cloak back, and rested his hand on the pommel of his sword. For a moment he thought of reaching into the wagon and lifting out his shield, but decided, regretfully, against it. It would be too bulky, and would impede his progress while leading the horse. It might be better to look brazenly confident than to look like what he was – one man alone, armed but frightened. For a moment he considered arming the slaves with what additional weapons he had purchased at market, but one look at them showed him how useless a hope that would be. The boy was talking to himself, the woman was wide eyed and terrified. She at least knew what was coming.

The warriors were upon them sooner than he'd thought, as though the river of time was against them and had chosen to flow faster. There were at least twenty of them, with cows tied alongside each horse, being dragged along the road with rolling terrified eyes. Several calves followed behind, unbound, desperately trying to keep up with their mothers. The war chief drew no cow with him, leading instead a riderless horse beside the one he rode on. He swung his beasts around to the front of the cart, and drawing his sword, smiled down on Gill, through a face and beard covered in dried blood. Returning from slaughter then, not just a raid. This was bad, very bad. The majority of cattle raids resulted in no loss of human life, but sometimes bitter rivalries between the tribes would burst out in bloodshed. These men had indulged blood lust in the recent past, and could do so again.

As Gill hushed his own dun horse he felt that strange absence of fear that sometimes came before a fight, and he smiled back at his would be captor. Two lumpy bags hung on either side of the riderless horse, stiff with blood. *The heads of the slain,* Gill mused, *brought back as trophies.* Like the gore on the man's face, the heads spoke of dangerous men. This taraigeacht would return to a hero's welcome. He wondered which group of unfortunates had been bested in battle by these pirates of the land.

"Little man," the warrior said, looking down on him. "Where go you?"

Gill looked up at him, and knew in his gut that this man was not from his master's Dirb Fine. His accent was wrong, and to Gill's knowledge none of his master's tribe were currently engaged in such bloody disputes. For Gill to state his destination as Foclut to the West would be suicide at worst. At best it would doom them all to capture. Each tribe distrusted another, and unless treaties were brokered a foreign tribe might as well have been a German or a Gaul. There was no loyalty beyond those of family, tribe, or foster kin. Gill considered his situation. The men might be tired from the battle, and simply want some fun on the way home. If so he could give them the woman, though he was reluctant to do so, since he had bought her to win back his master's favour. He couldn't give them the boy, since he was already designated to replace the last sheep boy. He decided, grimly, that if it came to a challenge he would not back down. Gill was a resentful man, bitter and often angry. He knew himself to be unlovely and unloved. But he was a brave man if nothing else; he could not bring himself to yield, even if he was killed outright. He could only hope that the men were in a hurry home, and wanted nothing but brief entertainment. Still – he wasn't that hopeful. The slaves, the horse, the dog, and the contents of the wagon were incentive enough, if one were needed, for these bloody men.

"I go where the gods lead me," he replied.

"And what if they lead you to your death?"

Gill looked up at the warrior, and found himself smiling, showing his teeth as his sword hand tightened its grip. "Then I will not go alone."

The horseman laughed. "I like you, Slave. It would be a shame to have to kill you. Tell me, what do you have in the wagon?"

Gill felt the name "Slave" twist in his gut like a knife. For years now that had been his only name, the title "Gill," or slave. He longed for the day he could win his name back, but suspected it would never come.

"I have nothing in the wagon," he replied. "All that is there belongs to another."

"Your master cannot think highly of you, to send you on the road alone. What did you do? Seduce his sister?"

The other warriors laughed; Gill felt the moment approach when to fight would be the only option. He let go of the horse's bridle, and stepped away from his interrogator, so that he would have more room to manoeuvre before his inevitable death. The war chief hadn't yet noticed his strategy, his contempt for slaves blinding him to Gill's careful positioning. The man was looking at the captives instead, a speculative expression on his face.

"What are these?" he said. "The woman looks well."

Gill took a breath, feeling his sweat cooling on his brow. Perhaps they would be satisfied with her after all.

"She's comely enough," he agreed.

The horseman grunted, and dismounted. Gill clenched his jaw. The man thought so little of him, he didn't even see him as a threat. For a moment the suicidal thought that he should kill the warrior where he stood flashed through his head. He quashed it. He might still get out of this without his own blood being shed.

The war chief, surrounded by his mounted men, was examining the woman. His fingers pinched her cheeks as he rotated her head from side to side.

"Does she bite?"

"Not men with swords," Gill said, and laughed. The warrior pulled her lips back, and she opened her mouth obediently.

"Good teeth," he said. "She's small, but strong." He lifted her skirt, then stood back, disgusted. "Faugh, she's bleeding."

The men on horseback laughed, then one said, "at least we know she'll bring babies."

The war chief nodded, then turned from her, his attention now on the boy slave. He looked him up and down, contemptuously.

"He's black and blue," he said. Gill said nothing. He felt keenly now how lucky he had been that the boy was in such poor condition when he'd bought him. He would never have got him for such a low price otherwise.

The boy had been a bargain, his bargain, which he alone had been clever enough to broker, and he did not want to lose his prize. Even if they took the woman... even if, gods forbid they took woman, horse, hound and wagon, he wanted to bring the boy back to his master. His master could bear the loss of some goods, and would know it had been his fault, not Gill's. Gill, however, would sooner die under the sword than return with the shame of empty hands.

"Why is he talking to himself?" the war chief asked. "What language is that?"

The woman suddenly spoke, her voice sounding clear and confident, to the astonishment of all present.

"He's praying in the language of the British," she said. "He prays constantly."

The war chief laughed. "His god hasn't been listening, has he?"

"The boy's wits are turned," Gill said. "He's not worth much."

The woman jutted her chin out, and with pride in her voice said, "This boy was worth more than a thousand men to his own people."

Gill could have strangled her. What was she playing at?

"Was he now?" The war chief continued examining the boy, with hungry eyes, and Gill's hand clenched again upon his sword.

"His Dirb Fine are famous in his land. His father and grandfather are both powerful druids, and he was the only child of his mother, who dedicated him on the day of his birth to a strange god whose followers say can raise the dead."

The man stood back and put his sword out, point touching the boy's chest. A tiny rivulet of red began to run from the broken skin. "This boy can raise the dead?"

Gill, suddenly realising what the woman was doing, joined in.

"His mother was a witch," he said, remembering the merchant's words. "She called down the crow on her enemies..." Gill carefully inserted his lie with a completely straight face, "and after they killed her, they had to strike the boy down, and bind him in iron chains for fear he'd raise her up again."

"You keep him in these irons because of his power?"

"I do," said Gill. Then, desperation making him crafty, he pointed to the dog. "You see the hound? We found him dead by the side of the road a week back. He was stinking and covered in flies. Even bound as he is, the boy raised him."

The war chief was now looking rather unnerved, and his men were no longer laughing. Everyone was gazing at the strange boy. In the silence his foreign prayers sounded increasingly unworldly.

"Why should I not take him to my King, to serve him?"

The woman laughed, contemptuously. "He won't serve your King. He goes where I go, and I will not go with you. I go to my own people, and as soon as I am recognised, I shall be loosed from these chains. This boy is my protector. Do you know why we walk this road alone? The warriors that were sent with us, brave men all of them, could not spend a night in his company. They saw things that would turn your blood to water. These men, your equal in valour..." she leant forward, and hissed the words, "they fled, every mother's son."

Gill knew that this story was a fabrication, from start to finish, but even he felt his skin begin to crawl. She spoke like a druid, as someone who had seen the future. He could almost believe that she was walking back to her own people, and that he was just the vanguard, not the captor. The effect on the war party was even stronger. The dried blood on their faces stood out more starkly as they paled, and the war chief was as still as a frightened bird in the moment before flight.

Suddenly the man forced a laugh. He lifted his sword and rested it on the surface of the neck iron, the long blade against the boy's bruised and bloody throat. The boy did not blink, nor did his quiet voice change in tone or pace. "These are children's tales," the war chief declared. Pressing the blade so hard against the throat that it bent the puffy skin, he challenged, "If I strike this boy's head from his shoulders where will your protector be then, Bhean Uasail?" His use of the honorific betrayed him: despite his bravado the man was frightened.

"I saw his grandfather, Potitus, taken in battle," she said, fixing him with a cold stare. "They struck his head from off his shoulders, and the old man stood up, took his head under his arm, and with one word slew the man that killed him."

Gill felt sick. This story he did not know to be a lie. He'd heard such tales before, and so too had the warriors. Everyone knew that it had happened, in days gone by, that a mighty druid would return from battle uninjured, although he'd been seen hacked to pieces the night before. Gill was not afraid to die. He was resigned to the fact that his life and death were not under his command. But he did fear that which moved under the skin of the world. He found his eyes fixing on the boy with dread. The war chief glanced and caught his expression. That, more than anything, seemed to finally make up his mind.

He withdrew his sword, and with a grunt remounted his horse. Looking down at the unprotected party, he saluted Gill with his sword, as though he were the captain of a mighty host. "You are a braver man than I, Slave. May the gods hedge you and me from all harm, and bring us safely to our homes."

He turned his mount, and with a shout put his heels to his horse's side; the whole party moving with a clatter and the road swaying as they galloped away. *They're not laughing now,* Gill thought, and smiled grimly. The story would spread along the road ahead of them, at every safe house along the way; travellers going up and down the road in both directions would bear the rumour. He realised that once this tale was known he would probably travel far more safely than if he had been himself surrounded by twenty warriors.

He should have felt relieved, but looking at the woman he only felt resentment. This was not his triumph, but hers, and somehow, strangely, the boy's. He had done nothing, but stand like a stone, unblinking, with a sword to his throat.

The woman was smiling, and Gill knew that she was probably waiting for a word of praise. Instead he walked around and hit her across the mouth.

"Don't go thinking you're clever," he said, "I know your tricks." He raised his hand and was about to hit her again, when he realised his wrist was seized. The woman was cowering with her hands over her face, and the boy had his arm, caught between the pincers of his bound arms. Gill stood back, cold as the dead with shock, and the boy let go of his wrist.

Trembling, the man went back to take the horse's head, and urged him to walk.

It was a very long time before he stopped shaking.

At the first safe house he came to they were turned away; the woman of the place spat over the threshold to keep out evil, when she saw the dog and the boy. The story had indeed run on ahead. Gill seethed. He had been looking forward to sleeping between walls. Instead he lay every night in the wagon, with goat leather raised above as a tent covering. Though he was reasonably comfortable, and knew he should feel safe, a new anxiety kept him awake.

He had come to hate the clever woman and the alien child. During the sleepless nights the shifting of the slaves beneath the wagon angered him. The clanking of the chains was an irritant in itself, and the woman grumbling in her sleep was bad enough... but oh, the boy! That stupid boy. If he had only stayed dumb! He hadn't paid any attention to his voice before they had been overtaken by the war party, but now it was like a toothache, a constant pain. The boy murmured day and night. How the woman could bear it Gill could not imagine. When he had first been told that the naked slave was talking to some maggot of a foreign god, it had seemed hilarious. That, however, had been before talk of the dead being raised. Gill seemed to feel the boy's odd gaze on his back, even in the dark, as though he were looking up through the slats at the bottom of the wagon, peering at him in the gloom.

On the fifteenth night of their journey Gill could stand it no more. With a sudden roar he thumped the base of the wagon so hard that the horse awoke with a stamp and a whinny, and the boy finally stopped. Furious, Gill pushed back the tent flap and swung over the side of the wagon. He grabbed the chain and yanked. Both woman and boy scrabbled out, the woman looking terrified, the boy simply dazed. Gill grabbed the boy by the hair and yanked him to his feet. Both slaves choked as the chain between the neck irons was pulled taut, until the woman managed to stagger to her feet. Gill took the key from his belt, unlocked the neck iron from the boy and threw him against the wagon. The boy stood shaking with his hands covering his groin. In a fury, Gill kicked him between the legs. The boy doubled over, and fell, causing the dog to yelp. Gill felt slightly better seeing the boy at his feet, and walked around to kick him again, this time on the slowly healing lacerations of his back. This wasn't as satisfying, and he snarled at the woman. "Go under the wagon." Her blood was still with her, and besides, he didn't feel like female flesh tonight.

Terrified, she obeyed, and crawled backward under the wagon. The dog stood alert, slavering with excitement. Gill struck him across the muzzle to keep him silent. He wanted no distractions. Then, grabbing the boy, he dragged him onto the wet of the bog. *I'll knock the praying out of him, show him who is really god in this world.* He threw him flat on the grass, and pushed his face hard into the earth, so that he would breathe and taste mud, so that his mouth would be too full of dirt to pray. The boy struggled, but chained hand and foot as he was he couldn't put up much of a fight. Gill waited until the desperate breaths began to whistle in the boy's chest, then he knelt between his thighs and pushed his legs apart. The chain at his heels restricted movement, but it was still possible to get in there; Gill knew from experience. The boy desperately arched backward and grabbed a breath. Gill struck him hard on the back of his head, his two hands clenched into a double fist. The boy went down with a splash onto the wet earth, satisfyingly limp. Undoing his belt, the man positioned himself carefully, then bore his weight down and in. The boy screamed. Gill laughed.

It was probably as painful for Gill as it was for the boy, but it was the boy's fault, after all. He had forced him to this, with all his praying. Vindictively the man bit the boy's shoulder, tasted blood. *Not enough,* he thought, spitting, and wrapped his two hands round his victim's throat and squeezed. Then, he was finished. He remained on top of the boy a moment longer to demonstrate his dominance, then got up and tidied his garments. He looked down at the boy, kicked him over onto his back, and sneered.

"Not praying now, are you?"

The boy's eyes were open to the moonlight, and blank. Gill smiled. He took the opportunity to kick him again between the legs, and the boy convulsed, then puked.

Good, thought Gill, contented. *He'll keep quiet now.*

He grabbed the boy under his arms and hauled him to his feet, dragged him back to the road, and threw him next to the cart. The dog was pressed flat to the wooden road, soundless, tail wagging, eyes rolling in fear. *Good; they should all fear me.*

"Woman," he commanded, and the female crawled out. "If he prays again, I'll kill him. Keep him quiet."

She nodded, satisfyingly mute, and he felt a profound satisfaction as he chained them back together at the neck. He climbed back into the wagon, dropped the flap, and settled back. Truth be told, he hadn't expected to enjoy it so much. The boy was nearly too old for him, and he was tall and strong looking. But still, it had taken the edge off his anger and anxiety.

Gill listened for a while to the noises of the night. The slaves made no sound at all. He congratulated himself on enacting strong discipline and drifted off into a happy sleep.

Chapter Five

After that night there was no more trouble. There were only a few days left of the journey, and they were finally within the master's tribal boundaries. Now that they were in safe country there was absolutely no chance of an attack, and Gill no longer had to feel beholden to the woman for her quick wit. He slowed the pace slightly, wanting to enjoy the last days of being his own man.

The first day the boy had not walked right, and stumbled so often that it made more practical sense for him to ride in the wagon. He lay very still. For a while Gill was concerned, and checked occasionally to make sure his cargo hadn't died. But the boy kept breathing. The second day he walked on behind the woman. Gill no longer bothered to observe them as closely. They were both so obviously cowed. He even took the leg irons from the boy to make it easier for him to walk. His ankles were swollen and bleeding, as were the soles of his feet. This was a boy who had been used to shoes, to soft living. Gill knew now that the boy would never run.

At some point during the second day the boy's lips started moving again, but this time noiselessly. Gill walked ahead with the horse, and so didn't notice the soundless rebellion. The weather improved and became quite warm. The boy's flesh reddened, blistered, then peeled in the sun.

On the last two evenings Gill commanded the woman to cook. He felt like sitting out to eat, enjoying the fire and the dusk. The dog brought back meat, obediently, which the woman cooked in the pot. When he had eaten his fill Gill settled back comfortably, and gave the leavings to the slaves and the dog. He felt quite munificent, and discovered that he was very much enjoying this last leg of the journey. Sated with good food he didn't feel any urge to take either of the prisoners again. The woman was still unusable, and to be honest, he'd not even desired the boy. He'd simply wanted him to know who was master.

Obviously the boy now knew.

Life should have been good, but on the last day of the trek his mood began to sour. Soon he would be back to normal life, and someone else would direct his every moment. The woman further irritated him by unexpectedly calling out.

"Master..."

"What is it?"

"We need water."

"Water? I've given you plenty of water. What do you want, to swim in it?"

"Not for me Sir, for Patrick, the boy is ill."

Gill stopped, and turned angrily to the woman. Even with the bulk of the wagon between them, she flinched. Yet despite her fear she held his gaze.

"How is he ill? He's been getting food enough."

"He's not made for this weather, Master, the sun has been cruel to him."

Gill sighed, and marched around to the back of the wagon. The woman's chain was fastened to the back end, the boy was fastened to her. He stood and inspected them, and felt a sudden queasiness in his stomach as he realised the woman was right.

He had known the boy was a red head, and had known he was catching the sun, but he hadn't realised the extent of it. The boy was shivering, despite the fact that he was blistered up and down his back and buttocks, largely on the right side. It appeared that these portions of his body had never seen the sun before. The British wore tunics, Gill remembered. The boy's legs were darker below the knee, as were his arms and freckled face. The rest of his body was milk. Gill cursed himself. He had seen that at the market when he bought him. It was common enough to break a slave by forcing nakedness on them, but perhaps he had overdone it. He should have put a tunic on him when the sun started to burn strong.

At least the front half was unaffected; no doubt because the wagon acted as a shield of sorts against the weather. The sun had been rising behind them as they travelled West, and moving in a northern arc over the course of the day. It was obvious now how the damage had been done.

Gill cursed aloud, and clenched his fist. The woman flinched. He gritted his teeth and relaxed his hand. Better not use his fists now. There was a real risk that he'd lost one slave. He'd better not mark the other.

"You stupid bitch," he said, showing all his teeth in a vicious smile. "Why didn't you tell me he was like this?"

"It was hard to keep up with the horse, Sir, and he was behind me. I didn't realise at first. Then when you paused a while ago, I turned and saw the state of him."

Gill chewed his lip and thought. Finally he made a decision.

"Both of you, in the cart. You, Woman, put the tent up, keep a shadow over him. I'll get water."

He marched off, muttering to himself, grabbing the bucket, and returned with it three quarters full. The tent was already up, and the boy was lying on his face, across the mattress.

"Don't make a mess in here," Gill snapped. "There's food, and wine and oil I don't want spoiled."

"I'll be careful, Master."

Gill watched, feeling somewhat redundant as the woman tore a scrap from her dress, and dipped it in the water. She carefully dribbled it over the boy's head; he turned his face, like a flower to sunlight. Gill shook his head, disgusted, as the slave started to suckle on the rag. When people were sick they always reverted to an infant state. This boy was very sick... not quite the triumphant return Gill had been hoping for. He felt rotten in his bones. He should have taken more care of the creature. What had he been thinking? He cast about in his mind for a way he could blame it on the woman, but realised he couldn't. "Master," the woman spoke, "I'll need more cloth. Do you have any?"

"What do you need it for?"

"To take the heat out of him, I need to soak rags, and apply them to the hot spots."

Well, at least I picked a woman with some knowledge of healing, he thought. *It's not a complete loss. The old Cailleach can't last much longer, someone will need to take over once she's gone.*

"Here," he rummaged through a box in the corner of the wagon. "These will do." He had set out prepared with a selection of rags in case he bought a woman. They always started bleeding at some point. This one seemed to have done nothing but bleed since they started the journey. If he hadn't known better, he'd have thought she did it deliberately to spite him.

"I can't use these, Sir."

"Why on earth not?"

"They're soiled sir, it could kill him."

He realised she was probably right. Any trace of woman's blood was a dangerous thing. Angrily he took off his tunic, and started to shred it. "Use this then."

"Thank you, Master."

He turned, and marched off angry. Her efficiency seemed like an insult. He was no longer in charge, and he wasn't even home yet. He'd lost control, and he could only imagine how difficult it would be when he arrived with a slave woman who wouldn't stop bleeding, and boy who looked like he'd been boiled.

There was no point putting it off though. The longer he left it, the worse it would be if he arrived and the boy had already died. At the farmstead he might get some medical treatment, besides what the woman could provide. With a grunt he urged the horse on, wishing with every step that there would be some sort of miracle before he crossed the boundary stones.

Finally they were in sight of home. Gill dismounted, and lifted the tent flap to inspect the produce in the wagon one last time.

"How is he?"

"Cooler. He's been drinking the water and hasn't thrown up."

"Good, good." He could see that the woman had put wet rags under the boy's armpits and groin, as well as across the angry bubbles of red on his back and buttock. The boy's eyes were still closed, but his throat was working as he sucked urgently on the water that the woman was providing through the rag. As one rag was drained she would snatch it from his lips, then provide another. At the same time her other hand was fluttering over the rags around his body, and replacing them as they absorbed the heat that radiated from his burning skin.

"He's not shaking so much."

"His heat is coming down."

"That's something," he said grudgingly. She glanced at him, and he saw for one brief moment the look of contempt in her eyes. Again, he wished he could beat her, but he was painfully aware of how precarious his position now was. His lip curled in a snarl. He could have spat. Instead, he turned his back abruptly, and over his shoulder delivered his edict.

"I'll need to clean you up. You're passing acceptable, but he's a mess." He said it as though it was her fault. There was silence, and he turned to glare at her, challenging her to disagree with him. "You'll have to get him clean. They'll want to inspect him." He spat over his shoulder. "I don't want to touch him."

She looked at him with a bitten down fury, as though she wanted to say something, but was afraid. He stared at her until she dropped her gaze. "I'll go ahead and let them know we're coming," he said, curtly. "You, clean him."

"I'll clean him, Sir," she replied, head bent submissively. He nodded, checked their chains, although he knew perfectly well they wouldn't be going anywhere, and walked on.

"Patrick," Fionula was speaking to him. He looked at her from far away. "Patrick, help me. I need to get you clean."

He was flat on his face, and naked. Realising his position he groaned and started to struggle. The Man would come and find him like this. Fionula couldn't protect him from the Man.

"Don't worry, don't be scared, he's gone. He's gone ahead to the farm. He'll not hurt you again, he's not allowed. Patrick, child of my heart, don't struggle, you'll hurt yourself."

Gradually he calmed down. He still felt limbless and weak, and very, very cold.

"Can you sit up?"

He moved, painfully, and felt the world rock. He realised that he was in a shelter, and suddenly started crying. Thank God he was out of the endless sun.

"Hush, hush." Fionula's voice was distressed. "Don't cry, light of my life, sweetheart, little boy, don't cry."

He sobbed himself out as she soothed him. He was sitting crooked, weight bearing on his left hip, with his head resting on Fionula's shoulder. She had her arms round him, lightly, and her hands were blessedly wet, moving up and down his burning back. How could he be so burning and yet so cold?

"When we get where we're going, there will be a person to tend you. A sort of a doctor. She'll know what to do. Here..." she lifted a metal cup, filled with water. Patrick recognised it as the Man's cup, and part of him recoiled from touching anything of his. But he was so thirsty that as soon as the cup reached his lips he started to gulp it down.

Fionula withdrew the cup. "Not so fast. Let it settle in your stomach." She looked frustrated. "I wish I knew where he kept his salt..." Then she brightened up. "There, that's where he keeps it. I recognise his bag."

Patrick's head was heavy, and he couldn't understand what she needed salt for. He tried to reach his hand to the cup, but she kept it back again.

"Wait, just a moment, this will do you good."

She opened a leather purse, and took out a pinch of white grains. "They keep him well enough," she said, scornfully, "that's good stuff. All the better for you, Sweetheart. Open your mouth."

He opened his mouth, then gagged as she put salt straight onto his tongue. Quickly, before he could try to spit it out, she put the water back to his lips and he drank.

"Good boy. Now, that's enough... just lie back down for a minute."

He lay across her, his eyes drifting shut. She started to put cold rags on him again; a blessed relief. He remembered the rich man in hell, and how he had cried out for one drop of water. He'd never known before what consolation one drop of water could give. Even as he thought it, he felt water dripping on his face, and he opened his mouth to receive the rapture of it.

"Good boy," she was still talking gently. "You'll do well, you'll be fine. That's right, you take your medicine, good boy…"

The water tasted now like tears, and his headache and shivering was subsiding. He wondered who wept for him, and saw an image of his mother, kneeling in his grandfather's church. "Mother," he said, and Fionula caught her breath. "Oh, my Son," she choked out. Patrick felt his mother's kiss on his forehead, and drifted off, still suckling, while somewhere women cried.

He flinched awake, then relaxed. Fionula was still with him, and the terrible thirst had eased. She was bathing him; he could feel the cool rags on his skin.

He was still lying on his front, and he felt obscurely as though he should be afraid of something, but Fionula had tended him as a small child, and she was a woman. She wouldn't hurt him. Through the slat of the tent he could see the sky dimming to a purple blue, and the first stars coming out. A cool evening. He whispered his thanks to the God of the cold pure heavens. Seeing he was awake, Fionula started singing under her breath, as she had done when he was an infant, to comfort him. She was singing in her own tongue, but her lullabies had never sounded threatening to him. As a child, though he hadn't understood a word of her songs, he had always thought her language beautiful. For a brief while it sounded beautiful to him again, and he could imagine himself a child, recovering from the spotted fever, perhaps, listening to his nurse sing as she made all things better. The water was cool on his burning skin, for which he was thankful.

Finally, realising he was thoroughly awake, Fionula started to speak, in a hushed tone. "He came back," she said, "but he's decided to wait till tomorrow to move on,"

"Where is he?"

Fionula laughed, low in her throat, and said, "sleeping outside with the dog. He realises you need the shelter more than he does."

"Where are we?"

"We're nearly there."

"Oh." Patrick couldn't imagine what 'there' was like, or what life would be like once this endless journey was over. Fionula was now carefully peeling strips of white skin from his shoulders.

"You have nasty blisters back here," she sounded concerned. "And you're still... I don't know, a bit scabby. From the flogging. It's hard to tell, the blisters are so big. I'll need to lance them if I get a chance. He probably brought clothes, to make you look presentable to the master." She sighed, and warned him. "Some masters want to inspect you naked, to check for strength though. They'll clothe you eventually. Remember, the clothes will sting when you first put them on... you need to be ready for that."

"Clothes?" Patrick had forgotten he was naked. A feeling of dizzy nausea rose over him. There was something he nearly remembered.

"Come on, Buachalin." Fionula was in a brisk maternal role. "You'll get over it. We all do." What it was that he would get over was left unsaid. After a moment's uncomfortable silence she continued. "It's a shame I can do nothing with your hair, but even if we don't have a chance to wash or cut the blood out, the scab will grow out in the end. It could be worse."

The following day the Man made them both walk. He was angry from the moment he showed his face. There was some shouting as he tried to dress Patrick, and he struck him across the face sharply when he discovered that Patrick had never worn pants before, and was simply too tired and confused to figure out which leg went where. Attempts to put a tunic on were equally fruitless. The man didn't want to take the neck iron or handcuffs off, and so Patrick finished the long trek as he had started it – naked. Fionula was pale, with black shadows under her eyes from the sleepless night. Patrick felt guilty to have caused her so much worry, and tried his best to keep up. Although he felt better than he had the day before, he staggered as he walked. Several times he stumbled, choking Fionula, who was walking sideways behind the cart so that she could brace him when he fell. "Don't worry, Patrick, we're nearly there," she reassured him. "I can see it from here."

At first sight Patrick didn't realise they had arrived, it looked so unlike what he expected from a farm. There seemed to be no organisation. The only stone building in sight had smoke emanating from it, and was evidently designed for living, not storage. Other than that, there were no stone buildings, and the dwelling places were round huts with reed roofs, like those of the poor woodcutters back home. They had passed several such settlements on the way, and he had assumed they were the villages of the poor. The huts were nestled together in a basin like valley, and behind them the earth swept up, like a bowl, steepling to a rocky crag. Fringed with forest to the right, and a glimpse of dazzling blue to the left, the mountain dipped precipitously to reveal the furthest sea.

Patrick stared. As the details of the scene began to arrange themselves in his overloaded brain he realised that this was indeed a farm. There was tilled earth in the low land near the huts, crops growing, cows wandering in the plain, pigs fenced off. The reality of it hit him, and his knees were weak with the knowledge: he was standing at the very edge of the world. Somebody had actually come to the lip of the world and built a farm. It was madness. The whole thing was so impossible, the scene so unlike his parent's farm, that Patrick couldn't quite believe the journey was finally over.

As he approached the nearest hut he shrank from the smell. He had never in his life been in such a building. Somewhere there was a bonfire, and the smell of roasting meat. He remembered stories of human sacrifices. It was reported that the Irish savages bound men and women up, hand and foot, put them in wicker cages and set fire to them. He remembered as a child an old soldier from this very island, one eyed and lamed in foreign wars, telling tales of delicious horror to the town's children on feast nights. They would all sit whispering and giggling, screaming with delight at the more gruesome details, as the man told them of the battles he had won, the heads he had brought home in a sack to throw at his chieftain's feet, and the men whose flesh he had feasted on.

For a horrible moment Patrick remembered the children at his parents' farm, heads struck off. His mind recoiled from it. Patrick had once believed that the ruined old soldier was spinning yarns for the sake of the feast, but now – smelling what he hoped was just pig flesh – he wasn't so sure.

The Man who had taken them this far seemed to be shrinking in stature the nearer he got to the homestead. He adopted an increasingly servile demeanour, and by the time he reached the door of the first hut Patrick had realised to his surprise that his captor was just as much a slave as he or Fionula were. He looked from the Man to the woman who had emerged from the door way. Yes. The Man was a slave. He was cringing in front of this woman. Patrick experienced a new dread. The Man had attained a fearsome stature in his mind, so whoever made him small must be a terror indeed.

The woman was tall, black-haired. She stood by the doorway of the hut, with her arms folded across her bosom. The wind whipped her hair backward, showing sculpted hard features, like one of the many faces of the Witch. Unlike Fionula this woman was well dressed, and from the way the Man deferred to her Patrick assumed she was the Mistress of the farm. She looked sternly at the Man, and spoke to him sharply. He responded in apologetic tones. She harrumphed through her nose, and turned to look at the two chained persons before her. She flicked her gaze dismissively up and down Fionula, seeming particularly displeased, then started to walk around them both. Fionula whispered, "stand still." Patrick obeyed without question while the woman continued her inspection. She seemed particularly interested in Patrick, and he closed his eyes, mortified that he was still naked. He flinched as she poked his back, and the woman laughed. She spoke to him gently, and suddenly he heard and felt the clinking as someone unlocked the neck chain. His whole body went tense, and a wave of sickness flooded through him with the unwanted memory of the last time the neck brace had been removed. He felt her fingers on his face, and despite himself he whimpered in his throat.

"It's alright Patrick," Fionula said, "she's not trying to hurt you." He stood shaking, aware that his face was wet as his handcuffs were removed. Then he heard a cracking sound beside him, like a slap, and Fionula cried out. Someone had hit her. For a horrible moment he thanked God it wasn't him. Beside him he heard the woman's angry voice berating Fionula. She responded in the barbarian tongue, in tones of deference and respect, and there was silence. Then the strange woman started to talk again. There was another silence. Then Fionula spoke to Patrick, in British. "The Bhean Uasail wants me to translate. You have to say something, so she knows you understood."

"I... understand."

More of the savage tongue, then Fionula reported:

"She says to open your eyes."

He opened them, and saw the woman standing in front of him, smiling. Her eyes were large, and very green, swimming in what seemed like a field of snow, hedged with soft black lashes, like winter fir trees. He found himself thinking of the mountain, and couldn't look away. She spoke again, then looked sharply at Fionula.

"She says..." Fionula paused, and took a deep breath, sounding distressed. "She says that you have beautiful eyes."

Patrick blushed, and dropped his gaze. He had been thinking the same thing of her.

"The Bhean Uasail says you're not to be afraid of her. She says that she's sorry you've been ill used. As long as you do what she says you'll be fine."

Patrick looked from Fionula to the strange woman, and blinked.

"Say something, she'll get angry."

"Tell her... thank you."

The woman smiled, then stepped forward and kissed Patrick on the mouth. He was too startled to move and she laughed. She turned then, snapped at the man and strode off.

The Man turned and glared at Patrick, like he wanted him dead. He barked some order, as though mimicking his Mistress and stalked away. Fionula took Patrick's arm and gently led him into the hut. "You can rest in here. You'll get food, and clothes, and medicine. Come on, dip your head now; the door's low for you... that's right."

Together they walked into the round hut. Patrick couldn't see a thing. Fionula was already talking with someone in the gloom, quite as though she belonged here, and Patrick sat suddenly, in a boneless collapse, without having had any intention of doing so. His limbs had felt disjointed. He didn't think he could move again.

There was a little circle of light in the centre of the ceiling. Patrick looked up, watched the dust spinning, motes of gold in the beam of light. He realised smoke was being drawn up from the fire beneath. As his eyes adjusted to the gloom he saw, hanging from the struts of the ceiling nothing but herbs and a dead goose. Not as he had half feared human heads hanging by their hair. Perhaps the old soldier had lied, after all. There were reeds on the floor; ash fenced in by a ring of stone. Beside the dead hearth sat what, at first, he took to be a heap of sticks. Then the angular silhouette spoke, and moved... and Patrick saw it was a Someone.

He gazed at it in dawning horror. This Someone was an old person... so old and decrepit that it's gender could not be made out. The creature scuttled toward him and in a flash he remembered the story of the old man withered to a cricket by age. He shuffled back on the rushes, painfully splitting one of the blisters as the creature approached. Whatever it was, it was as old and desiccated as anything he had ever seen; the thin high stream of foreign cackle issuing from its shrunken lips made him flinch with fear. The face was completely collapsed round a toothless cavern of a mouth, and the nose beetled over it like a claw.

When he was a very little child, one of the household slaves had told Patrick the story of the cricket – that the goddess of the morning had once loved a mortal man, and begged Zeus to give her beloved the gift of eternal life. And eternal life the man was given. He withered with it, and shrank, and wept for death, till the goddess could no longer look at him, and locked him away in a cage. When he was shrivelled enough he crept through the bars, and hid in the long grass. And the lover still twittered at the dawn, singing his adoration in the dry voice of insects, while the goddess rose in the pink of the morning and never looked his way. The young Patrick had endured nightmares for weeks before he confided the source of his fear. His grandfather had been angry to hear that he had been indulging in pagan stories with the slaves, and had persuaded his parents to sell the woman concerned.

And here he was, a foreign slave, faced finally with a creature straight from his nightmares.

The floor lurched up around him, as the wrecked face thrust itself toward him. Mercifully the world went black.

Fionula apologised. "I'm sorry, he's not been well. I hope he won't be too much work for you."

The old woman cackled. "Don't worry, sweetheart. I've seen them all come and go. He'll either toughen up and survive, or lie down and die. It's up to him which he'll do."

She inched closer to Patrick's prostrate form. "Could you build the fire up, Child? I'll need some light, and the fire will clean the needle."

Fionula did just as the wise woman told her, feeling obscurely comforted to be in such a familiar situation. She had hoped, when they arrived in an Irish port, that she might be bought by a member of her own tribe. It did occasionally happen. She could have gone back to her father's people then, and been finally free. But she knew the chances of her being recognised were slim; it had been more than twenty years, after all, and she had been so young... hardly anyone could be left who would recognise her. But she remembered this kind of woman. The Cailleach could have been her own grandmother.

"He's been through it, hasn't he?" The old woman examined the boy carefully. "Could you tell me what happened?"

Fionula paused, considering what she should say.

"Ah, don't worry yourself; it won't get back to the big folk. I just want to know because sometimes it's the spirit that's hurt, not just the body. Anything you tell me can help."

Fionula decided to trust the woman.

"He's the only son of British aristocrats, highborn. Actually, that's what his name means... his parents were so proud of him. Patrick. It means something like our Uasail... high born, an aristocrat."

The old woman laughed, but not cruelly. "Well, poor boy, he's fallen on hard times. So, he's never worked a lick in his life, has he?"

"No. I mean, not real work. He's done book work, as the Romans do. He's learned to read and write, and he speaks British, Latin and Greek. I think he's not fond of his studies, though he likes the Greek. Many people speak it where he comes from, and many of their best story tellers come from the Greeks. The Latin wearies him, it's just book learning, and he sees no use for the mathematics. He prefers... well, I mean he used to prefer, to swim, and climb trees, and kick the bladder round with his friends. But even though he's such an ordinary boy, his family had dedicated him to some foreign god." Fionula cocked her head, pondering. It seemed there was something important there. "His mother had been childless for many years. She prayed to this god of theirs, and then this boy was conceived. Apparently she dedicated him to her god, out of thanks."

"I heard something about it, that the boy's got powers. The story's all over the country." The old woman looked amused. "I suppose you exaggerated, did you?"

"It seemed the only way to scare off the warriors."

"You're a quick girl, that's certain."

"It is true though that his mother dedicated him to her god."

"Well, he seems like a stingy god to me, if he only gave her one."

"Yes, and a powerless god, now that he's allowed the boy to be stolen from her."

"Is the woman too old to have another child?"

"I think so. Her womb was a cold and rocky place. I was surprised she carried this one to term."

"She'd lost others?"

"Yes, many, both before and after."

"Ah," the old woman sighed. "Poor woman. It's better sometimes to have no child. The loss of them can be such bitterness in your old age."

Fionula turned her head and blinked wetness from her eyes. The old woman looked at her sympathetically, and tutted.

"You've lost children yourself?"

"I have," she replied.

"May Brigit grant you children to warm you in your old age, and keep the wolf from the door."

"Thank you, Mother," Fionula replied. Then, to turn the conversation, she said, "it's been a long time since I've set a turf fire. They used wood where I was, and the man who brought us here set the fire for us when we needed one. I can't get it going, could you do it for me, Mother?"

"I can that, Daughter. Come here, I'll show you."

Fionula sat back on her haunches, and watched as the old woman got the fire going. She felt transported back in time, comforted by speaking her own language, and being understood, by sitting with a wise woman who called her 'Daughter,' and even the familiar smell of the turf. Despite the brutality of the capture, and the transport, and the long road here, she now felt safe. As the fire caught and the homely smell of it strengthened she smiled at the old lady. "Thank you," she said, "I'll try again next time."

"You were a long time in the mongrel lands?"

"I was so." Fionula had forgotten the term, it came almost as a shock to her.

"Is this boy a mongrel?"

"I think not," Fionula shrugged. "His family claimed ancestors three hundred years back who fought the Roman oppressors. Their aristocracy are often like that. The lowborn intermarry, but the highborn keep their bloodlines pure."

"His hair and features looks like one of ours. A red child, like a fox, but big boned like a wolf. And yet he speaks their language, and follows their god?"

"He learned their language in their school, but he speaks their old language at home. Their language is not completely unlike our own. And their legends are the same."

"But he follows the Roman god?"

Fionula paused, considering. "His grandfather claims that their god is not Roman. That their god is the god of the whole world."

The old woman sat back and laughed. "Are they all so daft in his country?"

Fionula laughed back. "It seems so."

"And is this one mad too? The Bhean Uasail won't be pleased if he is."

"Oh... well, that's a pity. I think perhaps he has gone mad."

"With the loss of all his hopes?"

"He saw things, when the pirates came. He saw what men do in battle.

"Did he fight? Or did he stand gaping?"

"He fought." Despite herself Fionula couldn't keep the pride out of her voice. Patrick may never have been the child of her flesh, but she had known him from the day he was born, and after the first few days she had been his wet-nurse. It had never been proper before to love him as her own, but the world had turned upside down. He was now a slave, and she could finally think of him as kin. Her own son. "He fought in a red mist like a proper Irish warrior," she declared.

"Well, if he has such strength in his bones, he may get well then."

"There is one thing though."

"What's that?"

"When he woke in the ship, his soul had gone out of him. He talked of being in the belly of a fish. And then when we arrived here, his soul was still walking abroad." Fionula leant toward the old woman and whispered. "He wandered in the lands of the dead."

"So, not all your story to the warriors was a lie."

"Not all. They do say that this god of his can raise the dead."

"You said the boy walked in the lands of the dead. What did he see?"

"He doesn't say. But since he returned he talks to his god."

"Does his god talk back?"

"I don't know. I do know that he never spoke to his god before, and his spirit never walked abroad before. Something has changed in him."

The old woman nodded, slowly. "The mother dedicated him to this god, you say?"

"She did so."

"It's a foolish thing, to offer someone to a god. When the gods take a man they take him all, body and soul. Did the woman not know the risk?"

"I don't know. I never bothered with their religion."

"You mentioned his grandfather, who also talked of his god. Was this an important man?"

"He was a... a priest. Held in high regard. And his father was also in their priesthood, though of a lower rank."

"So, the boy is a hereditary priest, is he?"

"He's not a druid."

"But he walks with the dead," the old woman repeated, thoughtfully.

"He has done, several times, this last few weeks. Never before."

The old woman nodded again. "You know, it's interesting. When Gill, arrived..." she paused and looked at Fionula's questioning expression. "Gill is the one who brought you here," she clarified, "when Gill arrived he told us that this one was the son of a witch. He knew none of this other story you tell me."

"He never asked," Fionula tossed her head contemptuously. "The boy's mother is no witch, I'll tell you that. She's one of those pious Christians that you find on that island, always talking about this invisible god of theirs, not letting people alone. She doesn't think people should worship any other god." Fionula shook her head in irritation at the memory of Patrick's mother. "A good woman, but quite mad. Not like her son is mad, just... she cannot see that people can have many gods, she just won't see the world the way it is." Fionula shrugged. At least she would not have to sit spinning, and listening to Patrick's mother, on the long winter nights, telling her stories that made no sense. "The woman is no witch," she repeated for emphasis. "The pirates who took us misunderstood. Patrick saw them dispatching children, and he ran to save them, or avenge them. I'm not sure which. The children's mother was there, and when her last child died, she stood and called down the Raven on them. They slew her where she stood, then struck down Patrick. I think they thought she was his mother. She was a slave of his family though."

"And you saw this?"

Fionula looked shamefaced at the floor.

"I've lived through such raids before. I've given up fighting."

The old woman nodded, pragmatically. Like Fionula she knew the folly of fighting. "He fought for foreign slaves though," she pointed out. "No blood of his. He's a brave boy."

"He is that. I wouldn't have guessed him capable of it if I hadn't seen it myself."

There was a brief span of silence while the fire crackled and caught. The old woman continued to feed the flames.

"You have no love for Gill," she stated.

"I have not."

"None of us do. I take it he is responsible for most of this."

Fionula didn't say anything, and the old lady continued. "I mean, who would ever expect a milk white red head to walk naked in such sun. The boy has sunstroke, on top of his injuries, and it's obvious that Gill has abused him. He's bleeding still."

"Don't..." Fionula gulped. "Don't tell anyone else about that. Where this boy comes from they don't assert ownership in that way. Or... at least they're not supposed to. There are those among his people who consider what happened to him a crime by the victim as much as the perpetrator. I've known men kill themselves for shame."

"Why?" The old woman clucked. "We women don't go so far, and we are the ones who have to bear the children." She shook her head. "Ah, well... as you say, they're all mad."

The fire was bright enough now, and she moved to the entrance and lifted the leather door flap, to let more light in. "Humph," she grunted, and rummaged through her tools before holding a sharp knife over the fire. "A needle won't be enough," she explained to Fionula's startled expression. "Now, my dear daughter, do as I say. Could you be kind and get me the rain water from the bucket outside? That will be the purest. And those broad leaves hanging above you there. And the salt is in the jar by the wall. Thank you... now." She sat back and considered the operation. "This will be painful for him, and he may struggle if he wakes. You're stronger than me, so I'll have to ask you to hold him down."

"Can we not just let him sweat it off?"

"No, I'm sorry, my child, but the whipping he took to his back has festered, and we need to drain the pus from the wounds. If not, it will poison him, and he may die of it. You say he has walked in the land of the dead, we need to go against death before it takes him. Feel here." The Cailleach grasped Fionula's hand, and placed it on Patrick's wounded back.

"I know, he's been burning up, but complaining of the cold."

"When we're done here we'll have to take him down to the river to keep him cool. The men will help you carry him, we have a litter. You'll need to build a lean-to and keep the sun off him. Keep splashing him with the running water, no matter how much he complains of cold."

"I'll do whatever you say, Mother."

"Good. All you have to do right now is hold him down while I make the cuts."

Fionula knelt at the top end of Patrick, and held his shoulders, and started praying to Brigid and Oghma that the patient wouldn't wake up. The old woman nodded in approval, and applied the hot blade to Patrick's back.

The blisters were the first area she attended to, and Patrick barely moved as the water spilled out over him. Rapidly the old woman cut around the wounded area, and removed the dead skin. She threw it on the fire, where it made a malodorous hiss and twisted into ash. She ignored the smell, and worked fast. The blisters extended in an angry splotch even down his buttocks and to the top of his right leg. The old woman tutted with sympathy as she removed the worst of it. "That could go bad easily," she said. "Normally sunburn isn't dangerous, but when it covers so much of the body, and when there's already uncleanness in the blood, as there is in the scars, it can be a serious thing."

Fionula was relieved that the old woman was treating her as an apprentice, and explaining her actions. She realised that she might learn something here. "Thank the god and the goddess that you are here to help him," she commented, sincerely, without any desire to curry favour. Again, the old lady nodded her approval. Prayer was always necessary in any operation.

"Thank the god and goddess that you walked in front of him, so that he only burned on his back. Had he burned on his front he would have had nowhere to lie in comfort. Now, this is going to be the difficult part. You see here?"

Fionula looked, and winced. The whip marks had been angry for a long while now, but the fat blisters had obscured quite how pus laden those scars had become. Now that the blisters were gone the scourge marks showed livid, long yellow and green ridges that stood out plump and poisonous amongst the raw red of the newly peeled skin. It was all too obvious how infected those injuries had become.

"There will be no choice but to cut these. I had thought a needle might relieve them, but we'll need to cut long if we want all the poison to drain out. And when we squeeze, he will probably scream and fight. Can you hold him?"

"Is there no other way?"

"He is not conscious, so I won't be able to drug him. And we should do this quickly."

"I can hold him."

The old woman nodded, and commenced the operation. As she had predicted Patrick woke up part way through, and began to scream.

Fionula held him down with all her weight, and wept, remembering the last time she had heard him scream. There was nothing she could have done, chained like a dog as she was under the wagon, but she knew in her gut that even if she hadn't been chained she would have been too terrified to have done anything. She had been cutting herself with a stone for weeks, to produce evidence of bleeding, in her efforts to thwart their captor from raping her. When he took Patrick instead she had been relieved that it wasn't her.

And now she pinned him down while he screamed. She felt like the rapist herself.

"It had to be done," the old woman reassured her, when they had finished. Patrick was still conscious, sobbing into the earth. "There was nothing else to do."

Fionula nodded her acknowledgement.

"Now that he's awake, you can give him this. He'll sleep."

"Thank you, Mother."

She leaned forward, and whispered to Patrick in his own language.

"I'm sorry, Master, we had to treat your back. It was festering, we were worried you would die." She hadn't called him 'master' since their capture.

He didn't turn his head to her, or speak.

"Please, Master, I have medicine for you. You need to take your medicine, it will take the pain away."

He moved, and looked at her. In the firelight his eyes glittered. "I don't want you to take it away," he said, "I deserve the pain."

"But I don't," she choked back tears. "I don't deserve your pain. I don't want to see you suffer like this."

After a moment he took the medicine, gulped it down, and lay flat on his stomach, closing his eyes against her.

"I'm sorry, Master, really sorry."

"Don't ever say it. I'm nobody's master," he whispered, "Not even my own."

"Just sleep," she said, "sleep and get strong."

There was a passage of silence, then foggily he said, "I think that God must have kept us together, Fionula, I would never have lived if it hadn't been for you."

Then he was asleep, and Fionula sat back, and wondered at what he had said. Even in the middle of all this, he clung to his god. She looked across at the old woman, who was now beginning to dress the wounded back. "I really do think that he's gone mad," she said sadly, and shook her head.

Conchessa was aware of the whispers. "The poor woman's lost her mind," was one of the kinder remarks. Others were less kind... women laughing at her because she'd lost her cherished child, the apple of her eye. She had always been considered too proud of her answered prayer, her son. She had even overheard one of the slave women saying, mutinously, "you'd think she was the only woman to ever have a child the way she carried on about him. Patrick indeed, what sort of a name is that to give a child? Highborn! And now she's the only woman in the world to have lost a child –" the sentence was cut off abruptly, and the woman's frightened face at the moment of discovery seared on her sight, like a glimpse in a thunderstorm.

That face, that frightened slave. Did her son look like that? What terrible thing had she become, for someone to be struck so white with fear?

She knew that the woman should be at least beaten, or better sold, but she was too heavy in her misery to take any satisfaction in punishment. Besides, perhaps the woman was right. Hagar heard from God as well as Sarah.

She tried to remember what wrong she might have done the woman; was she Sarah to this slave's Hagar? But nothing came to mind. Her thoughts all kept turning, and returning to Patrick. Where he was, what he was doing; he was hungry, or cold? Was he sold to good people, or to evil?

But oh, one thing she clung to, no matter how mad the world thought her. Her son was not dead. He was coming home.

CHAPTER SIX

The first night passed like a dream. Patrick was carried out of the round hut, to a bright stream in lush green woods. Fionula and two strange men wove a shelter, and placed him under its shade, and then knelt and started splashing water over him. Whatever medicine he had been given worked in his blood against the fever, and made the world a strange place. Everything felt like a child's story, something he would have been told when his first teeth came loose. After a while Fionula left, and the men continued to splash him. It was the first time she had left him since they had been taken, but before Patrick could panic she returned and took over from the men.

Through the long watches of the night at least one or other person remained by his side and kept him wet. Mainly Fionula, sometimes the old bundle of rags that Patrick now knew was an ancient woman.

At one point he looked up and saw that the Lady of the place was kneeling over him, pouring moonlight from a silver cup. Behind her, over the stream, in the woods, he could see fog rising in the form of a wolf that twisted into a snake. The Lady smiled at him as she poured her moonlight, showing red lips and red tongue, and sharp white teeth. A whole generation marched in chains through the endless fog into the jaws of the Giantess. He cried out to God, and the world shrunk back to normal dimensions. The Lady stepped backward over the silver water, fading from sight, and he felt relieved and bereaved at the same time. Then Fionula took the Lady's place and he gasped with relief. Clutching her hand he started to babble, urgently, warning her about the wolf, the snake, and the teeth, the Giantess chewing, the woman on the water;

moonlight poured from a cup. "Hush, hush my child," Fionula said, and he slept, dreamt of his weeping mother.

The next day he was well, but weak. Fionula was sleeping alongside him, and after a moment Patrick smiled to see that she was not chained, and her clothes were no longer rags.

"May the God of the bright morning shine His face upon you," he said, and she woke, startled.

"Bright morning to you too." She looked at him and smiled back. "I didn't realise you called on Lugh in your prayers."

"I do not," he declared, in good humour. "The God of the bright morning isn't some little sun god, He's the God Who made the sun."

Patrick was strangely happy today, and although he still believed that God was against him, he also knew that He was good. A terrible God could still smile. He felt God smiling today.

"Well, whatever you say." She yawned. "Your heat came down toward dawn, and you slept easy. I'm glad you're back."

"I've not been gone."

"You have so. Do you not remember what you saw in the night?"

He remembered the moon in a cup. "Ah," Patrick shifted uncomfortably. "Did I tell you about it?"

"You did. Do you know what it meant?"

Patrick wrinkled his brow, and puzzled. "I'd not thought about it." He gnawed his thumb anxiously. "Maybe I shall have to ask God what it means." *God might choose not to answer me though*, Patrick thought. *Why should He? I never listened to Him before.*

"Now, take my advice, and don't you go asking your god for anything," Fionula urged him. "Look what he's done to you."

"This isn't His fault," Patrick was appalled that she'd think such a thing. Although God had permitted it, surely it was not *His* fault. Patrick was the sinner, after all, and his Grandfather had warned him often enough that the wages of sin is death.

"You said it yourself," Fionula insisted, "when you first landed here. 'Wrath of god,' you said. I didn't believe a word of it at the time... but look at all that's happened to you. And you've changed since we got here.

Your god's done something to you." She raised a hand to his forehead and tapped between his eyes. Patrick blinked at the oddity of the gesture. "It's your mother's fault," Fionula continued, her voice low. "She should never have given you to that god of hers. He's vicious."

Patrick went pale with shock. "Don't speak against God like that."

"What, or he'll do to me what he's done to you? Drive me mad and send me wandering naked and beside myself from one end of the country to the other?"

"God's not responsible for the acts of evil men."

"Perhaps," she sounded unconvinced. "But he's not safe. This time two months ago you didn't believe in him yourself, you flicked wax at the old priests and teachers when they droned on and on at you. Now, don't deny it," she pointed her finger at him as though to stop him, although he had made no move to deny it. "I saw you... and I laughed too. Who could help laughing? There wasn't any sin in that; it was just a boy having fun. But now look what your god's done to you. He's got you seeing the things that eat the shadows, things that nobody can see and not go mad, he's got you talking to him as though he was the only thing in the world that mattered."

Patrick had a pained expression on his face. "But, Fionula," he paused, and struggled for words. "He *is* the only thing that matters."

She sat back, horrified. "He's driven you mad." She shook her head, and stood, brushing her skirt. "Stop. Don't say anything. I don't want to hear about your god."

Suddenly Patrick laughed.

"What? What's so funny now?"

"When we first got here, you said to me, 'whoever heard of an invisible God,' and told me He had no power. Now you're scared of Him."

"Why's that funny?"

"I just remembered something my Mother said..." he climbed stiffly to his feet and smiled down at her. "'The fear of God is the beginning of wisdom.'"

The early days didn't prepare him for the reality of being a slave. Having been so ill he was initially only given light work to do... he learned later that it was women's work, more specifically the work of old women. He sat and carded wool by the river, under the watchful tutelage of the old woman who had so terrified him when he first arrived. Between her careful ministrations, and what attention Fionula could give him between her new duties (which remained a mystery to him) he gradually began to pick up words in the language. In fact, he thought, though it was harder than Greek, which he had picked up as an infant, it wasn't quite as difficult to learn as Latin had been... it seemed to have the same rhythms and pulses as his own native British. Every now and then there were surprises when he would find a word or expression that was almost the same. Sombrely he mourned old Simon, who would be alive still if not for him. The ancient grammarian had painstakingly taught him, or attempted to teach him, amongst other things, the rules of language. Patrick realised now how useful such knowledge was, and regretted his insolent indolence.

The old woman, far from being a creature from his nightmares, turned out to be something of an ally. In the light of day she was simply an old crone, not some stick hag or living skeleton as he had at first feared. Patrick felt ashamed of his superstitious dread of her. She took professional pride in him, seeing his recovery as proof of her powers.

One day as she was changing the dressings she let out a long sigh.

"I'm sorry boy, I can't keep you here for much longer, you'll have to go up the mountain soon."

Patrick teased the sentence apart in his mind, and plucked the sense out of it. Haltingly he replied, "the mountain? Why do I go there?"

"You were bought to be a sheep slave. You are nearly strong enough now to go up the mountain."

"I don't know what a sheep slave does."

"You'll learn," she said grimly. "I'm sorry."

Although the days had become easier, the nights remained times of fear. The Man who had assaulted him turned out to be Gill, the foreman, the keeper of the slaves. Although he worked mainly with the master, and was considered of a higher status than the rest of the slaves, he nevertheless slept in the hut with all the workers, both of house and field.

For a while Patrick remained subject to nocturnal relapses, even when he seemed to be perfectly recovered during the day; this did not make him popular with the other slaves. After his first public delirium they whispered against him, and looked at him with a mixture of distrust and fear. Patrick knew that he must seem foolish and mad, and was ashamed. Night after night, although he fought his fear, it still rose, hallucinatory and terrible in the dark; it rose and consumed him.

When he first slept in the hut he remained feeble and in pain. Fionula, who had arranged his bedding had been summoned out of the hut by a female slave at some point. Patrick tried to follow her – he couldn't bear to be alone here – but found himself too weak to move. The old woman talked to him in her dried leaf voice, but at this point Patrick did not know her, or her language. He tried to calm himself down, but couldn't stop his heart from choking him. His heart hammered in his throat; for some reason his mouth tasted of mud, and he forgot that he was recovering. *I'm going to die,* he thought. *I'm going to die, and I'll not have made a good Confession, I'll die with my sin on my head, and I'll always feel this burning, this terror. This is just the beginning of the agonies.*

Then, to add to his horror, as night fell outside, the room began to fill with people.

First one man came in, glanced at Patrick, laughed, made a disparaging comment to the old crone, then two women came in, neither of them Fionula. After them a man and a boy, both smelling unmistakably of fish, and after that three more men. The room was becoming crowded. Patrick started to shake. He couldn't understand a word anyone said, and they were all looking at him. In his family home he had slept in a stone room, on a raised pallet, with a straw stuffed fleece for a mattress. He had never shared the chamber with more than one person at a time. Sometimes his mother when he was a little boy, or sometimes a slave woman, Fionula usually, when he had a fever. *This* room continued to fill up, and he lost count of the occupants. He would never sleep in a room so crowded. All the air seemed to be full of the stink of human flesh.

Finally Fionula returned, and sat by the fire. She didn't look at him, and she spoke to the other inhabitants of the room. Patrick realised she was introducing herself. Her voice had the cadence of story to it, and her audience were rapt. One of the men gave a cheer, then the others also started to applaud... not in the Roman way, gently flapping the tail of their garment, but in a raucous noisy way, like the poor of Britain. They slapped their hands together, palm on palm, and shouted their approval. One of the men leant across and slapped Patrick's shoulder, not having seen the rawness of it. Patrick flinched, and the man looked puzzled, taking his hand away wet. The old woman said something, and crossed from the far side of the fireplace, to sit next to Patrick and reapply his dressing. The man looked apologetic, and said something, Patrick assumed "sorry." He didn't know how to reply. At last Fionula spoke to him, in her normal tone of voice.

"I was telling them about our capture, and how you fought bravely, like a proper son of heroes. And then I told them of how you rescued us from the taraigeacht..." she paused realising that he didn't know the word, and cast around for a British substitute. She shrugged, and translated inaccurately, if in the correct spirit, "I mean the land pirates. If you keep your head you'll do okay."

Patrick was puzzled. He couldn't remember fighting like the proper son of anything, much less a hero, and couldn't see that he'd played any role in the strange episode of the warriors on the road. On that day he had been feverish and ill, and he had almost wondered if the whole experience had been one of his dreams.

"Why did he slap me?"

"That was a gesture... you know, a pat on the back. Well done. He didn't realise you were hurt there. The old mother told him off, and he apologised."

"Tell him... that's alright."

Fionula spoke again, and the man grinned. Patrick closed his eyes.

"Why are there so many here? Is it feeding time?"

"This is the living quarters. The slaves sleep here."

"So many?"

There had been many more in the belly of the fish, now that he thought of it, but that seemed such a long time ago...

He blinked, and began to tremble, realising that his mind was slipping again. "Oh God," he said, "don't let me go away again tonight."

"What are you doing?" Fionula hissed. "Stop talking to your god."

"It's happening again," he whispered feverishly, "I can feel myself going."

Fionula sucked her breath in, anxiously, then turned and spoke to the old woman. Turning back to Patrick she said, "she's going to make you some medicine. It should help you sleep."

He looked at her puzzled. "Why are you here?" Where were they? He couldn't remember.

She groaned. He had that look on his face.

"You're here too…" Patrick whispered, "oh, that's bad. That's very bad. So it swallowed you too?" He pushed his head into the ground, and started to pray, urgently, into the rushes on the floor. Fionula looked concerned, and started to speak to him. From a very long way off he heard her voice.

"Patrick, Patrick, what swallowed me? What are you talking about?"

"We're in the belly of the Monster."

"Oh, by the great mother, don't go there again. Patrick, you're not in a fish, you're in a house, on a farm, in Ireland."

"Not a fish," he whispered. "A snake, a great black snake. Oh God, God have mercy on me. God have mercy on us all."

Fionula looked around, and shook her head apologetically at the other inhabitants of the room. She said something, and the old woman clucked, bent over her bowl preparing a mixture. But for Patrick the scene was becoming increasingly unreal as he sank deeper and deeper into the belly of the snake. When the Man walked over the threshold of the serpent's teeth Patrick screamed.

CHAPTER SEVEN

After a time, Patrick got better. The old woman was right; despite his night terrors he was strong enough to do more than card wool. Even so, she kept him under her care for as long as she could, and the period of his recovery was a peaceful time that he would remember with regret in later years. Twice she had drained the pus from the whip marks, but the open blisters never got infected, as she had originally feared, and eventually they healed over, with tight new skin. He was able to wear a tunic without it burning, and he had even got used to the ridiculous pants these people wore.

"Who had the idea for these things," he grumbled, the first time he managed to put them on without tripping over. The old woman pursed her withered lips in what might have been a mocking smile, and said, "the horsemen. And you'll be glad of the warm legs in winter."

Bad news came soon enough. A few weeks after their arrival Fionula came weeping to him as he sat by the river carding wool, and told Patrick that she would no longer be sleeping with the main body of slaves.

"Why, what's happened?"

"The master wants me."

Patrick groaned. "I'm sorry... is there nothing we can do?"

"No, I can't keep cutting my leg. The women here know that trick. One of them has told him."

"Why would anyone tell him that?"

"I suppose so that he'll leave her alone."

Patrick shook his head, disappointed more at the betrayal of women than the cruelty of men. He'd learned to expect the latter. "I'll pray for you,"

"What, to that god of yours? What will he do for me?"

"I don't know."

"You're a good boy Patrick. Oh," she keened, sharp like a bird. "What will happen to you now, without me to look after you?"

"Don't worry about me."

"At least you have the old mother to look out for you now."

"What's her name, by the way?" Patrick knew it wasn't the time to ask, but it had been bothering him. "I don't know how to ask yet in Irish."

Fionula looked embarrassed. "She doesn't have a name."

"What? How can she not have a name?"

"She's been a slave all her life, nobody thought to name her. Some of them call her Morrigan after the battle goddess, or Cailleach, which is her title as a wise woman and doctor, but I call her old mother, since it's a less fearful name than those others, and I think she likes it."

Patrick shook his head in anger, doubly angry that Fionula was being taken from him in this abrupt and violent way, and that any human being could live a nameless life. "What's the master's name?" he asked, bitterly.

"Declan," she said, with a contemptuous curl of her upper lip.

"I'll pray for you, Fionula" he promised. He took her hand, and squeezed it. What could he do to comfort her? He cast about in his head for a story.

There it was. "There was a woman once called Sarah," he said, his voice dropping into story. "Very beautiful she was. She was taken from her husband by the King of Egypt."

"What happened?"

"The wombs of all the women in the Kingdom were closed, and the King could not touch Sarah. So he returned her to her husband, unharmed."

"Would your god do this for me?"

Patrick looked at her, and something fierce came over him, chilling him to the bone. Instead of answering her he clasped his hands together, wrist to wrist and palm to palm, as though they were still cuffed. Sinking to his knees he looked up to heaven. "God," he pleaded skyward, and closed his eyes. "Father God, please, don't let the man Declan touch Fionula. Don't let this man touch your daughter Fionula."

There was a silence and Patrick came to with a shock. He felt as though something strange had happened, as though he had given a promise that wasn't his to give. How could he make poor Fionula hope that the man wouldn't assert himself on her? It was the man's legal right, nothing could be done about it. What on earth had Patrick been thinking? He blinked, sickened by his own stupidity, and focussed his eyes on Fionula again. She was staring at him, with something like awe.

"You called me a daughter of your god."

"You are so."

"Inion Dia? How can I be his daughter?"

"He made you. He saw you in your mother's womb, He knew you before the world was made."

The woman stood in the dappled sunlight beneath the trees, and put her fingers, shaking, to her lips. "A daughter of God?"

Patrick closed his eyes in shame. Her hope was the worst thing; he knew he'd betrayed her. When she was raped tonight it would be his fault, she would never believe in the King of Heaven now. "A daughter of God," he said, wretchedly. When he opened his eyes she was gone. Still kneeling, he groaned, and prayed from a breaking heart for his friend Fionula.

That night the Bhean Uasail came smiling to the hut, and called him out.

"I came to thank you."

"For what do you thank me?"

"My husband thought to take a lesser wife." Patrick nodded, anxious for news of Fionula. The Bhean Uasail smiled, and laughed. "I hear you withered him."

Patrick raised his eyebrows. "I didn't do anything to him, my Lady."

"Your kinswoman tells me that your god does not approve of men taking many wives."

"That is true. A man should love his wife like he loves his own flesh, and be prepared to die for her. So the book of God says."

"Well, I like this god of yours. It seems he fights for his women. Your kinswoman Fionula will be returned to you soon."

"Thank you my Lady."

"I may come for you again."

Patrick didn't know what to make of that. He simply bent his head, and said, "my Lady."

She smiled in a way that made him uncomfortable. "When you're a little older perhaps."

As she walked away from the hut Patrick saw Fionula in the distance coming toward him. The Bhean Uasail had called her his kinswoman, and as he watched her break into a run his heart leapt with joy, knowing that she was now a sister of his in the Lord. Her hair flew out behind her like a triumphant banner, and she was laughing as she ran. He threw his arms around her, and hugged her hard, spinning her off her feet and kissing the top of her head. For the first time he realised how much taller than her he was, this woman who had walked at his side like an angel. He felt very tenderly toward his guardian, as a son would feel to a mother, or a brother to a sister. She was his kinswoman indeed.

"Thank you, thank you, thank you..." she was breathless with running, joy radiating out of her like heat from a fire. "Your God is wonderful! You must tell me about Him."

That night, before the Man came to silence them all, Fionula breathlessly told the story of her rescue from the master's attention. The women leaned forward sympathetically, the men sat uncomfortably with their legs crossed, trying not to draw attention to themselves. Fionula was so excited that she talked loudly, bright and swift. Patrick could barely follow her speech in Irish, and she would glance at him apologetically and translate so that he could keep up.

"I was terrified, as you can imagine. I mean, I know you've told me that he's not a harsh man," she glanced to the other women as she spoke, "but at my time of life I've had enough of being used like that. I mean, I must be thirty and some five or six by now. And there's always the risk of a baby, and then who knows what will happen to the poor child? And every one of them could kill you. So, I was scared, and of course there's always the Bhean Uasail here, you can tell she wants him to herself... and well, why shouldn't she? She had him first." The women nodded, and Fionula continued.

"Anyway, so there I was, and he just stood there and told me to take my clothes off so he could have a look at me, you know the way they do, and I kept thinking of what Patrick told me about the King of Egypt." There was a brief intermission while she explained the story of Sarah to her listeners, then she continued. "And I thought, if God could stop a man like *that* from taking a beautiful woman... for this woman Sarah was beautiful... wasn't she so, Patrick? You said she was beautiful?" Patrick agreed that indeed, she was very beautiful, it said so in the book of God. "Well, if He could stop the King of *Egypt* from taking Sarah, He could surely stop this farmer from taking me. And may the Lord God strike me dead if this isn't the truth, I looked at him when he told me to take off my clothes, and I said to him, 'I can't do that, my Lord. I have another Master, and I belong to Him.'"

The women sat back with a shared gasp of astonishment at her audacity, then began to laugh and clap.

"And he got up off the bed, angry with me, and raised his hand. I thought for sure he was going to strike me. But then he stopped dead in his tracks, just looking at me... and I could see his eyes getting bigger and bigger, and fear in his face. So I just stood there, and he sat back down, and said, 'What Master are you talking about?' And I said, the God of Patrick, the God Who's above all the other Gods, Who made the sky, and everything in it, and the earth, and the water, and every living thing.'"

"And what did he say?" one of the women asked.

"He didn't say anything at first. He just sat looking at me, then he shouted at me, 'out, get out, and take your terrible God with you.'"

The women again laughed and applauded, but the men it appeared were not nearly as enthusiastic about the story. Patrick noticed them edging away from him, and giving him looks of distrust. It hardly mattered though, Fionula was safe. Having finished her story, she now turned around, and again flung her arms round Patrick. "Thank you."

"Thank God," he replied.

And then something happened that he would remember all his life, right to his deathbed. As an old man, looking back on the shape of his years, he would sometimes see this moment as clearly in his prayers as if it were happening in front of him, as though it had been snatched out of the ordinary passage of the days and pressed, like a flower, between the pages of a book. Fionula got to her knees, lifted her hands, and prayed. Right there, in front of her country men and women, without any shame, a child talking to her Father. And Patrick, who had been so afraid of God, who had felt so crushed and terrified beneath the weight of His gaze, knew at once that he too was beloved. Young and old, Patrick would pray, for the rest of his life, and be drawn back to this moment out of time. The time he knew. As a slave, and as an old priest he prayed, tears on his face and his heart so big with beauty that he thought it would break in his chest.

That night there were no horrors. Even the Man who had so terrified him was diminished, and Patrick saw only Gill, a lonely, bitter slave sleeping at the door; not a giant, or a demon at all. He even pitied him, and found himself praying for him, that he might be forgiven his sins, snatched from the eternal death by the Mighty God Who delivered his children. For the first time since he had landed in Ireland Patrick slept like a baby, safe in his mother's arms.

It was just as well, for the following day everything changed.

Conchessa woke crying in the night, and Calpornius, half sleeping, threw his arm over her, trying to comfort her. She shook him off, and rolled far over to her side of the bed, her back turned stonily toward him.

After a while she slept again, breathing more easily. Calpornius, however, realised he could not return to sleep. Not tonight. Sighing, he got out of bed, and walked across to the window. Sitting on the ledge he looked West. Somewhere out there his boy might still be alive, and there was nothing he could do to help him. More than anything he wished he could take comfort in God, as his wife and father did.

Conchessa blamed him. He knew it, though she didn't outright say it, yet he felt the cold truth of it in his bones. He should have been there. He should have done – something. And so, Conchessa hated him. There was nobody else for her to rage at; all the clumsily unspoken affection of the years was turning sour. If he could only pray, perhaps his wife would forgive him; if he could only believe that Patrick was coming back.

If only he could only be as unreasonable in his hope as she was.

When Conchessa woke again, she saw her husband sleeping by the window, with his hands clenched in a double fist on his lap. Her heart softened, at what she took to be a gesture of prayer.

She looked West, to Ireland, and prayed for her son, wherever he was.

CHAPTER EIGHT

"Up, get up boy."

Patrick woke with a shock, and saw the Man standing in front of him, a switch in his hand, and a cruel smile on his face. He scrabbled to his feet anxiously, and positioned himself in such a way that the central pole of the hut stood between him and the Man.

"That won't help you boy, the master of the place wants you outside now."

The other slaves had started to awaken, Patrick could hear the women starting to whisper. He forgot the pity he'd felt for the Man when he had prayed the previous night. As his chest began to tighten with fear he remembered only that he had been brutalised by him. His heart was beating like a drum, and sweat had broken out on his skin. Like an obedient slave he said nothing, but did not move.

"Well, it's all the same to me." The Man grinned wolfishly, and grabbed Fionula by the hair. "If you don't come out, I'm sure the master will be happy enough for this one to take your punishment instead."

"Leave her alone," Patrick whispered, "I'm coming."

The Man let go of Fionula's hair, kicking her to the rushes. Patrick bent his head beneath the threshold and stepped out into the early dawn. The sun was still below the horizon, and the air was very chilly. The master of the place was standing under a spreading beech tree. Patrick had never seen him so close before. He was a tall man, taller than Patrick, with blunt features, long chestnut hair that looked black in the early morning, and a rust coloured beard flecked with silver. He had murder on his face. Automatically Patrick started to pray. The master's blue eyes bugged in his head, and he roared at him, "Stop that!" At the same moment the Man struck him from behind, bringing the switch hard into the crook of his knees so that his legs folded and he went sprawling on the wet grass.

"Bind his arms," the master commanded, and Patrick suddenly had the horrible fear that they intended to rape him. He twisted on the earth, and threw himself at the Man's legs. The Man, not expecting Patrick to fight, fell over on his back, sending up dust and shouting in surprise. Patrick jumped to his feet and made to run, before being tackled from behind and hitting the ground once again. He looked up, dazed, and saw one of the horse slaves standing over him, grimly satisfied. This was one of the men who had looked so uncomfortable the night before. It suddenly dawned on Patrick that he had no friend here, other than the women. Every one of the men could be relied upon to see him as a mutual enemy, a potential threat to their virility – regardless of whether they were slave or free. He tried to think of some way to plead for pity, but all the scraps of language he had gathered together scattered, and he could only say in British, "oh God, oh God, help me."

"He's still praying," the horse slave cried out to his master in alarm, and kneeling on Patrick's chest struck his mouth. "Stop that," he said, as Patrick twisted and bucked to free himself, still calling out to God. "Stop that right now." Someone else had grabbed his legs to keep him from kicking. Patrick closed his eyes, and wondered if he was finally going to be blessed with death. With a sudden sense of release he went limp. "If you want to kill me, then kill me, God," he whispered. "Just help me to bear it." Rough hands grabbed his arms, and wrenched them over his head; his wrists were bound together. He heard someone say, "string him up." He recognised the phrase because the old woman had used it, asking him to string up chickens and rabbits for the pot. *This is it then,* he thought, as he was dragged to his feet. *Maybe the stories are true and they'll cook me.* "Oh God," he whispered, "help me to stand it, don't let me dishonour you in my death. God give me strength."

"He's still praying," the horse slave said, in a voice approaching hysteria, "Somebody stop him praying."

There was a blow, and the world went red before fading to black. The horse slave had his wish. The praying ceased.

Patrick woke to a new and terrible pain. His arms, shoulders, upper back, and lungs were burning. He opened his eyes and tried to scream, but couldn't get the breath for it. His arms were over his head, and he seemed to be swinging. The rest of the slaves were standing in a semi circle, looking at him. The master had gone. Patrick took swift sharp breaths, and frantically swung his feet, questing for a place to stand. Finally, on tiptoe, he managed to find a patch of earth to rest his feet. It eased the pain in his chest and he was able to breathe more easily.

He realised that not much time had passed. The sun was still below the horizon, and he could see the blackened grass where they had fought and struggled in the dew. The women were weeping. The men were looking uncomfortable, trying not to meet his gaze.

Patrick could feel someone's presence behind him. He heard breathing, and realised it was the Man. He tried to turn around to face him, but lost his foothold and swung instead, burning. When he finally put foot to earth again the Man was standing in front of him. He held the slim wooden switch in his hand, and started to slowly strike it against his palm.

"The master would like you all to see this," he informed the assembled servants, reminding Patrick, incongruously, of the narrator at a comedy. "He would like you all to remember what happens to those who displease him."

Carefully the Man took a couple of steps back. Then he rushed at Patrick, and struck him with the switch. The pain was excruciating, and with the first blow he wet himself. His head arched back, and all his breath was gone. He couldn't believe anything could be as bad as the first strike, but each blow compounded the agony. He prayed earnestly for death.

Death did not come.

Hours later they cut him down. At some point a merciful woman had come and put a block of wood under his feet to ease his stance, but even so, by the end of the ordeal he could barely keep his balance, his whole body was in so much pain. He didn't move when they finally released him and carried him into the hut. That night there was no storytelling, nor laughter, nor applause. The men and women were lined up on different sides of the hut, like opposing armies. The women circled Patrick, as though defending a fallen warrior. The men sat, muttering, in grim but guilty triumph on the far side of the fire. The women took it in turns to sit by him until dawn, the old mother clucking like a hen as she rubbed life back into his arms, while tears got lost amongst the wrinkles of her ruined face. Fionula did not sleep at all, but noiselessly wept. When he could speak Patrick tried to comfort her, but to no avail. Mute, she shook her head, and shook her head. She was convinced that this was her fault, and nothing could console her. In the end Patrick commended her to God, having no energy to speak or think. He lay dumb, and exhausted, sleepless with pain until dawn broke over the farm.

Gill took an especial satisfaction in relaying the news to the praying brat that he was being sent out into the fields to tend the sheep. The boy stood before him, his arms hanging slack by his sides, with that infuriatingly passive gaze that had so annoyed him on the journey from the market. "Anything to say, Holy Boy?"

The boy said nothing. Gill knew perfectly well the brat was afraid of him. His body was clenched as if expecting a blow. *Good, the slave knows his place,* Gill thought. "So. You know all about sheep, do you? No questions?" He laughed, scornfully, and turned to go.

The old Morrigan spoke out.

"How's he supposed to work the sheep? The boy's never known such work, he'll lose himself or half the flock before the week's done."

Gill glared at her. "Let him speak for himself if he needs to know something."

"Are you as foolish as your face? How can he speak after what you did to him yesterday?"

Anger suffused Gill's features, and his hands clenched. He could do nothing about this woman's insolence. She had attained the sort of years that made her immune from punishment. If he touched her he would bring a curse on his head; he and she both knew it. He took a deep breath, calmed himself. Forcing a smile he nodded his head to her, conceding the point.

"I'm not a fool, Old Mother," he said, respectfully. "You know we've brought in a sheep slave from beyond the woods. He's being hired out to us until the boy knows the job. I'm sure you'll agree that's an acceptable solution."

"Pity you didn't think of it last year. The poor little German boy wouldn't have been taken by wolves."

"Well, Mother, we don't all have your wisdom, to be sure. We live and learn."

She looked at him scornfully, and he wilted under her gaze. Grunting he made a dismissive gesture. "I've got plenty of work to do. You make sure he's out to meet the sheep man by the time the sun is crowning the hill." He walked off briskly, as though dismissing her. As soon as he was out of sight, however, he stopped, and thumped fist to palm.

"May her bones rot," he cursed, "why is there always some old crow-dog of a witch everywhere I work, thinking she owns the place?" That was the kind of thing that could take all pleasure out of the day. He shut his eyes, forcing himself to regain control of his emotions. He reminded himself of all the positives. After all, things weren't as bad as they had been after the last boy died - he was back in favour, and that British brat had been put in his place. There were plenty of things to be glad of. "Everything is good," he reassured himself. Hearing it aloud he felt better. He opened his eyes and smiled. Yes, things were good. The brat was finally being put to work, the women were afraid, the men looked up to him. He started to walk again, this time whistling.

Things were just as they should be. All was right in the world.

CHAPTER NINE

Patrick had learned that the sheep were kept high on the mountain. It made it harder for potential raiders to carry them off, and a sheep could bring wealth from land that had no other use. You couldn't grow food on the barren top, but a sheep could grow fat in the summer, and bring wool, and meat and cheese. The main dangers to them from were accident, the extremes of winter, wolves – even the occasional bear. Patrick's family had kept sheep. Never once had he given a thought to the sheep boy. Thinking of it now he realised that he hadn't even *known* they had a sheep boy. When he asked her, Fionula assured them that they did. Patrick was ashamed of his ignorance. He had never realised before how sheltered his life had been. All the while he had been sulking over his studies, skipping school so that he could run with his friends to the comedies, mocking his grandfather's efforts in the Church, teasing his mother, ignoring his father – all that time they had been protecting him from such a life as this.

Patrick trudged past the tilled land, and began to clamber over the rocky patches, as he made his painful assent. Gill had beaten him soundly, excruciatingly, but carefully. Although the weals on his back stung, the man had not drawn blood. The pain of being strung up was the main part of his punishment. Gill knew how to inflict pain, without destroying the master's property.

"Keep your eyes open, you'll see the shepherd," Fionula had told him, as he stiffly prepared himself for the journey. She looked dull eyed and wretched, speaking to him in British, before giving him the word in Irish. "But don't call yourself 'shepherd,'" she warned, earnestly. "If it gets back to them, they'll be angry and think you're above yourself. A shepherd is a freeman who owns his sheep. You're a sheep boy; you're going to see a sheep man. He'll tell you what to do."

Patrick had nodded, then kissed her chastely on the cheek. "I'll see you soon, Sister, á Shiun," he said to her in Irish, and walked off before either of them could see the other crying. He had no idea what his duties would involve, and was not even sure where his food would come from, or where he would sleep at night. His whole upper body ached. His back and torso still burned and when he tried to raise his arms they flopped like wet cloth, dropping to his sides, slack and useless as dead fish. His wrists were swollen and bleeding where they had been bound, the recently healed injuries from the cuffs opened once more. He was relieved to find his fingers still moved. He supposed that this must mean there was no permanent damage, but all he wanted to do was sleep. Even that had been denied him the night before, his anxiety and pain having been so great.

He came out of the soft bowl of land that contained the tilled earth and dwelling places, and began the ascent of the rocky incline that led to the sheepfold. From a distance it hadn't looked terribly steep, but weakened as he was he quickly lost his breath and began to struggle. Doggedly he followed a narrow, uneven path that had been trodden out by the sheep. He could see the sheep already, white dots on the green, at a fair distance, above and ahead. Amongst them he had spotted a small figure that was, no doubt, the man who currently tended the flock. Patrick put his head down, determined, and painfully inched up the hill.

As he made his way he began to pray. It was a relief to pray aloud, as all men prayed, as he had done in the days before the Man beat silence into him. He was tired, so tired, and could not form words easily, and so he prayed simply, as the Lord had taught his disciples, as his mother had taught him on her knee. Struggling up the path he turned each word over in his mind, like the precious stones that they were, and gradually fell into awe, marvelling that he'd never noticed before how beautiful and strong this prayer was.

'Our Father...' *Yes, He is our Father,* Patrick realised, slipping on a rock, and landing hard on his right knee. *He belongs to us, and we belong to Him, and He loves us. A father can be angry with his son, and can chastise him, but a father can never stop being a father, and a son can never stop being a son.*

'Who is in Heaven...' Patrick rested, caught his breath, looked up at the sky, so blue it hurt his eyes. Heaven... *He is looking at me from Heaven now.*

'Holy is Your Name...' *Holy...* Patrick closed his eyes, and heard the gulls calling, and remembered his grandfather reading something from the Book of God, that the birds cried out to God and He answered them. He wished now – he wished – *If only then I had the sense of a wild gull,* he wished, *and known to praise Your Name.*

'Thy Kingdom Come...' *Come soon.* Patrick squeezed his hands in urgent prayer. *We're chained to the world; shatter those chains.* He continued to climb, the sweat of his brow drying in the freshening wind.

'Thy Will be done...' That one... that one was a mystery. Patrick turned his mind to the problem. He had *never* done God's will. Nobody did – everyone sinned. *And yet... who can do other than Your will? Even Judas did Your will.* Patrick's breath caught with sudden knowledge, and he shivered. *Even the devil, when Christ was nailed to the cross. How could there be resurrection without death?* With a shock Patrick realised that even when he wilfully rebelled he had done God's will. Despite his rebellion, maybe even because of it, Patrick now knew the Living God. Whether anyone obeyed Him or not, God had all things in His hands.

'On Earth as it is in Heaven.' Patrick's gaze dropped from the heavens, and looking at the vibrant grass, he listened to the bleating of the sheep – nearer now. *Earth.* Then he turned his face back up to the dizzying sky, and smiled. God's Will *would* be accomplished on earth, he knew that now... for God was God, and what He desired would be accomplished, despite all the malice of the devil and of man.

'Give us this day our daily bread.' Patrick was suddenly overwhelmed with shame that he had doubted for a moment that God would feed him. He remembered the first food that he had eaten on this island, when Fionula had said, "take, eat," and he, obedient, had broken the bread of bitterness, the Lord's Supper. *Thank you, Lord, for the bread of life.*

'And forgive us our sins...' Patrick was panting with exertion now, so he paused for a moment to catch his breath. Closing his eyes, he remembered his sins; in particular *that* one which had preceded the raid on his parents farm. He felt himself shrivel inside with sorrow, and wondered if his family knew. If so, they would consider him damned, not knowing that God had snatched him from his sin. It seemed impossible to him that just over a month ago he had so despised the God of everything that he could have done such a terrible thing. And afterward, his final argument with his family, and poor old Simon coming to talk sense into him. His sin reached up to heaven. No wonder he had been hounded across land and sea, and brought to this. And yet... and yet, not a God of wrath, but of mercy. Mercy...

'As we forgive those who sin against us...' Looking at his bruised and bleeding wrists Patrick remembered the Man, and the Master of the place, what they had done – all the things that had been done to him since he arrived on this island. *None of that is anything,* he thought, *compared to what we did, when we laid hands on the Son of God and nailed Him to a cross.* Christ had forgiven Patrick. *Please, God. Let me forgive them. And if I cannot forgive them, at least let me want to forgive them.*

'And lead us not into temptation...' Patrick knew how weak he was, and how easily he failed when led into temptation. The weight of his sins would crush him, if not for God. *Lord,* he whispered, *don't let me suffer any temptation that's too great for me to bear.* He knew he couldn't stomach it if he did anything that brought dishonour on his Lord. *Please, God. For your Son's sake, don't let me sin against You.*

'But deliver us from the evil one.' Even as he felt his heart sinking with shame at his weakness, at the secret sin which brought him here, he knew that God was a strong and mighty deliverer. Patrick saw in his memory the Snake, and the Giantess, and the grinding teeth flashing in the moonlight, but knew that God was mightier. God would deliver His children from all evil, as He had delivered His children out of Egypt.

"AMEN!" Patrick cried out suddenly, and smiled. They could take everything from him, and they had. He had been naked, and hungry, and out of his mind – yet God had still been with him.

He thought of his lessons, which he had so resented, Simon or his grandfather reading to him from Scripture, and wished again, profoundly, with all his heart that he had paid more attention. "Lord, if you sent me another teacher, I swear I would listen; I would eat Your words like bread. They would be honey on my tongue and strength in my bones."

As he spoke, something rose up in his memory, as though God Himself whispered it to him. Neither height, nor depth, nor hell itself could separate him from the love of God that is in Jesus.

Despite his weakness he knew his body to be light and free beneath God's good heaven. As his prayers continued to fall from his lips he saw in the distance a man with a staff standing among the sheep. Knowing nothing about him, Patrick thought immediately of the good shepherd, and without even realising it his prayers flowed into song.

The man's name was Victoricus, and before long Patrick knew that he was the answer to his prayers. It struck him with wonder that God had answered his prayer for a teacher. That even before he had voiced or felt the need, *this* man had been waiting for him on a foreign hill.

At first sight he was unimpressive. Much shorter than Patrick, broader in the shoulder, and tough. He was a surprisingly ugly man. Even his bald head was wrinkled; sun-browned and spotted with age. His face was nearly as wizened as the old mother's, covered in a wiry white beard, and one eye was milky with blindness. His hands were large, blunt and strong. Wrapped around the shepherd's staff that he was leaning on his fingers looked like knotted roots, themselves almost part of the wood. His muscles were bunched and wiry, and his skin was very brown. He looked amused as he saw the boy approach.

Patrick had stopped singing as he got nearer to the man, and cast about in his head for a suitable greeting. The man smiled, and spoke first, in Latin.

"God's blessing to you, young scholar,"

Not realising that the wind had carried his song ahead of him Patrick was startled to hear the language of the Empire being spoken here, literally right on the farthermost edge of the inhabited world. Puzzled though he was, he replied automatically as he would have done to a school teacher.

"God's blessing to you, Master,"

The man laughed.

"They haven't beaten your manners out of you."

"Not yet. Sir, who are you? How come you to be speaking Latin?"

"How come you to be singing it? And most beautifully might I add. It reminded me of years gone by." The old man smiled, and his one brown eye peered kindly from the wrinkled face. "I'm Victoricus, and like you, boy, I'm a slave. I was captured, it must be at least thirty years ago now. I've lived as a slave for as long as I lived free. But I remember where I came from, and I talk to myself in my own tongue, and recite stories, songs and poems to myself, because I have no desire to lose what learning I ever had. That's how I come to be speaking Latin to you." He leant forward to Patrick and put his finger to his lips. "Listen," he whispered, "you know all sheep speak Greek, don't you?" Patrick looked at him solemnly, and the old man broke into laughter. "Oh, you green child!" He dropped his Latin and spoke in the people's Greek. "I'm teasing you! Come here, tell me about yourself. What do you know about sheep?"

"Well... I know wool and milk and meat come from them. That's about it."

The old man grunted. "At least now you know they understand Greek, so that's a start. Well, you're lucky, you've come just after shearing is finished, and all the lambs are growing. I'll have a little time to get you settled before the hard work begins in winter."

It was hard enough work as it was. A major aspect of the job seemed to be preventing the sheep from wandering off the edge of the cliff. They appeared to have an almost suicidal desire to explore the most dangerous crags, and so Patrick spent much of the first few days in a stumbling trot (the nearest thing he could approximate to a run at this particular point of his recovery) trying to head them off before they plunged to a watery death.

"Why don't we just build a wall, or a fence or something?" he asked, as he stood breathless and sweaty next to Victoricus. The old man looked far calmer than his young protégé. Where Patrick chased the sheep Victoricus called them, and they would turn gently toward him and amble his way. When Patrick called them, the best he could get was a long stare before being ignored, and the worst was that the sheep concerned might take fright and run in exactly the wrong direction.

"A fence would be a very sensible thing to build," Victoricus agreed.

"So why don't we build one?"

"Your master doesn't see the point of it. He's never tended sheep, and doesn't see why he should make our jobs any easier. Besides which, he claims it would be too much bother, an additional expense, and would take his slaves from all the other important jobs he has for them."

"Can I ask a question?"

"Go ahead young man."

"How come when you call the sheep they come to you, and when I call them they fly off like a flock of gulls?"

"The sheep know my voice." The old man looked at him mischievously. "Have you tried calling them in Greek?"

Patrick laughed, then shrugged, and called.

"Come here you cloth eared ninnies, the cliffs are dangerous... did you not know sheep can't fly?"

The sheep stood looking at him ponderously, then turned their backs and wandered off.

"They don't like your accent," Victor joked. Patrick smiled ruefully. For some reason, the old man reminded him of his grandfather. He sent up a prayer for his family, then trotted off to head the sheep away from the crag.

Potitus could not put it off; he had to return to the work of the parish. He could not indulge his grief any longer. It hurt him that he'd collapsed into sorrow and neglected his flock, even though he knew it was only natural that he respond this way.

As well as losing the apple of his eye, young Patrick, on whom all the family's hopes rested, he had lost his best friend, Simon, who had gone to appeal to the boy's conscience. Potitus tried to imagine Simon surviving a raid, and fresh slavery in Ireland; his heart balked at it. The man had been old and ailing. He mourned Simon as one dead, knowing he would see him in heaven.

But as for Patrick... Potitus could not bear the fear that he had died in his sin. He could not stand the hope that he had survived. The hope was worst. His mind would flicker back to it, as he would flick a tongue to an aching tooth, or pick a scab still healing. Every moment something reminded Potitus of his lost grandchild. What must the boy's poor mother be going through?

His daughter-in-law seemed, to the public eye at least, to have recovered herself well. Enough at least that she could run her household as before. But his son... Potitus loved his son, and knew him better than Calpornius had ever guessed. Potitus knew that his son still struggled on alone. He knew that the man did not pray; although he assented to all the credos of the church, even as a deacon, he did not yet know the living God.

And now there was nothing else for Potitus to do other than get on with the work of the Church. There were people to be welcomed into the faith, baptisms, weddings, and the constant beautiful mystery of the Supper. All these things must continue, even though his heart had stopped.

Entering the church for the first time since it's desecration he blinked back tears. It had been how long... two, three moons? In that time Calpornius had done what was necessary, and the women who worshipped there had kept it swept, and cleaned, and prayed quietly. Conchessa had been here, praying for her boy. She did not know what had been done on that altar, in a flagrant act of rebellion. Calpornius had seen it, but did not know that his son had been the culprit.

Oh, what had possessed the boy to sin so? What had he been thinking to commit such a sacrilege? Potitus' heart still flinched at it, fearful that Patrick had died with his sin on his head. What a terrible final act of rebellion that would be.

Would have been, he corrected himself. Conchessa had a point. She had prayed so earnestly for a child, why would God answer her prayer only to let the boy die in his sins?

Perhaps the whole family was being condemned for idolatry. It was possible to love a child more than God, after all. Perhaps they were the culprits, and had loved Patrick too much...

"Stop thinking on it," he spoke aloud, and shook his head, as though he could scatter the obsessive thoughts from his skull. The women had dressed the church for the baptisms later that day. White flowers adorned the plain altar, and a lamp glowed in the centre, smelling faintly of olive oil, and banishing the gloom. He tidied the dropped leaves and petals, and knelt. Heavily he bent his head, planting his elbows on the wooden surface of the altar. Forehead pressed to the cold grainy wood, hands folded over the back of his skull, he prayed.

Then, in the stillness after prayer he waited to hear from God.

He waited a long time, and his thoughts wandered. He had known when he first became a deacon, and every step of the way since then, that to serve God's people was hard work. He could not turn now to his Master and say the work was too hard.

Through the silence one word rose to the surface of his mind, floating on the darkness like a petal. He had his word from God.

He got to his feet stiffly, knees popping. He spoke the word aloud. He had one duty only.

"Endure."

Chapter Ten

The immediate benefit of all of Patrick's toil was that he worked so hard that he slept well at night, with no nightmares or visions. The first night he was so tired that he never made it back down the mountain. He lay on the earth outside the sheep pen, and the next thing he knew it was morning. Despite the fleece Victoricus had thrown over his young protégé, Patrick awoke to discover himself covered in dew. After that the old man made sure that he left in time to reach the slave quarters by dusk. "You might as well sleep in the warm and dry, while you still can. Winter will be on you soon enough."

The worst effect of his duties was that they often forced him to miss meals, since he would leave early in the morning, and return so late at night that often the food from the communal pot was gone by the time he got to the hut. It gradually dawned on him, however, that this did not have to be an unwelcome hardship. After some thought and prayer he decided to follow his Grandfather's example, and began to fast to the Lord.

This was eventually to cause some consternation, not just amongst the other slaves but even among the "big people" when they realised what he was doing. Fionula, who had gradually been gaining stature in the kitchen (a part of the homestead he'd never seen), had taken to bringing him scraps of food – bread, cheese or dried fish, that she would pass to him, hidden in a twist of cloth at the end of the day. On certain days he would thank her, but tell her that he didn't feel like eating. It didn't dawn on him that his refusal to eat might worry her, since he felt strong and healthy enough. However, one day she found time climb the hill, with a message from below.

On seeing Fionula Patrick paused gratefully. Bending at the waist and resting his weight on his knee he took the opportunity to catch his breath. He had been running to keep track of the large ram, who had been amorously bothering the lame ewe.

"The Bhean Uasail is worried about you," Fionula declared, as soon as she was in hearing distance. "I told her you're not eating, and she's sent me with this for you." She unwrapped a bright yellow cloth, and revealed the contents... peeled boiled eggs, a piece of ham, soft bread, cheese, and an apple. Patrick was taken aback by this largesse.

"Thank you," he panted, and rubbed his forehead with the back of his hand. "Do you have water?"

"Yes," she proffered a bottle, and Patrick drank, careful not to get carried away and empty the bottle. He neither wanted cramp, nor to leave her thirsty. There was water near the woods, but she probably didn't have time to find it. Handing the bottle back he smiled, then apologetically pulled a face. "I'm afraid I can't eat that."

Fionula looked concerned. "You're not ill, are you?"

"Not at all. I'm fine." He was about to tell her that he wasn't hungry, and then he realised that this would be a lie. He crinkled his forehead, casting about for something to tell her. It was a difficult question: Jesus Himself had said that people should fast in secret, but also that they shouldn't lie. His moral quandary was solved, however, by Fionula herself, who suddenly guessed his secret.

"You're fasting, aren't you?"

He looked at her apologetically, and made a little shrug of assent.

"I know you tell me about God whenever you can, Patrick," she said in tones of exasperation, "and I do love Him, but I could never understand why your people fast to Him. Why would He ask you to fast?"

"I can't explain it," Patrick admitted. "I just have to do this." He peered into the distance, and spotted Victoricus. "You could bring the food to Victoricus," he said, "Though he lays traps and provides his own food, I'm sure he'd be glad of some dainties."

Fionula looked unhappy. "The Lady commanded me to only give the food to you. If I gave it to someone else it would be like stealing."

"I'm sorry to disappoint her, but I can't eat that." He smiled at her, then bent forward and gave her a quick kiss on the crown of her head. It had been an unexpected pleasure to see her in the day. "You're looking well. I'm glad of it." He straightened, and saw that the ewes were straying too near the woods in their efforts to avoid the ram. The woods, he knew were wolf territory, and though they were more dangerous in winter, he didn't feel happy to see the sheep so close to them. "I'm sorry, I have to go now. They'll get themselves lost if I don't catch them." Quickly he sprang off, and forgot about the food as he concentrated on the sheep instead.

Fionula stood watching him, with the expression of a mother observing a foolish child. "Romans," she declared, although she hadn't thought of him as Roman in a long time. "Not Romans," she corrected herself. "Men! Never thinking of anyone else." Grumbling she turned and began her descent again. "I climbed all this way for nothing!"

When he got back that night he realised that something was wrong, the moment he lifted the leather door flap and bent his head through the entrance. The slaves were looking at him distrustfully. Fionula was already sitting by the fire, and there was no trace of irritation on her face, only anxiety. She looked up at him, with frightened eyes, and began speaking to him in British, as she always did when she wanted to keep something private between them.

"I'm sorry Patrick," her words were rapid and clipped with fear; "I didn't know what to do. She was angry when I came back with the food, and she's going to want to talk to you."

"She didn't hit you, did she?"

"She did not. She no longer hates me that way, since her husband leaves me alone. But she was very angry. I don't know what she'll do."

Patrick felt wretched. Why hadn't he just taken the food, and hid it? Or brought it to the old man? Why make a fuss about it? "I'm sorry," he apologised, "I wasn't thinking..."

"I know that," Fionula said bluntly. "But now she thinks that you're fasting against her, as a challenge."

Patrick opened his mouth to ask a question ("what on earth does that mean?" sprang immediately to mind) but before he could speak he heard soft footfalls outside the hut.

"She's here," Fionula whispered. Patrick was still standing by the doorway, slightly bent over beneath the low roof, and peering round he could see every eye was on him. *Please God, don't let them thrash me again,* he prayed silently. Saying nothing he pushed back through the door flap and exited the hut.

The Bhean Uasail was standing there with a basket, covered with the yellow cloth.

"Holy Boy," she said, "I hear that you are fasting against the house. I've bought you food, and ask pardon for any wrong done to you."

"Lady," he said, truly puzzled. "I'm not fasting against your house. I don't understand what you are talking about."

"Before you were sent to work with the sheep you received a harsh beating for protecting your kinswoman. So I have heard. Is this not why you are fasting against us?"

"My Lady, it is not." *What is this 'fasting against' that she's talking about,* he wondered. There was obviously some kind of misunderstanding here.

The woman looked flustered. "What else is there? You've been treated as any other slave. That is simply the law. There must be slaves, or the world will fall into chaos."

Patrick nodded, silently affirming that this was so. *Until the Lord returns and breaks all chains,* he thought, but did not say. To say such a thing would sound like rebellion, something so dangerous it would turn the world on its head. He was unsure enough of his footing as it was. He might one day be able to speak to this woman of the coming Kingdom and the King – but today was not that day.

"Is it the manner of your capture? Is it the discipline of the men? It's not my business how my husband or his man treat the male slaves, but if they've harmed you..."

Patrick flushed with shame. The idea that she thought his fasting could have anything to do with the treatment he had endured at the hands of Gill made him sick. Though he still sometimes woke in fear of the Man, it only lasted an instant these days. The keeper of the slaves had simply become less fearsome, since Patrick now spent most of his time on the pasture with the sheep and hardly saw him. He knew Gill might have power to beat him, but he knew also that the power was delegated, that Gill himself could only do what the master told him to. "No, my Lady, I'm not fasting against you, or your husband, or your house, for any reason."

"So why are you fasting?"

"I'm fasting to my God."

She blinked, and took a step back. Then unexpectedly she laughed.

"To your god? Your complaint is against him?"

"I have no complaint against Him."

"So, you are not accusing us?"

"I am not." He felt like Theseus in the maze. He should have gone into this conversation with a thread, he thought, he couldn't puzzle his way out of it. "I'm not accusing anyone," he reiterated. "I'm simply... fasting. God has called me to fast for a time."

She looked at him concerned. "You're a strange boy. You love your god, and yet you're sitting at his gate fasting against him. Why would you anger him?"

"I wouldn't anger Him. I don't understand what you're saying."

"Ah, it is a terrible pity," she said, and her voice became soft as butter. She reached out a hand, and touched his face. "The slaves are right. You look like you're turning into such a fine strong man, and yet your god has ridden you to madness."

Patrick was momentarily speechless. He'd never heard of such a response to a religious fast before. As it happened, he had fasted long enough, and had thoroughly intended to eat something tonight, but now he felt he couldn't in all conscience allow them to think he'd been reasoned out of a foolish choice.

"My Lady..." he felt the weight of the foreign language on his lips, and stumbled over the words, "I'm not mad."

"Will you sit and eat with me?"

"Not tonight, my Lady."

"Your god won't let you?"

"There's no compulsion, my Lady, I simply choose not to break my fast."

"Not with me?"

He swallowed, and blinked. He was afraid of the consequences if he offended her, but he could not now back down. "Not for anyone would I break a vow to God."

"I see," she said gently, with a condescending pity in her eyes. "You are under gaese. Goodnight, poor Holy Boy," she said, and turned to go. "I hope you'll eat tomorrow."

All this talk of food had made Patrick feel far hungrier than normal at the end of a fast. But more than anything, he was simply confused. As he stooped to go back into the hut he felt more keenly than ever since his capture that he was in an utterly alien culture. He had no idea what on earth the woman had been talking about.

When he did eat, he supplemented his diet with whatever he could find on the steep slopes. There was plenty of sheep milk, of course, which he found surprisingly palatable. In addition to that, the old man showed him which leaves and roots were good, how to soak worms in salty water, so that the earth came out, and how best to cook snails in butter and wild garlic. He warned him not to eat mushrooms. Patrick knew that there were witches in the Empire who used mushrooms in their religious rituals, and he was more than happy to avoid them. Despite his best efforts there were days when he gnawed bark for hours at a time to stave off hunger.

Despite the hunger though, there were wonderful surprises. During his forays into the forest for firewood there were discoveries of honey, and honey was better than gold. After dividing the spoils with Victoricus he would bring the remainder into the valley, where the other slaves rejoiced in it. For a while even the horse slave would forget his distrust and smile at him. The old woman would make candles from the wax, wrapping them around rushes, an astonishing innovation that he had never encountered before. The fragrant smell of their burning mingled with that of the pungent turf, and made even the hut seem luxurious. With his eyes closed he was in his grandfather's little church, watching the glowing gold of the oil lamp on the altar. Christ was light in the darkness, leading His people through the dark flood, and Christ's presence was a sweet aroma that filled the air, not seen, but perceived and known to those that loved Him. At such times Patrick felt that all he had to do was open his eyes, and he would be home.

On the mountain there was plenty of pure running water, springing straight from the earth, in which he would bathe his hands, feet and face. He drank straight from the head, as the sheep waded lower down in the shallow stream.

Later in the more fruitful autumn, berries and nuts from the woods were a welcome addition to his feast days. He bitterly regretted that he had no idea which day was Sunday, the day that the Lord rose, but even though he worked seven days a week he picked one day, arbitrarily, to be his day dedicated to the Lord. On that day he would rise earlier to go to the pasture, and rejoice in the morning. "The Lord is risen," he would say, as he turned to face the rising sun. When the Lord came, that was the direction from which He would come. "'As the lightning flashes from the East to the West, so will be the coming of the Lord.'"

The day he had chosen for Friday was always a fast day, because that was the day on which the Lord had died, and on his Saturday he fasted too, because the Lord had been in the ground. But on a Sunday he would eat well, and bring bread up to Victoricus, so they could break it together. On one such Sunday, as he was leading the ram by his horn from the edge of the forest, he found a nest lying hidden in a bush, with a single, out of season egg lying alone. Pitying the mother he left it untouched.

Fasting seemed to be good training for hunger. On days he ate he was actually hungrier than days he fasted, though at times he feared he would always be hungry. He wasn't aware of it himself, because it was happening gradually, but he was getting taller, filling out in the shoulders; his muscles, though thin, were hard and wiry. One day he found himself early in the morning passing the master, and he realised to his shock that he was now a little taller than him. His voice was also beginning to change, cracking high, and lurching low, with no control. Although he continued to pray constantly when he walked alone, he didn't sing so often, since even to himself his voice was strange.

He was also getting more accustomed to the sheep, and they were more accustomed to him. Now when he called they came more often than not. He informed Victoricus that he'd been mistaken, and all sheep spoke British. The old man had become a true consolation to Patrick, particularly when he realised that he knew the Book of God. Even after all his years in captivity, Victoricus cherished the stories, and would recite them, word for word. When Patrick wasn't running around after the sheep the Victoricus would tell him tales from the old and new Scriptures, and Patrick would laugh, delightedly, at some of the bizarre twists of fate that God allowed His people to go through.

"God has a sense of humour," Victoricus told him. "Did you know that Moses had a stammer?" "He did not," Patrick declared, though he knew his friend wouldn't have said it if it weren't true. "Did he really?" And Victoricus told the story of how Moses surmounted all odds, including his 'uncircumcised lip' to best Pharaoh and all his magicians. Patrick lapped it up like milk. There were times when he was down in the valley, speaking Irish with the other slaves, when he felt as though his own lip was uncircumcised. It seemed to him at these times that he knew Moses, that the Patriarch sympathised with his stammering tongue. Patrick had known these stories from his mother's knee, but never before had he loved them so much. His mother had intoned them reverently, in a manner which seemed increasingly dry to Patrick as his childhood had worn on. Victoricus, on the other hand, told the stories with gesture, motion, and many different voices. Pharaoh was arrogant, with the high nasal intonation and supercilious attitude of a Roman official, whereas Moses' stuttering Latin, as Victoricus acted him, was British in accent, and when he spoke to the Israelites he did so in Patrick's mother tongue, as though the Israelites were his own close kin. Despite Victoricus' age he would energetically re-enact battle scenes, dramatic escapes, or David dancing 'like a madman' to the distress of his first wife. The parting of the Red Sea proved a particular success. Victoricus held out his shepherd's crook as though it were a staff, and the sheep parted before him, like the divided ocean. Both man and boy fell over laughing at the comical looks of alarm on the puzzled woolly faces.

At other times Victoricus would talk of the miracles of Jesus, or of His Passion. On those occasions his acting talent would slip. With a broken voice he would recount the story, and more often than not both he and his one man audience would end the tale in tears. Patrick wondered if the old man had ever been an actor, or an orator, but didn't want to ask. Acting was considered a dishonourable profession for a Christian, as was politics, and he had no desire to offend someone who, as the months progressed, he was beginning to love like a father.

One day, while he was cradling a ewe on his lap, examining her hooves and scooping out the muck with a curved pick, Victoricus came toward him gloomily.

"I've had word," he said bluntly, with no cheerful preamble or greeting. "I'm to go back to my master for the winter."

Patrick's heart sank. He had hoped, earnestly prayed, that he wouldn't lose Victoricus so soon. "I won't know what to do," he said. "Do you *have* to go?"

"I'm afraid I do have to go, Son." He took Patrick's hand, and squeezed it distractedly. "Don't worry, you will know what to do. You know how to clean their little wounds now, to make sure they don't get worse, and you can trim their feet. They've come to trust you, and they won't wander so far in the snow."

Patrick looked away, almost angry. He was ashamed of himself. He knew he was selfish, that the old man shouldn't be up on this hill anyway at his time of life, but he had come to rely on him.

"Son," Victoricus said gently, "it will be well for you. They don't fear you anymore." He sighed. "Your two great dangers are wolves and the weather. The wolves can get desperate when it's freezing, and they sometimes come right up to the sheepfold, so you'll have to be prepared to fight them off."

Patrick nodded his understanding, dumbly.

"Remember what I told you," Victoricus continued, "Mark the points I showed you with your urine, as the wolves do. That will tell them the place is protected, and it often works to keep them out."

"I know, you told me that." Patrick thought it a very strange practise, but Victoricus knew more about wolves and sheep than he did. Things that would have seemed impossible, even crazy when he was in Britain made a strange sense to him now.

"Whatever you do," Victoricus urged, "you will have to be careful not to get lost in the snow. Also, if you can't see far in the weather, be very careful not to go over the edge of the cliff. Better to keep the sheep penned in for days on end than have them stumbling around in a blizzard. But you know all that."

"I know. I'll be careful." Patrick blinked tears from his eyes, as he continued to clean the ewe's hooves.

"If you do get caught out in the snow, huddle in under the sheep for warmth." The old man smiled sadly. "But... don't get caught in the snow."

Finishing his task, Patrick let the ewe go, and got to his feet. He hung his head. "Father," he said, and his voice caught. "I'll miss you."

"And I you, Son. I'll see you in spring, when the lambing starts. Pray for me."

Patrick rubbed his cheeks, finding them wet. "You know I will."

"As I will pray for you." The old man put his arms around him, and they hugged. Then Victoricus sighed, handed the crook to Patrick, turned and walked away.

The family had settled to a new kind of normal. Calpornius was immersed in managing the estate, trying to rebalance the books after the great financial losses the raid had brought upon them. In the first shock of the disaster he had almost overlooked the pecuniary problems; the loss of Patrick overshadowed all else. Now he hid in his work, as though by keeping busy the empty space at dinner could be filled. As deacon, he also helped his father when duty called for it. Potitus had shouldered his burden again, continuing to faithfully serve his congregation. Conchessa had finally stopped weeping. She ran the household as tightly as ever, but she no longer smiled, or laughed, or told Bible stories to the slave women as they sat spinning by the fire.

Calpornius lay awake most nights till early in the morning, oppressed by the wall of his wife's back, turned against him. He would listen to her breathe, to her calling Patrick in her sleep. She woke early these days, and would find her husband ill rested and heavy eyed. They were both tired all the time, but so accustomed to exhaustion that they barely noticed it anymore.

They did not talk. She continued to pray. He felt further away from her with each passing day.

His father dined with them often. He made awkward small talk, describing the lives and prayers of his parish, as though Calpornius was in the least bit interested. But he always knew when to stop. *My father's greatest virtue,* Calpornius thought, *is that he knows when to be silent. When to distract with tales from the town, when to offer comfort.* Sometimes Potitus even made Conchessa smile.

But for the most part, Calpornius found the greatest comfort was to be in silence. Perhaps it was as well that he and Conchessa rarely talked. If they said too much then what was left between them might fracture irrevocably; he did not think he could live with that. Silence remained.

Silence remained, and snow swept the landscape, and frost settled. Everything was hushed by the white drifts.

It would never be summer again.

Chapter Eleven

It seemed as though when Victoricus left he took the last of autumn with him. The following day the weather turned cold. Patrick no longer went back to the slave quarters to sleep. As the only sheep slave his duty was to stay with the flock and guard them with his life. He had been given a spear, in case of wolves, but wasn't sure if he could use it. It reminded him unpleasantly of the night he was captured.

The sheep pen was a high wall that looped around on itself into a circle, with a narrow doorway, wide enough for only one sheep to pass through at a time. The wall was woven tight between upright wooden poles, each sharpened to a point at the top, and the weaving was coated in daub. Patrick supplemented the spikes on the top by stringing twists of rose and blackthorn between them. He knew it wouldn't keep out a determined wolf, but it might make them think twice. That was worth a few pricks, he thought, and the hours of fearful wandering in the neighbouring woods. Since he was alone now he looked for thorns in the night time, when the moon was bright and the sheep were penned in. The woods were a strange world to him; he could have sworn there were phantoms peering at him from the trees, perhaps the dryads of the Greeks. It was all worth it though. After long effort he finally stood back surveying his handiwork, sucking a cut in his thumb.

Foremost amongst Patrick's jobs was the maintenance of this wall. Every morning and night he would walk around it, making sure there were no gaps through which foolish sheep could escape or sly wolves get in. Once a week, two men from the valley would climb the mountain, dragging a hay load with them, to replenish the stores of food for the flock. This would be deposited in a ramshackle lean-to in which were also stored various tools; an axe, picks for the sheep's feet, the shearing blade, a small, sharp knife for trimming them, a long slim blade that Victoricus had told him he didn't have to use yet, a skinny long tube made from bone, sharpened at the edge, used to puncture the abdomen of a sickening bloated sheep, in order to let the air out. These items and the waxed rope took up much of the space, and when the feed came up the mountain there was no room left. On rainy nights Patrick would sometimes wake up resenting inanimate objects, thinking of the tools, more valuable than himself, sheltered in the dry, while he lay shivering on the wet cold ground.

The two fishermen who most commonly brought the feed up the mountain had also found an object for their resentment... unfortunately it was Patrick. Struggling up from the valley with a heavy load was not something they appreciated, although now that the fishing season was over they were often put to hard physical labour. For much of the spring, summer and early autumn they could feel like freemen, working pretty much under their own authority. Although not quite slaves, they were bondsmen, and in winter they felt the pinch of servitude. The sheep slave was an easy target for their resentment. As well as feed for the sheep, they also delivered Patrick's weekly portion of food. On several occasions he saw them pause in their assent, and eat from his rations on the way up the hill. They didn't even try to conceal their thefts, as though they were daring him to make something of it.

Patrick said nothing, not because it came naturally to him, but because Jesus said to turn the other cheek. One of the ewes was still giving some milk, so at least he wouldn't completely starve. Instead of rising to their bait, he would quietly report to them if he needed extra provisions or tools for the maintenance of the wall, or if medical supplies were required for an injured or ill sheep. They would pass on any description of symptoms, and the old mother in the valley would mix together a poultice, or medicament, and send instructions up with the youngest boy, Finn, named after his blond hair.

This boy was honest, and would sometimes smuggle dried apples, cheese or fish up the hill, since he felt sorry for the "Holy Boy." Patrick liked the boy too, and wished that he was not a slave, or if a slave, at least a slave in Britain, in his father's house. There at least he would not be beaten or abused by men like Gill, and he would have good food, someone to teach him his letters. After several weeks of worrying about it, he sent the boy down with a wooden frame to the old mother, and asked her to coat it in beeswax. Puzzled, she complied, and when Finn brought it back up Patrick introduced him to the writing tablet. The boy delighted in this new toy, and on his infrequent visits would sit with a sharp stone, inscribing it with spirals, and stick figures of sheep, little coracles, tall trees. Patrick thought that maybe in the spring he would teach the boy to read and write... though he wasn't quite sure what good it would do.

Apart from these visits he saw nobody, from one week to the next.

Sleep was difficult. Patrick would drop a bar across the entrance of the pen, then lie in front of it, so that the sheep couldn't wriggle through the gap and leave in the night. At first he was always waking. Having enjoyed deep sleep in the slave quarters it was strange for him to get used to constantly startling awake, as some sheep or other tried to test his resolve, and the strength of the makeshift gate. After a few days of the new regime they got used to him, and he was able to sleep better, though still uneasily. Night noises, owls, and wolves in the forest, kept him awake. The wind came in from the sea, incessantly, in a way that could not be felt in the valley below, and sometimes, once every week or so, Patrick heard great men marching in the wind above him, or horses screaming, and hounds, and the sound of battle. At times like this the sheep moved uneasily, and he kept his eyes tight shut, covering his head with his arm as he prayed aloud to the Risen Christ, Who alone was greater than whatever unholy things rode the night.

It wasn't only the unseen armies that kept him awake. Having initially found sleeping in the slave quarters claustrophobic, he now missed the sound of other humans sleeping. Even on quiet nights when the wind did not scream so loudly he found it hard to sleep.

He had no word for this pain that he could speak to himself, but the fact was... It was a simple hurt. He was lonely.

There was, however, one benefit of sleeping with the flock rather than in the slave quarters. He had two fleeces, one to lie on, and one to lie under. For a while at least, he was warmer than he had been in the hut. However, the first night that it rained, he could have wept with exhaustion. It wasn't just that it was wet, it wasn't that it was just cold. It was both these things, but the greater insult, it seemed at the time, worse than anything else was the fact that everything stank of sheep. He didn't smell like a man anymore. *If the wolves find me,* he thought angrily, *they'll probably eat me first, thinking me mutton.* Patrick found himself hating the whole world, himself, the earth, the sky, the stupid itchy fleeces, the endless rain and the bleating sheep.

One morning as he got stiffly to his feet, he forgot to pray. Following the flock out to the pasture he had a sudden overwhelming urge to simply rush to the edge of the cliff and fling himself off it. He shook his head, shocked by the sudden impulse. That would be a terrible sin. He started to pray, counting his Pater Nosters on his fingers, although he no longer believed that his prayers could reach heaven under this unrelentingly grey and wintery sky. God had turned His back on him. He remembered his prayers on this same barren slope, earlier in the year when he'd almost been able to forget he was a slave. He had been able to sing then, spontaneously, for sheer joy. What a fool he'd been, not to see the way things really were. He was nothing but a lost soul, stuck on a rocky spur of land, facing the sea at the very end of the world. Whipped by rain, wind and sleet, he might as well be the poor dead thing his parents no doubt believed him to be. He remembered when he first arrived on this island, that for a while he had thought he had died and gone to hell. There were times as winter came upon the land that he longed for death, no matter what came after. He walked like an old man, hobbled, and the cold got into his bones.

The only consolation he had, beside the infrequent visits of Finn, was Fionula. After the first month she came, like the answer to a prayer, and though she couldn't stay long, she lifted his heart for those brief periods. She warned him that she couldn't visit often, but when she did come up, once a week or so, she would almost always manage to bring him a small crock of soup or stew. On other occasions she would bring dried apples from the winter store. He would horde these gifts as though they were gold, and eke them out, like a miser, making them last. The ewe's milk finally failed, and he was hungry all the time. Although he maintained his weekly fast days from sun up till the following dawn, and carefully preserved his portions, he made up for this caution by eating his allotted rations swiftly when the time for food arrived. He felt somehow that he was skimping on his duties to God. But he was so weak and cold that food consumed most of his waking thoughts.

The first day that snow came, Fionula arrived before it hit.

"I made you a pair of shoes," she said, "put them on quick."

He sat on a boulder, and started to pull the shoes on. They were like leather socks, lined with fleece, and he struggled to pull them over his foot, which had broadened, and grown hard. He hadn't worn shoes since he'd been on this island, and these shoes felt strange and constricting. He knotted them with thongs at the top, to stop them from sliding off his legs, and looked up at her. It occurred to him that he couldn't remember the last time he'd smiled. Then it hit him that he couldn't remember the last time he'd spoken, other calling a sheep, or saying his prayers. He had simply accepted her gifts, wordlessly bolting his food down, then lying on the floor and covering his face with his arm.

"Thank you," he said. He tried to say something else, to express his gratitude to her, but it was too hard. He seemed to have forgotten the art of speech, or perhaps it was just that there was something in his throat, like dry bread, choking him. Instead of speaking he took her hand and squeezed.

She seemed to understand, and kissed his head. "I'll see you next week, Patrick," she said, lifting the empty soup crock. "If God wills it."

With many such signs Patrick knew that she continued in the faith, and he should have been glad of it. But in his heart he was beginning to fear that *he* was no longer in the faith, and never had been. It was no wonder he could barely speak to another human soul. He felt as if his own self had gone out of him.

CHAPTER TWELVE

The snow was hard, harder than he had thought possible. When the wind blew the first flurry of white in from the sea, visibility dropped to almost zero. The white flakes whipped against him, and shredded like shards against his skin. Wearing a fleece as a cloak, Patrick decided that the sheep were far safer staying in their pen than venturing out into that blizzard. They grew restive. The ram in particular became distressed, and started to butt and bother the ewes. Patrick managed to find him in the flock, and dragged him out by his horns, so at least the females could get some peace. Putting a loop of rope around the ram's neck he tied it to one of the fence posts, then dragged a bale of hay to form a barrier against the snow. The ram bucked and bleated, and at some point Patrick was kicked in the head by him. Patrick cursed, thinking for a moment he was blinded, until he realised it was only blood running into his eye. Then he remembered he had cursed, something he hadn't done since his conversion. Realising his error he cursed again, bitterly, and hit himself on the forehead where the ram had clipped him.

It was too much. It was all too much. He tipped his head back, looked up at the blind sky, opened his mouth so wide his jaws cracked and ached. With snow falling on his tongue and in his throat he screamed. He screamed until his voice was raw.

When he had finished the ram had also worn himself out, struggling against his bonds, and Patrick sat curled up next to the obstinate animal, who leaned against the bulwark of the hay. Pulling one of the fleeces over his body he buried his head in the ram's wool, and tried to remember being comfortable and warm, in a room with a roof and a fire. He rested his hand on the ram's forehead, in the dimple between the horns. Wearily he scratched the animal's skull in a soothing, circular fashion, in a way he knew the beast liked. He leaned against the warm fleece, even if it was damp and riddled with fleas. He twined his fingers through the wool and prayed for both of them, for him and the ram. For him, and all the sheep. For all of them, for everyone.

Patrick decided to name the ram David. The ewes also had personalities and names, but it was David with whom he most identified. David, like him, was frustrated by captivity and the weather. The snow lasted a week, and in the end Patrick contemplated actually sleeping in the pen for warmth. The only reason he didn't was that he feared he'd be trampled and hurt, possibly even killed. *Killed by sheep.* He huffed an unexpected laugh, watching his breath smoke into the frigid air. That would almost be funny, he thought wryly, after everything he had been through.

Most nights, Patrick attempted to light a fire. He had built up a store of wood in the previous months, and Fionula brought turf once during the worst of the snow, heroically braving the weather. The fire was not just for warmth, but also to deter wolves. Despite his best attempts though, the fire was too quickly destroyed by the snow and wind, and rarely lasted even the first watch. In all this David was an ally. Patrick would keep him out of the pen, and lie between him and the wall when the wind was really bad. David seemed calmer for the space, and the ewes, though not happy, managed better alone.

On Patrick's chosen Sunday the snow finally stopped falling, and he let the sheep out for the first time.

He almost immediately decided it was a mistake. For a week they had eaten within the confines of their pen, slaked their thirst with snow, and lived in their own droppings. They had been confined so long that they sprang from captivity like young lambs, and ran everywhere. Even the most obedient of them was unresponsive to his call. With dread Patrick imagined every worst thing that could happen... nightfall, sheep in the forest tempting the wolves, a ewe falling over the cliff, one of them stumbling in a rabbit hole and breaking a limb. The landscape looked strange and different in the snow. It would be too easy for someone, even himself, to trip over an unseen obstacle and break a bone.

"Oh God," he prayed, "please don't let them run into danger."

Fortunately hunger brought them back. In the winter there was nothing for them to eat on the mountainside. Having cleaned the accumulated muck of the previous week from their pen, and thrown down a layer of hay for fresh bedding, Patrick ostentatiously started to put out their food. They came trotting eagerly toward him, their fleeces smoke grey against the snow. It amazed him, looking at them now, that he had ever thought them white. He closed his eyes with relief as he counted them all returning. Thirty seven, and the ram.

Patrick thanked God as he pushed each sheep, one by one, into the safety of the fold. He could have sworn that David was acting as a shepherd, and rounding up the ewes for him. He grinned at the ram, and gave him a friendly scratch on the forehead. The ram leaned into Patrick, and rubbed the length of his body alongside him as the last ewe was secured in the pen. Patrick knew enough of sheep that he recognised their equivalent of a hug when he saw it. As he dropped the bar across the entrance he realised from the ache in his face that he was smiling... for the first time in how long? Just getting away from the sheep pen for a few cold and wintery hours had made him feel like a person again. He closed his eyes, and asked God to forgive him for his bad temper and faithlessness, before huddling against the ram, tucked under the fleece for the night.

Winter continued very difficult. At one point, when a later snow was melting, Patrick woke in the night, feverish and hot, struggling to breathe. It had been a very long time since he had seen the Giantess, or the Snake, but tonight he heard the Giantess out there, beneath the cliff, crashing and grinding on the edge of the world. He knew also in his bones that the Snake was in the forest, waiting to devour first the sheep, then the shepherd, then the people in the valley below.

Fionula found him in the morning, as he counted the sheep one by one out of the fold. Recognising he had a temperature, she tried to persuade him to come back to the farmstead. He wouldn't come. For one thing, he knew that a sheep boy who was derelict in his duties was beaten as a matter of course. For another thing, he didn't think he'd make it down the path. More importantly, the sheep were out now, and there was nobody else there who knew their names, how to call them back home, or how to steer them away from the perils that were obscured by the snow. Patrick remembered the crying of the black ewe, Mara, when she had broken her leg that summer in a hidden hole. Then he'd had Victoricus to help him tend her, now there was no-one but himself to help the sheep. He daily filled in every hole he could find, fingers freezing as he tried to make the iron ground safe, but he knew there would always be more. Leaning on his staff he told Fionula that he couldn't bear to think of one of his sheep picking up a serious injury at this time of year. Worried by his gasping voice she urged him to reconsider, but he was adamant. He would not come.

In the end Fionula persuaded the Bhean Uasail to prevail upon her husband for another hand to help until Patrick recovered. For nearly a week young Finn was up on the mountain top with him. Patrick did better during the day, but was glad of the boy's help in rounding the flock back home as the dusk came in. Between them they distributed the food, and when the sheep seemed to have eaten their fill, Patrick would call them by name. Checking them for injuries, with Finn's help, he gently urged or bullied the flock back into the pen. The lad was scared of the wolves, and though the old mother had warned him not to sit close to the sick man in case he caught the disease himself, he still lay right next to him under the fleece, his back to the ram. Although he was a big boy now, on several occasions Patrick saw him sucking his thumb.

The first night of Finn's stay the wind whipped up savagely over the crown of the hill, keening like a woman for her dead. Patrick wrapped his arms around the child, who hung on for dear life as the Slua Dubh galloped above them. The boy was crying, and Patrick whispered to him feverishly to close his eyes. Finn ground his knuckles into the sockets and moaned with fear. Everyone knew that looking at the Dark Host deprived you of your reason.

After that first night the boy was as scared of Patrick as he was of the wolves. He had heard the man in the darkness, talking to invisible people in a strange tongue, crying out in Irish against a female giant, and toward morning, speaking of a monster in the wood. Finn dreaded to think what he was talking about, or who he had been talking to when he spoke the mysterious language of the island to the East, or the even stranger language in which he prayed. The boy recognised the prayers, because he knew the word 'Amen.' The women had started to use it when they prayed, and he also knew the word 'Paternoster', from Fionula, though he didn't know what it meant. Whatever power Patrick had spoken to was terrible enough to keep the Slua Dubh away.

Finn now knew something important, the name 'Christos,' a name of power. This must be the foreign god that the men said had driven the sheep slave insane. It was true, the man clearly was mad, but the boy was glad to have him on his side. In spite of his newborn fear of Patrick, he still crawled into his arms at night. The mad man held him as gently as a mother might, while the wolves howled in the woods, and the boy dreamt unquiet dreams. When the day came that Patrick's breath no longer crackled in his chest like burning wood, Finn was sad to know that he would have to leave him. But even so, when the men came up the slope with the feed for the sheep, Finn ran ahead of them on the return, glad to leave the terrors of wolves, and worse, behind him.

Winter wore on, and Patrick no longer imagined the spring. He lost one of the ewes, Mara. She had slid on the frost, and as he had feared broke her weakened leg again. Although Patrick splinted it, and did his best to keep her alive, she cried so hard that, when Fionula came, he asked her to get one of the men up to put the poor creature out of her misery. He had a blade for the job, but knew he could not do it himself.

The next morning the horse slave and the Man came to the top of the world, and between them they butchered her. Then the Man took his switch in his hand, ordered Patrick to remove his tunic, and flogged his back for his mistake. Patrick had known this was coming, and didn't put up any fight. He didn't think there was any fight left in him. Even with his eyes shut, his sight was full of blood on snow. It felt as though someone else was being flogged, and his assailant even seemed to be weary of it.

That night Fionula mounted the slope with mutton soup, and Patrick wept. He told her he couldn't eat it, and she wordlessly gave him bread and an apple instead before making her way back down over the bitter earth.

No wolves came near him that winter. When the world had shrunk until there was no tomorrow, spring came. He woke one morning and the air felt different. The snow had all but melted, only patches of it remained. As he let the sheep out, they sprang gladly over the grass, and looking up he saw a figure he'd never stopped praying for. He was coming out of the forest, leaning on a staff, smiling to see the sheep. He was greyer, if anything, than he had been, and just as ugly, but still the most welcome sight in the world. Patrick straightened, and felt an unaccustomed sensation in his chest. Joy.

He lifted his hand, and his voice.

"Victoricus," he cried, and started to run.

That night Patrick walked into her dreams, as he did often. Conchessa groaned, as she began to wake, and desperately yearned to return to sleep. He was running, a fat cheeked toddler, and held his arms up to her. Then she was awake, and angry with the birds that had woken her from the dream.

When Patrick had been little, he had loved the sounds of birds, she remembered, and in spring would practise their cries, to see if he could persuade them to come to him. Of course, they never did.

What was he doing now? Did he hear birds sing?

She carefully eased her way out of bed to avoid waking Calpornius. His face was wet. Perhaps he dreamt of Patrick too.

She felt such pity for her husband, but did not know what to do with it. She didn't dare talk to him anymore, because she was afraid she would weep. She had seen how much he hated it when she cried. He even saved his own tears for sleep, so that he would not know his own weakness. She wished she could kiss him. She wished she could taste his tears.

Instead, she knelt by the bed, bowed her head, and began to whisper her prayers. Her husband groaned in his sleep, and rolled, covering his eyes with his arm, as if to shield his sight from the early morning sun.

CHAPTER THIRTEEN

In the flurry of hugs and exchange of greetings Patrick finally understood how much he had changed. Firstly, he noticed with a shock that his voice had finished breaking. He had not heard himself over the winter months. Even when he had spoken he didn't listen to himself. It came as a shock to him when he heard his voice in his chest, so like that of his father.

Secondly, despite the hardship of the winter, he had grown even taller, though leaner, and he now towered over Victoricus.

And thirdly...

"You stink, lad," Victoricus laughed. "Time you got yourself clean... I take it you haven't had a chance to change your clothes all winter?"

Patrick blushed. Still unaccustomed to conversation, let alone jesting, he couldn't think of anything to say. Victoricus looked at him sympathetically.

"It was a hard winter," he said. "The first one is always worst, not everyone survives it. I prayed for you every night."

"I prayed for you. Sometimes I thought I saw you coming out of the wood."

"Sometimes I dreamt I came to you. Perhaps you saw me then."

Patrick nodded. Many things were possible under God's big sky.

"Now, go on with you, wash yourself, get the oil out of your hair. I'll see about sorting it out when you get back."

Patrick felt dislocated and odd to be leaving his sheep in another's charge, but he obeyed, and walked over to the spring. The water gathered in a still pool beneath an outcrop of rock, before spilling out and running down the mountain in a frothy, white and silver stream. Patrick knelt and looked in the pool. For the first time in a long time he saw his reflection. What he saw shocked him.

His father's face looked out at him, but not his father as he had ever known him. His father was a clean man, neat, who kept his hair cropped short at the sides in the Roman fashion, and his crown shaved to show his allegiance to the church. Also, in the Roman fashion, his father shaved his face. His grandfather had a beard, but Patrick had never known his father to have one. If he'd had a beard, it would have looked something like the face in the pool... but his father was better groomed and fed; fuller in the cheeks, not so wild in the hair or haunted in the eyes.

Patrick examined his hair. He hadn't thought about it, but now he cringed, sickened. Instead of curling, as it had when he first climbed this mountain, it had matted into thick red ropes, so that he looked like Medusa, or even, he shuddered at the thought, one of the sheep he had been protecting. He had not known that human hair could bind itself up like that. It was oily and grimy to the touch. Suddenly he was overwhelmed with his own stench and sweat. Repulsed with himself he stripped off his ragged tunic, and began to wash. He used a flat stone to scrape the worst of the filth off his torso and arms, and tore his ragged nails with his teeth. But despite his ministrations he was bitterly aware of how foreign to himself he had become.

He thought of how, in another world, he would have gone to the baths from his parent's town house, at least once a week, and how he would be anointed in oil, sitting in warm water till his skin was pink, while a slave scraped the muck off him with a strigil. Perhaps it was having heard his father's voice coming from his own mouth, and seeing his father's face in the pool, but the memories rushed over him, and they were as painful as anything that happened to him yet on this island. As he scoured himself of grime he thanked God that his parents couldn't see him. He had no idea what he could say to excuse himself to them. The whole mess and sorry stink of it seemed to him to be his fault, and he was almost angry that Victoricus had arrived, and reminded him that he had to be human again.

Victoricus seemed to understand. He cut the worst of the ropes out of Patrick's hair, and left them lying by the wood. "Some creature may use them to line their den", he said. "Everything has its purpose."

Patrick was still ashamed that, left to his own devices, he had become something so wild. He said nothing. The old man talked gently, pointing out the places where snowbells and bluebells were poking out of the remaining snow. Just as his departure had bought the winter, so his arrival heralded the spring.

At the end of the first day he suggested that Patrick go down to the valley.

"Stay down there a few days, get your strength back. You need sleep, good food, and a change of clothes." Patrick felt obscurely alarmed.

"There's no need for me to go down," he said. "They'll send someone up eventually."

"Son," Victoricus said, patiently, "I know how hard it is, when you've been alone so long, but you need to go down and be with people again."

"I'll be with you."

"You'll be with me enough, during the lambing and sheering. For now, go down and make sure they remember you. Otherwise you'll forget how to talk to people, and you'll always be living alone on a hill."

Patrick conceded defeat, and that night bade farewell to his sheep for the first time in four months.

There was still some snow and frost on the slopes, but the weather grew milder as the descent softened and eased into the valley. He smelt the scent of cooking rising toward him, fresh bread. Hunger rose up in him, so fierce that his mouth flooded with saliva and he almost fell. The nearer he got to people, the more anxious he became; with every step he fought the urge to turn around and run back up the hill. Dusk was beginning to fall, and the shadows seemed strange to him, down here in this depth, where even the air had changed.

"Oh God, help me," he whispered, "I can't do this, help me do this, God, please..."

God answered his prayers. The first person to notice his arrival was Fionula. He didn't think he could have borne anyone else. She was sitting outside the only stone building in the place, where the "big folk" dwelt, accompanied by the Bhean Uasail. Although the shadows were lengthening, the women were still working in cloth. Fionula was sitting with some kind of frame in front of her, on which she'd been weaving. The lady was knitting... not as the fishermen did, socks and garments, but some lacy thing, fine floating stuff that only the rich would use.

Fionula broke off her conversation with the Bhean Uasail, and stood. A smile spread across her features, and the Bhean Uasail, turning to see what had caught her attention, put down her lace.

"Patrick," Fionula cried, and ran to him. He opened his arms, and enveloped her in a hug. He didn't think he could speak.

"So," the Bhean Uasail said, smiling, "the warrior returns from the war."

Patrick looked at her, and struggled to think of a reply. She lifted an eyebrow, an arch expression on her face. "You've grown," she said. "It seems that you are now a man."

Again, Patrick looked at her mutely, then looked back at Fionula. "Say something, Patrick." His kinswoman prodded him in the stomach. "You could at least say hello."

"Greetings, Ladies," he said, then stopped, feeling foolish. For some reason he had spoken in British. He tried again.

"Hail..."

That was no good. That was Latin. Helplessly he looked at them. He understood what they were saying, but he couldn't remember how to reply to them. The Bhean Uasail laughed, at last understanding.

"And there I thought you were being insolent. Poor Holy Boy, you've not spoken to anyone all winter. You've forgotten the tongue of men, with all your commerce on the hill with sheep, and giants and the black host."

Patrick bit his lip, and swallowed, looking at her.

"Oh, Finn told us all about it. Everyone knows what can happen up on the mountains when the wind is wrong. You did well to lose only one sheep." She put a hand on his arm appreciatively. "After you've eaten, and remembered your tongue, you'll have to tell us all about it."

"Oh Lord God help me," he said in British, and looked at Fionula. "What's there to tell? They'll think I'm mad."

"What does he say," the Bhean Uasail inquired, "will he tell us of his encounters with the Slua Dubh?"

"I think not, my Lady," Fionula said. "Not yet. I think more than anything, he needs a change of clothes and a good meal."

"Well, you can arrange that." She looked at Patrick and smiled again. "Now that spring is here, I hope you'll stay a few days before you have to return to your lonely watch. Your kinswoman has been good company to me, and for her sake, I would be kind to you."

Patrick managed to find the appropriate words. "Thank you, my Lady," he said, his tongue thick and stumbling, as it had been when he first spoke Irish. Awkwardly he bowed his head.

"Good, good. I'll see you soon." She picked up her knitting again. They had been dismissed.

Fionula bowed to the Bhean Uasail, then taking him by the hand led him to the slave quarters. Patrick felt a tremendous relief to be away from the black-eyed gaze of the unnerving Lady. He could feel her still watching him, a weight between his shoulder blades. He could picture her nimble fingers, working, spider like, across the lace.

"I'm glad to see you safely back," Fionula confided, in British for his sake. "I've been worried sick about you."

"I'm well now."

"Is it true what the boy Finn said?"

"I don't know what he said."

"The Slua Dubh. We hear them sometimes, even down here. Are there truly spirits up on that mountain?"

"There are spirits everywhere."

"Weren't you afraid?"

"God protected me," he said, then smiled ruefully. "But I was afraid," he conceded. "I was very afraid indeed. I'm not a very good Christian."

"Oh Patrick, you silly boy," she said fondly, then stood up on tiptoe to kiss his chin.

Chapter Fourteen

When he first came into the large hut the men and women were lying down for sleep, but his arrival caused such a stir that, in spite of his reluctance, he sat up late into the night, answering questions. The presence of so many people, and so much noise made him dizzy, and the smoky interior of the hut gave him a sense of unreality. He was surprised to find that even the men seemed pleased to see him. It was something of an event for a sheep slave to come down from the mountain; they always had something to say.

The first person to question him was the old mother. Her questions were purely pragmatic, with no spiritual components at all. She wanted to know how he'd managed to keep warm in the snow, and nodded approval at his makeshift arrangement, lying behind the hay, and the ram, with a fleece under and over him. "But you probably took that chest complaint because you were wet all the time," she pointed out. "There should be some kind of way to keep you warm. Why they don't build a hut for you outside the pen I don't know."

One of the fishermen interjected. "It's been asked in the past. You remember... oh, what was his name... the sheep man five, six years ago? He even started building one, but the master found what he was about and had him beaten."

"Why would the master beat him for that?" The young woman who asked, Niamh, was sitting with her hand folded protectively across her belly. It wasn't showing yet, but Patrick could tell from the gesture that she was pregnant. "It makes no sense," she continued, and pouted. The fisherman smiled protectively and put his arm around her. Patrick guessed he was the father. He tried to remember the man's name, and after a brief struggle retrieved it. Colm.

The fisherman shrugged, and replied, "I know it makes no sense, *you* know it makes no sense. Everyone sitting here knows it makes no sense. But as far as the master is concerned everything has to be done the way it's always been done. He would think it was a waste of time."

"It might save a life," the old mother said. "We've lost more men up that mountain... The boy who was before you Patrick, he was taken by wolves, but I think he would have been gone in the spring anyway." Her voice grew sad and reflective. "There has been many a man who just jumped."

Patrick glanced away from his interlocutors guiltily. Fionula caught his gesture, and said sharply, "Patrick, did you think of it?"

"It doesn't matter," he said in British, "I don't want to talk about it."

"What?" Niamh asked. "What did he say?"

Finn suddenly piped up. "There's a monster up on that mountain. She tells you to jump."

Everyone stopped and looked at the boy, then looked at Patrick for confirmation. He blinked in the smoky air and shook his head. He repeated in Irish. "I don't want to talk about it."

It was the worst thing he could have said, because suddenly almost everyone was speaking at once, asking questions about what he had seen on the mountain and in the woods. Patrick looked pleadingly at Fionula, but she couldn't rescue him from the questions, which came from every side. The old woman looked at him with a wry expression on her ancient face, and laughed. "I'll say goodnight then," she commented. "I know all about them up the hill, I don't need to hear it again."

Patrick covered his face with his hands, and prayed for a bit of peace, but his audience seized even on his gesture of prayer, looking for significance. In the end there was no way to avoid it. Patrick just took a breath, and began to describe the winter to Fionula; in British, since it was easier to think that way. He didn't touch on his loneliness or despair, and was brief and sparse in his description, but Fionula spun the story out. It did in fact make the story more credible to her listeners, since he seemed so reluctant to tell it that they hung on every word. Occasionally Patrick looked at her crossly when she embellished too colourfully, and she was forced to correct herself. But he was surprised that most of her guesses were accurate. In particular, she described the riot of the wild hunt across the night sky more keenly than he could have done, and he couldn't fault her description of the Giantess chewing at the bottom of the cliff. He wondered if perhaps she had seen and heard these things too.

When he had told as much as he could stand of the story Finn chipped in, with his description of the days he'd spent up "on the top". This story came as a surprise to Patrick. He knew the boy had been with him when he was ill, and he remembered some of what he talked about, but he had chosen to forget the worst of his illness.

The boy told, as colourfully as a travelling Ollam could have done, of the night that the dark gods rode over the stony sky, and Patrick had covered him with a fleece, warning him to close his eyes. Then he told how Patrick had prayed out loud, to Christos, and how Christos stood against the hunt, and they had fled back to the West. Later, Finn said, a howling came up out of the sea, like the wolves of the forest, but bigger, and louder, and more terrible than wolves. And Patrick had talked out loud, commanding the wolves and the Giantess to get back to where they had come from. "So she marched back into the sea," the boy stated, as though he had seen it with his own eyes, "and the wolves with her." Then there was the Snake that came out of the forest. Everyone knew that this island had no snakes in the natural, but there were other Snakes, far worse, that lived in lakes, or pits, or caves. Fionula butted in at this point, affirming that Patrick had come against the Snake from the moment he set foot on Irish soil, and that, when she had first found him feverish by the sheepfold he was talking of the Snake, and how it intended to devour the flock. "This was the day before Finn went up," she reminded them. "It was fighting the Snake that made him ill," was her earnest conclusion. Everyone nodded. This made more sense to them than the old mother's contention that it was the weather that had beaten him. Patrick was a young man after all, and young men didn't just sicken. There was always something else behind it. Finn bounced up and down eagerly, and crowned the tale by saying, "and even though the Snake came right up to the sheep pen, Patrick kept praying, and rebuking it, and telling it to get back in the name of Christos. And the thing went back into the forest, slithering over the snow."

He smiled at Patrick with shining eyes, then looked at his audience, radiant with pride that he'd lived such an adventure, and survived to tell it. To be sure, he'd told the story before, but never had anyone believed it so completely as they did with the hero of the tale sitting next to the fire.

Colm looked at Patrick with a wary admiration. "What do you remember of it?" he asked. Patrick had sat through Finn's account feeling thoroughly ashamed. Although he couldn't deny anything, because his recollection was so fractured, he felt as though these stories were not about him, but someone else.

"I'm sorry," he said, "I don't remember much of it."

"You wouldn't," Niamh pointed out. "They say people have to forget these things, they're too terrible to live with."

"But you remember the Snake, and the Giantess," the boy asked, in hopeful tones. Patrick nodded, slowly conceding the point.

"I remember the host riding across the sky," he admitted, feeling safer to mention them under a roof. "They would come across sometimes at night, and frighten even the wolves of the forest."

"And you drove them off in the name of Christos," the boy said triumphantly.

"I didn't drive them off at all," Patrick chided. "I don't have that kind of power."

Finn looked deflated.

"Christ has the power," Patrick explained, and the boy immediately brightened up.

"He's your god, isn't he?"

"He's the only God," Patrick said, feeling more comfortable with this subject matter. "All the others are small little things." Lifting his hand he made a tiny gap between his index finger and thumb, to show how just small. "Even though they're big to us, they're tiny under His feet."

"Even the Giantess?"

"Even the Giantess, and the Black Host, and the Snake."

There was silence in the hut, as Patrick's audience absorbed his words. The idea of a God who was greater than the Black Host was a new and terrible concept. It was Niamh who broke the silence.

"How can anything be greater than the Slua Dubh?"

Patrick closed his eyes, and remembered his Grandfather reading to him when he was a small boy. He smiled in the firelight, as God brought the verse back to his recollection.

"It is written," he said, with sudden authority, "that God gave Jesus, that is the Christ, a name that is above all other names, so that at the name of Jesus every knee should bow, and every tongue confess that Jesus is Lord. He is greater than the Black Host, and the Snake, and the Giantess. He is greater than the earth, and the sea, and the sky, and everything that is in them. He is greater even than death itself, because He defeated death and rose alive from the grave."

After this pronouncement there was silence, and the fire popped and hissed in the centre of the room. Patrick felt a great surge of exhaustion rise up in him, abruptly, and he swayed where he sat. His head spun, and he covered his face with his hand.

"I'm sorry," he stammered, swallowing down nausea. "I have to lie down."

"Good night," Fionula said, and covered him with a blanket. She looked round the room. "We all need to sleep, look outside, it's the middle of the night. Some of us have to get up with the day."

Patrick was unconscious before she'd finished speaking. The other occupants of the room, however, took a long time to get to sleep, and there was much whispering and speculation in the dark. Finn in particular tossed and turned, his head full of story and adventure. When he finally slept, he slept well, dreaming happy dreams, of giants, and heroes, and an invisible Father who carried Him on His shoulders as a shepherd would carry a sheep.

"Son," Potitus stood in the doorway. "You need to take a break."

"Not yet," Calpornius was angrily scratching out sums on a wax tablet, feeling like a student again. He was loathe to waste precious parchment on his mathematics, and was trying to make sure the books were balanced at least in his head before he committed anything to the permanency of ink.

"You've been in here for hours," the old man came in, and put a hand on his son's shoulder. "You've not eaten, you've not drunk enough. No wonder you get headaches."

Calpornius paused in his calculations, and looked up startled. He didn't think anyone knew about his headaches... well, apart from the Greek slave who ministered to the health of the family. He would not say anything of course, he could be beaten for betraying a confidence. Calpornius was not as lenient as his wife in matters of discipline. He never beat a man more than he himself had been beaten as a child, and his father had not been severe, but Calpornius' consistency in these matters ensured that the male slaves at least were obedient. Conchessa had charge of the women, and how she handled them was her affair.

Potitus pulled up a stool and sat next to his son.

"It's obvious you've been neglecting yourself," he told his boy. "You forget, I raised you after your mother died. I know every expression of your face, and certainly what you look like when you get a headache. You're doing it now, pinching your nose between the eyes, and I've seen you rubbing your temples. Besides, I saw your urine just now as the slave girl took it. It's very dark. You will make yourself ill if you are not careful."

"But Father, this needs to be done."

"I'm sure it does, but need it be done now? Do you really think it is more important to you than food, or drink, or your wife?"

Calpornius flushed at the perceived criticism.

"I don't put my work ahead of my wife."

"When did you last speak to her?"

He turned his face from his father, and stood, abruptly.

"This morning," he replied, though he wasn't certain that a brief greeting was entirely what his father meant. When had he last really spoken to Conchessa?

"Go take a cup of water, Son, and sit with your wife." His father spoke gently. "If you can't think of anything to say, at least hold her hand."

There was no hope for it now, all the numbers he had been puzzling over had flown out of his head. And besides; he did have a headache, he did miss his wife.

His shoulders drooped as he gave up the resentment he felt at his father's interference. The old man was almost always right.

He turned and kissed his father's cheek in filial obedience. "Thank you," he whispered, then went to look for Conchessa.

Chapter Fifteen

Patrick slept for the next day and night, waking only briefly for food and to relieve himself. He had not realised he'd been so tired, and felt dimly as though he should apologise to the people around him, whose work continued unbroken.

The old mother was waiting to get his attention on the morning he woke fully for the first time. "I've got orders for you," she said. "You're not to go up the hill for a few days yet. The Bhean Uasail and her husband will want to hear your stories of the winter, and I'm to make sure you're clean and in fresh clothes when you go to them."

Patrick was mortified. "I can't tell that story again", he said. "It nearly killed me with shame the first time, and I'm not at all sure that I was battling giantesses and snakes the way Finn told it."

"I'm sure you were battling monsters in the high places," the old mother said, "though not, as you say, the way Finn told it. And the dark gods do ride up there, so that part's certainly true. However, if you can't tell your story, you have no choice but to live with how others tell it. We all need story or the world makes no sense."

Patrick looked at her. "I have no idea what you're talking about."

"Of course you don't. You're a man."

He shook his head. "Are all Irish women crazy?" he asked.

"Only the wise ones," she laughed. "Which is to say that you are right, we're all crazy. Now, go wash yourself. You'd make an onion cry."

You should have smelled me before, Patrick thought wryly, sniffing himself. Somehow he didn't feel quite as ashamed of his odour as he had done when Victoricus had pointed it out. *Perhaps,* he thought, *Victoricus was right, and I did need to come down here.* He couldn't remember what he'd been so afraid of now. The old woman threw a waxy block at him. "Go to the sea," she said, "and rub yourself with this, then scrape it all off. You'll feel a lot better for it."

"We use oil, in Britain," he said, "but I do know to scrape."

"Good. I'll see you when you get back. Now that I've seen how much you've stretched I can finish the new britches." She looked at him mischievously and laughed. "You were glad of the warm legs, I'm sure, this winter."

"I was so," Patrick admitted. "They're not such silly clothes after all."

It had been a long time since Patrick had stood on a beach. This beach was both familiar and strange to him. He had watched if for three seasons, from a height, and here he was, right next to the pulse of it, watching the waves as they sighed in and out.

A year, he thought. *A year since I stood on a beach.* A year since he had stumbled out of the slave ship onto the Irish shore.

He could barely remember how he'd come here. Closing his eyes all he could see were flashes of memory, broken bits and pieces that made no sense to him. His dead teacher sitting opposite him, as though invigilating some terrible exam. Somewhere in the line ahead of him, a woman had dropped dead, and he suddenly, vividly, saw again one of his captors pulling her body up by the hair while a comrade hacked her head off. He realised now that this was probably easier for them than untying the neck brace and breaking the chain. The captives had been forced to step over her body as they were marched to the slave market. The memory confused him. It should have made him sick, but thinking of it now, he felt nothing. He couldn't understand his lack of feeling, nor the fact that he only now remembered it. How could he have forgotten a thing like that? How could it mean less to him now than if he'd heard it in a story?

"What's wrong with me?" he asked. The wind snatched his words away, and gave no answer.

Patrick opened his eyes, and gazed out across the ocean. It was remarkably blue. All the winter long it had been as grey as a steel blade, but now it had changed its aspect for the spring. The waves lapped the against the seashore like a friendly dog. The world changed so easily. Despite all this beauty, there were things that he had seen which he could never forget. And God had seen it all. What must the heavenly Father think, when He saw His children commit such cruelties?

Patrick stripped, and began to pray. He left his clothes in a heap, and tender footed it across the shingle, until he reached the sand. Gingerly he covered himself in the grease, then ran into the sea.

The shock of it took his breath away. For a moment he thought the cold would undo him, then heat returned to his limbs as his blood asserted itself against the waves. It had been a long time since he had swum... something of which his father had never approved, but which his grandfather, strangely, did. He had learned to swim as a small boy, not in the sea, but in a local river. It was possibly his grandfather who had taught him. He couldn't remember. This was the first time he had ever swum in the sea.

It was exhilarating. The waves, which looked so gentle from the shore, lifted him, as though he were flying, then dropped him with a swoop, before lifting him again. If he had known more about the sea he would have felt that he was in danger, but he had no such fear. All he felt was relief. He had become so used to tightness and pain that he had stopped noticing it. Now he felt his muscles release, and the aches easing out of his body, and he twisted and spun in the water, laughing and whooping with the sheer pleasure of it. The water was so clear that, when he held his breath and swam beneath the waves he could see his shadow flying beneath him, undulating along the ripples of sand. Fish glinted in green sunlight, and scattered before him like jewels. Breaking the surface and taking in a triumphant breath he thought that he would never want to swim in a sleepy river again. The pulse of the ocean was a revelation.

Finally hunger caught up with him, and thirst. He reluctantly left the briny water, and hobbled back to his clothes. Shivering he scraped the grease off with a stone, and was surprised how much dirt he removed. Underneath, the skin was pink and clean. The last vestiges of the terrible winter sloughed off him. He closed his eyes, and thanked God for the sea.

It seemed a shame to put on his dirty clothes again, and so he wore as little as possible, pulling on his britches, and bundling the tunic up under his arm. It was later than he'd thought. He started back along the path he had come by, chastising himself for his lack of foresight. He should have bought his boots with him. He'd worn them all winter, removing them only when his feet were wet, when he would turn the boots outside in, and dry them by the fire. The only parts of him that had not grown tougher in the winter were the soles of his feet. He thought again of his first days in Ireland, and how his feet had bled. At least they were not yet as soft as that.

The path curved round the base of a steep slope, the foothill of the crag on which he had spent the winter. Walking with his head down, to make sure he didn't tread on anything too sharp, he almost bumped into someone. He sprang back with alarm, then stumbled an apology, when he realised it was the Bhean Uasail. To his shame he issued his apology in the wrong language, and then when he tried again he stammered like a fool.

The Bhean Uasail laughed. Patrick blushed, mortified. It seemed to him suddenly that she was always laughing at him for something, and he felt a stirring of resentful pride. Why was everyone always laughing at him?

"So, Holy Boy," she said, in tones that seemed to him mocking, "I've been watching you. You truly are mad, you bounced up and down in that water like a grey seal."

"I was only swimming, my Lady."

"I've never seen anyone swim like that. Were you born in the water?"

Patrick clenched his jaw and looked away. This woman never seemed to talk anything other than nonsense. How was he supposed to respond to a question like that?

"You seem embarrassed. Are you ashamed of your talents?"

"I am not sure what you're talking about," he said. "It's no talent to swim, I just went to wash the winter off me."

"You enjoyed yourself," she pointed out.

"I did so," he admitted, reluctantly, wondering whether a slave would ever be allowed any pleasure in life without someone coming to chastise them for it.

"I enjoyed it too," the Bhean Uasail said, and smiled at him, coyly. All of a sudden Patrick understood what her sly seeming comments and gestures had been about. He went white with shock, realising that she was flirting with him. He clapped his hand to his mouth and looked at her with horror. Then, before she could say anything else he bolted, as fast as he could run, toward the slave quarters. The Bhean Uasail gawped incredulously after him, hands on her hips, as flabbergasted as the fleeing slave.

The whole incident was later to become as much one of the stories they told about poor Patrick as the tales of his adventures on the roof of the world. Colm and the other fishermen were also on the beach that day, for the first time since they had weighed the curraghs down at the end of the fishing season, the previous year. While they were examining how well the skins of their boats had weathered the winter their attention was unexpectedly caught by the antics of The Holy Boy. The youngest of the two lads, Finn, who had just started out with them today, noticed the sheep slave first, and assumed, not knowing any better, that his bizarre behaviour was normal.

"I won't have to go into the water will I?"

Colm tousled the lad's hair. Children said the strangest things. "The plan is that you stay in the boat."

"I mean, not like *him.*"

The men looked where the boy was pointing, and silently took in the strange spectacle. None of them could swim of course, since nobody in their right mind would tempt the ocean by treating her with such disrespect, and at first they couldn't figure out who the tiny white figure was, or what on earth he was doing.

"It's the Holy Boy," Colm said, "you can see his red hair."

"Do you think he's trying to drown himself," Caithail asked, getting anxiously to his feet. His resentment of the British slave had dissipated with winter, particularly in the glow of hero tales around the fire. He watched the bobbing figure apprehensively, wondering if they would be in time if they ran down there and tried to fish him out.

"He's doing a poor job of it, if he is trying to drown himself." Colm stood staring, trying to make out what was going on. "If he'd wanted to kill himself he could have jumped off the cliff. And why would he take his clothes off to do it?"

"He is mad," Caithail pointed out. "Who knows why he does anything?"

They carried on staring, then Colm stated what everyone was thinking.

"He's swimming!"

At this point they were all standing, squinting incredulously at the lone figure, in the ocean. He looked to them odd and comical, bouncing up and down, occasionally diving under, then springing back up again. They knew of course that some men could swim, but they had not actually seen it done before.

"That looks like a strange sort of thing to be doing by choice," Cathail speculated, "wouldn't you get cold?"

"Well, he seems to be enjoying himself."

The youngest boy then proffered the suggestion that perhaps Patrick was a selkie. Colm looked at him scornfully and clipped him round the ear. "Don't be daft," he said, "you're as mad as he is. Only women can be selkies."

After a while they lost interest, and carried on with the more important business at hand.

The next time they noticed the strange sheep slave was as they were finishing for the day. "Hey hey," Cathail said, looking up, and grinning. "See who's coming? It's herself."

The men looked up, and saw the Bhean Uasail walking down the path. She was dressed in her finest, the black flood of her hair loose, adorned with ribbons and beads. She walked tall and loose in the hip. Patrick was walking toward her, with his head down, wincing as he carefully positioned his feet over the shingle.

"He's not seen her," Colm said.

"She's seen him. I'd say she's been feasting herself with a long good look at him." Cathail laughed. "We all know what *she's* been thinking."

Of course, they all did. It was no secret that the master and the Bhean Uasail had been unhappy for years. It was the lack of a child that seemed to be the trouble, though it was neither partner's fault. They both tried enthusiastically enough, usually after a blazing row. However, after five years there was still no child, and it was a source of increasing astonishment to all observers that they hadn't simply gone their separate ways. It was a mismatched marriage from the very start, he being nothing but a middling wealthy farmer, married above his station, and she being of noble blood. Quite what the story was behind their union remained a mystery to all observers. They must love each other, the women suggested, and sighed. The men just laughed, and thought the answer was rather more basic than that.

The couple did indeed seem to want to stay together, and there were various avenues open to them under Irish law. Both man and wife were entitled to look elsewhere for a child, and any such offspring would be treated as a legitimate heir, if the other partner agreed. The master had sired offspring on several slave women, but as they had all been girls, the problem remained. The Bhean Uasail, on the other hand, was choosier than her man, and hadn't yet picked a mate to sire a child on her. For years the slaves had been speculating on who the lucky man would be. There had been rumours that she was considering someone of her own station, but it never came to anything. And yet from this distance it was beginning to look possible that her choice had fallen on Patrick.

The fishermen all stopped what they were doing, and watched the scene unfold with bated breath.

"He looks annoyed," Colm mused.

"Well, that's not normal," Cathail said. "What man wouldn't be flattered?"

They all muttered their assent, even the youngest boy, who was too young to really know what they were talking about.

Suddenly there was a burst of incredulous laughter. "I told you he's mad," Cathail said, slapping his leg for emphasis. "Look at him, running like a hare from a hunter!"

"She won't be happy," Colm shook his head. "Oh dear, oh dear... she won't be happy at all!"

Chapter Sixteen

Under the circumstances, Patrick got off lightly. His first fear was that he would be accused by the Bhean Uasail of some terrible crime, as Joseph had been when he refused Potiphar's wife in Egypt. One thing he had learned this last year was that, no matter what you lost there was always more to lose. He was probably going to be thrown in some terrible dungeon, or worse. His fears however proved to be without foundation. The Bhean Uasail, even though she was obviously wanton, and had no idea of God's commands, was not a liar.

When he got back to the hut the old mother was sitting outside, putting the finishing touches to his britches. He breathlessly told her about his narrow escape, and couldn't understand why she rocked backward and wept with raucous laughter.

"What?" he asked. "What's so funny?"

"I wish I could have seen her face. Oh, she can have any man for miles around, and she picks the one man who won't have her. Did she not know, mad as you are, that you'd be as useless to her as a stone boat? She'll be a fury when she gets here..."

"Well, can you give me my new clothes so I can head up the mountain?"

"I don't think heading up the mountain will do you any good. She'll probably fly up there on a black thunder cloud and kick you off the cliff."

"You mean she's a witch?"

The old woman laughed louder. "If she wasn't this morning, she will be now. Oh, child, you silly child, whatever you do, don't add insult to injury and run up the hill. She'll never forgive you then. You'll just have to explain it to her."

"What's there to explain? She's married."

"So, she's married. What's the problem?"

Patrick stood there dumbfounded. "What do you mean what's the problem? That *is* the problem. She's married."

"So another man can't touch her?"

"That's exactly right. Another man can't touch her."

The old woman stopped cackling, and craned her head toward Patrick, like a bird examining a carcass. It suddenly struck him that despite her cleverness in stitching she was nearly blind, and was working largely by touch.

"Come here," she said, "let's get a look at you."

Patrick sat opposite her, and let her peer at him. She put her hand up and felt his face.

"Well, who would have thought it?" she said in a tone of wonder. "You actually believe what you're saying."

"Well, of course I do. I wouldn't say it otherwise." Patrick's shame, alarm and confusion were combining to make him feel foolish and childlike. He couldn't negotiate with these people; they were just too strange to him. He was becoming rather worried that he might cry.

"So, is that the law where you live? One man must have one wife, and one wife must have one husband, and that's all there is to it?"

"That's all there is to it. It's God's law. Is it not so here?"

"I thought you knew. So, you mean to tell me that in your country men and women live their whole lives like swans, and only ever have one mate?"

"Well... not exactly," Patrick reluctantly admitted. "Some men do betray their wives, and some wives betray their husbands. And sometimes one or the other will run away. And if the husband or wife dies, the survivor can remarry."

"Our people don't have to lie, or run away when a marriage dies its death. So, how is your law any better than our system?

"I don't know, I don't even know what your system is. I only just heard of this thing a moment ago, and it makes me sick."

"You'd better not tell the Bhean Uasail that." Tugging sharply on the last of the thread, the old woman held up Patrick's britches. "That should do you now."

With indecent haste Patrick hurriedly changed his trousers, and began to pull the fresh tunic over his head. It looked like he wasn't going to heed her advice and planned on running up the hill regardless.

She sighed. "Listen, Son, let me talk to her. I'll explain that in your country the men who serve your god are under gaese not touch any man's wife, except their own."

Patrick had heard the word before, and hadn't understood it then. "What's 'gaese'?"

"You really do know nothing, do you? It's when someone takes an oath, a solemn vow. To break your gaese is to curse yourself. You have taken such a vow for your god. Is that not so?"

Patrick considered it. "It's not quite the same," he said, "because the reason I don't break my vow isn't for myself, it's for God, and it's not that He compels me, but..." he shrugged helplessly. "It's the best way I can think to explain it."

"You let me do the explaining," the old woman said. "You don't want to do any more damage."

The Bhean Uasail was indeed extremely displeased with Patrick, and took his refusal as a personal insult, which from anyone else it would have been. In the end, however, she accepted his explanation, though grudgingly. "I suppose this is part of your strange fast to your god," she said. "He seems determined to deprive you of all joy." Patrick was tongue tied, and so nervous he couldn't think of anything to say. The Bhean Uasail glared at him, then made a curt, flicking gesture with her hand. The slaves were dismissed. Heaving a sigh of relief Patrick admitted to himself that the old mother's knowledge of local custom had indeed saved the day.

Apart from the laughter of every slave in the place when he got back to their quarters, there was one immediate benefit of his 'fast.' He was not asked to attend the evening meal of the 'big folk' and recount his stories to them. It seemed he had exchanged one embarrassment for another. Even Fionula thought the story was funny.

"You don't understand us yet, Patrick," she said. "What you did was unheard of. The poor woman will never live it down. And all she wanted was a father for her child."

"What's wrong with her husband?"

"Well, you see, they've been trying for years, and nothing's happened. There's either something wrong with her, or something wrong with her husband, and neither one of them wants to admit it."

"My parents waited eight years before God gave me to them."

Fionula paused, and pondered.

"You know," she said, "I'd not thought of that. I only came to them when your mother was expecting you. But yes, she told me she had waited a long time and prayed hard for you. You're right… anyone would have thought your mother was barren, until you came along."

"Well, perhaps you should tell your Lady to pray to God. He's the one Who opens the womb."

She nodded, thoughtfully. "You know, I'll do that. Patrick, could you do me a favour?"

"If I can."

"Could you pray for them too? They're so unhappy, and they so want a child."

Pray for his captors?

Patrick remembered the woman standing in the path, and for the first time felt sympathy for her. He knew how much women could hunger for a child. She'd gone about it all the wrong way, but how could she have known any better? The few laws he knew of this barbarian land were enough to turn anyone savage.

"I will pray for God to open her womb," he said. "Tell her I'm sorry that I offended her, but that though I can't do what she asked, I can pray."

"Good lad," Fionula patted his wrist. "Now, if I were you, I'd get some sleep and head up tomorrow, while the weather stays fair. She'll like your soft reply, and the moment you are back in her favour she'll be asking you about the spirits on the top of the world, and I know you don't want that."

Even Victoricus knew what had happened, though he at least had the sense not to find it funny.

"How does everybody come to know about this?" Patrick asked, as they patrolled the height, carefully observing the sheep. "Does nobody have anything else to talk about?"

"Oh, I'm not mocking you, Son," Victoricus said, "though I'm sure most of them in the valley thought it was terribly funny."

"They did so. Even Fionula laughed."

"They have strange customs, these Irish," Victoricus shook his head. "Even when they have a child, they only keep it for the first seven years. Then they swap it with another tribe, and raise the neighbour's son or daughter as their own until they come of age."

"What would they do something like that for?"

"Well, from what I understand, it started a very long time ago. When warring tribes would sign a peace treaty they needed some way to make sure the other side kept the bargain, so they would take each other's children as hostage. If one side betrayed the other, the children's lives were forfeit."

Patrick was appalled. "That's a terrible thing, how could a parent do that?"

"It was a point of honour among them, a sign of good faith. These are proud people, who hold honour as their highest good. Most of the time the system worked... very few tribes broke their treaties when their children's lives were at stake. In the end, it probably benefited society. The children would grow up caring both for their natural parents, and their foster parents, for both their blood tribe, and their honour tribe. Sometimes it could even end a war... blood brothers would see each other on the other side, and embrace instead of killing each other. Now it's just part of the way things are, custom, not hostage taking. That custom is how some of the larger coalitions have grown in strength, and believe it or not, folks do say that things are more peaceful now than they used to be. There are still many war parties, and skirmishes, but life has improved for the freeborn man and woman."

Patrick looked down into the valley, at the loose scattering of huts, and the stone house in the centre.

"You know, I've been here a year, and I hardly know a thing about how these people think," he said. "I keep making a fool of myself, and they think I'm mad, because I don't understand what they're talking about, or why they do what they do."

"It took me a long time too," Victor said. "I was older than you when I was taken. You already speak Irish better than I do."

Patrick was surprised. "You don't mean it?"

The old man nodded. "It was hard for me to learn," he admitted. "I speak British well enough, but it wasn't my mother tongue, as it is yours. Your language springs from the same source as these Irish. A long way back you come from the same grandson of Noah."

Patrick had not thought of it that way. Victoricus smiled, and continued. "I suppose if they thought about it, they might consider you 'Fine', distant kin. You find these Irish strange, yet only a few hundred years ago you lived just as they do." A flicker of pride crossed the old man face, then was repressed. "My people had men voting, and arguing politics and philosophy, hundreds of years before Rome had a senate, or an Emperor, or any of us were born."

"They were still men stealers," Patrick pointed out. "They still are. Like the rest of the world, they take slaves."

"That's true," Victoricus sighed. "And of course our grand culture fell. Men try to build their mountains, and God knocks them down like a children's tower in the sand. Even my name I owe to a Roman master. I was born a slave, you know."

Patrick hadn't known.

"I worked hard, and earned my freedom, and somehow found myself in Britain, a very long way from my mother's people. I remember the day I was made a freeman." His face twisted wryly. "I'm glad I didn't know then what was to come. Sometimes I wonder why God allowed me to be taken. I came to know Him late in life, and wanted nothing more than to honour Him by becoming a priest... yet before I had a chance to complete my studies, we were raided, and everything I'd planned for went up in smoke."

Patrick bent his head, and kept a respectful silence. For all of their closeness over the previous year, Victoricus was a private man, and had never spoken about his life before slavery. It was a shared understanding between them. Both men knew that the pain of bondage was too raw a wound to be examined carelessly.

Victoricus looked out to sea, and continued talking, wistfully. "I thought for a long time that I had displeased God, dishonoured my profession in some way. It says in the books of God that He fights against His enemies, and I wondered if perhaps I was His enemy. It seemed that He was fighting against me. In the end I had to submit. All a man can do is live each day as it comes, praying that He will give strength for the next. And I find that life, even a hard life, is liveable, if you live it for Him." He looked at Patrick to see if he understood. "Does this help you?"

"It does," Patrick said, then, cautiously admitted his deepest fear. "I also believe at times that the Lord is fighting against me."

"Why so?"

"I never believed in Him. Right up until the day I was taken. It's not just that I didn't believe, I mocked Him. And I... I sinned against Him. In an hour, less than an hour." He looked away, remembering his Grandfather's church. Who found the sacrilege? he wondered. *Did they know it was me?* He shook his head. He did not feel able to confront his sin just yet. Victoricus' good opinion meant too much to him. "God took me, with my sin on my head," he admitted, sadly, "and He crushed me. I still don't know why He didn't kill me."

"Perhaps He has something for you to do," Victoricus said.

"What can I do? A sheep slave, stuck on a high hill?"

"Look what God has already done," Victoricus pointed out. "Your kinswoman, Fionula, she tells me that you were the one who showed her the Living God. And the boy, Finn, told me yesterday that Christos is the power that made the world, and that He is stronger than the grave. While he was up here, I told him about the Lord's death and Resurrection."

Patrick felt his face stretching in a foolish grin. "The boy is a believer?"

"I think so." Victor grimaced, "I tried to teach him the Lord's Prayer, but I imagine the lad will have had to correct my grammar."

Patrick laughed, "I'm sure it's not that bad," he said.

"Have you ever heard me speak Irish?"

"I have not."

"Think yourself lucky." The old man shrugged, and continued. "What I mean to say is this. God works through the weak things, and the broken things, and the things of no account. When I first heard you coming up from the valley, singing to the Lord, it felt like a curtain had lifted, and the Lord finally showed me what my life was about. Patrick, whether you are a slave here until you die, or whether He delivers you, He will use you to His glory."

Patrick blinked back tears. The old man thought so highly of him, and yet he knew himself to be so low. He could hardly confess his crime to this good kind man. It would break his heart.

"How can He use me to His glory?" Patrick whispered. "I'm nothing."

"Listen here, Boy... what is the first of the Ten?"

"'I am the Lord thy God, thou shalt have no other God but me.'"

"That's right. And what do you see in that command?"

"Well, just what it says. I am not to worship any other God."

"That is true. What else?"

Patrick shook his head, at a loss. What else was there? "I don't know."

"He says 'thy' God, not 'your' God. He's not talking to many people at a time, as in a crowd, He's not ignoring each little man. He's talking to *'thee.'* You, alone in all the world. He's not just speaking to Moses, and Aaron, and Israel, nor just to the priests, or a congregation in some stone church on a hill. He's talking to you, Patrick. He's always been talking to you. God is 'thy' God. He speaks to you, face to face."

Patrick felt himself shaking, and he whispered. "I know this."

"What else does the first commandment tell you?"

Patrick shook his head, humbly. "Tell me?"

"You didn't quote the whole of it. What it says, in full, is this..." The old man closed his eyes, leaned on his staff, lifted his head, and declared: "I am the Lord thy God, Who has brought thee out of the land of Egypt, out of the house of bondage. Thou shalt have no other god but Me.'"

Patrick's knees went weak, and he sank to the ground.

"Patrick, remember, whatever happens, that God does not bring us into slavery, He brings us out of it. I think I know now that I will never be free from man's tyranny while I live, but I do know that God brought me out of the house of bondage. I am a free man today, even in chains, because I know the God Who bought me." He looked down at the kneeling Patrick and smiled. "Give me your hand. Get up, Patrick. Look up, and rejoice. Our Saviour draws near."

CHAPTER SEVENTEEN

Spring was as busy a season as winter had been, but in a different way. David the ram, like his namesake, had taken many wives, and most of them were pregnant. Before Patrick was ready for it the first of the ewes went into labour. Without quite knowing how it had come about he found himself kneeling at the back end of a sheep, utterly at a loss. As a male he had never before seen any mother, human or otherwise, delivered of a baby, though he had heard it often enough. When these things happened (as they did several times most years) his mother would rise to the occasion, like a queen. He thought of her now, bustling into action, organising the slave women and, with brisk efficiency, banishing every man from the place. Their job, after all, was to sit outside and pray... although those of a less religious bent had a tendency to partake of liquid courage instead. The men were more than happy with this division of responsibilities. The screams of a woman in labour, particularly a first time mother, were more than enough to remind them that this was a purely female mystery.

Patrick was therefore not at all prepared when Banbeg's contented ruminations came to a sudden halt, and her bleating took on frightened and urgent tones. By the time he got to her, her water had already broken. His first reaction when confronted with all that gore was horror. He was very nearly sick.

Victoricus, having seen many a young herdsman through this initial response, resorted to pure pragmatism, and refused to indulge Patrick's squeamishness.

"It's not their fault the whole thing is so messy", he said bluntly. "If you think this is bad, be glad that you've never had to deliver a *woman's* child."

"But there's so much... mess."

"Well, take your tunic off then, the woman who made it for you won't be happy if you ruin it before spring is even over."

Patrick took his tunic off, and swallowing the bile that kept rising in his throat followed Victoricus' brisk instructions. The man reminded him, bizarrely, of his mother.

"It would help," Victoricus pointed out drily, "if you'd keep your eyes open."

"Wouldn't it be better if I watched you do this the first time?"

"It would not. The best way to learn something is to do it, and you'll be putting it off forever. Besides, you're lucky, this girl is young and healthy, I brought her to birth last year. Since she's dropping first, you might as well go with her. Better to start with an easy one."

"Easy..." Patrick raised his voice incredulously. How could this be easy? He was up to his elbow in horrible juices, the mother's contractions were crushing both his hands and the baby's head, and he didn't even know how many she had in there. "Oh, Lord God, help me, help poor Banbeg... urgh, oh by Heaven, that's vile!"

"And that has to be the strangest prayer I've ever heard," Victoricus, despite his carefully calculated attempts to be gruff, started to laugh. "You're doing fine. Just keep turning the head..."

With a sudden spurt the baby's head emerged, with a pop, and look of surprise.

"His eyes are open," Patrick marvelled, "he's looking at me!"

"What a thing to be your first sight in the world," Victoricus joked. "He'll probably decide to go back in."

Despite this jesting prediction, the birth proceeded more easily after the head had been released, and within moments the whole body had slithered out. Patrick sat back on his haunches, astonished, forgetting his gruesome hands, and despite himself joined Victoricus in laughter. "I don't believe it... look at that, she did it! Thank you God!"

The mother was already turning, nuzzling and licking her lamb, which, incredibly to Patrick's eye, was struggling to stand. Despite the mess, and the ugly throbbing umbilical cord which still dangled from the mother's rear, he found himself dazzled by the beauty of new life.

"Stop gawping for a moment." Victoricus took Patrick's sticky hand, and pressed it under the mother's belly. "You feel that?"

"What am I feeling?"

"A soft space, you ninny. You're in luck, she's only carrying the one. Now all you have to do is wait for the afterbirth. She'll eat it... now don't look like that, it will make her strong, and help her give milk to her baby. Try to get a look at it before she eats it, to make sure it isn't torn. If it's torn, she will sicken, and you'll be left with a motherless lamb. But Banbeg is healthy, and her labour was short, so she'll probably be fine."

It was just as Victoricus predicted. By the time Banbeg had delivered and consumed the afterbirth the lamb was standing, suckling eagerly. Patrick couldn't get over how beautiful the little girl was. As he cooed over the beauty of her pink little nose and delicate ears Victoricus smiled indulgently. "You sound like the lamb was your first born son. If ever you do marry you'll be a doting father. We can be sure of that."

Patrick's heart sank, thinking of how unlikely it was that he would ever marry. Even if he were ever to be free, he had concluded that he would never risk bringing a child into this world. And having seen how painful labour was, even to a sheep, he couldn't imagine asking a woman he loved to accept the danger of childbirth.

He kept his thoughts to himself though. Some truths were his alone.

In the end thirty-three ewes gave birth, with fifty-two lambs between them. Of the lambs that were born, seven died, mostly the weaker of twins. The worst death was that of a single giant of a lamb who became stuck, killing the mother. Patrick sobbed convulsively as Victoricus introduced him to the uses of the long, thin, flexible blade. Grimly the old man instructed him in the dreadful duty of dismembering the unborn infant in order that he could be born, a piece at a time. The operation was not a success. The mother died with her son.

Two other ewes died during the lambing, a week apart from each other, leaving offspring. On both occasions Victoricus dressed the orphans in the skin of dead lambs, in an attempt to fool a bereaved mother into accepting them. One young mother quickly accepted the tiny imposter, and allowed him to suckle. Within a few days they were able to safely remove the coat. An older ewe, however, refused to fall for the ruse, obstinately turning her back. The little orphan staggered around after her, burdened down by the sad coat of her dead child, plaintively bleating, while the intended mother continued to walk away, and away.

Finally she turned and rushed at him, and Victoricus scooped him up before she could trample him.

"It's no good. She won't fall for it; we'll have to look after him ourselves."

Life became a constant round of milking the childless mother, and trying to keep the little lamb alive. Dipping a rag into the milk for the lamb to suckle on, Patrick thought of his illness toward the end of the long march across Ireland. He wouldn't be alive if it hadn't been for Fionula's patience and skill. It became a point of anguish to him that the lamb should live, and he prayed constantly that God would spare him. After the first three days the lamb's eyes were brighter, and he gambolled and skipped around Patrick's heels, as though the man was his mother. Seeing the lamb's devotion, Patrick's heart was glad. *Perhaps this is why God took everything away from me*, he thought. *A motherless lamb will always love the shepherd.*

He called the lamb Nathan.

As well as their duties of care to the orphaned lamb, the new members of the flock needed constant supervision in order to learn which areas were safe, and which were not. The lambs skipped with such alacrity into so many different kinds of danger that Patrick wondered at times how any of them survived. Nathan was the only one of the lambs who had the sense not to run into trouble. He was as obedient as a well trained dog.

Inevitably, perhaps, one little lamb managed to fall from the cliff. Fortunately there was a sharp wind coming in from the ocean that day, and when Patrick lay flat and looked over the edge he could see the little creature had landed on an outcropping ledge, about twenty feet below. The mother was so distressed that she had to be taken and tied up in the pen, and her cries echoed shrilly, bouncing over the landscape, as though she was not one desperate mother, but twenty.

Patrick and Victoricus had their first real fight, arguing as to which of them should hold the rope, and who would be better suited to climb down after the lost lamb. Both were angry enough that the quarrel was soon bilingual, Patrick shouting in British, Victoricus in Greek. Both men thought they should be the one to descend the cliff face, and both had good reasons for their choice. Victoricus pointed out that Patrick was far and away the taller of the two, and therefore probably weighed more. Patrick insisted that he was built of twigs and feathers, having starved over winter, and Victoricus had obviously eaten better, and was, beside, a solid oak of a man. Victoricus, not wanting to concede the point, declared that he was older than Patrick, and having lived longer had fewer years to lose if he fell. Patrick snapped back that he had more years to endure if he didn't. Finally Victoricus insisted that he had scrambled on those cliffs alone in years gone by, and that he would be the best choice to go down to the ledge. Patrick fastened sharply on the phrase 'years gone by,' and learned that Victoricus had last made this suicidal descent twenty years earlier, and that on that occasion the lamb had only dropped a dozen feet.

"I don't mean to be insolent," Patrick asked, his tone belying his words, "but did you have two good eyes at the time?"

Victoricus was hurt. "There's nothing wrong with my sight," he said. "I can see just fine out of one eye, that's good enough."

Patrick remembered his tutor Simon teaching him from the Greek physicians, explaining that a one eyed man could have difficulties judging distance, and balancing. That had been one of the more enjoyable lessons he remembered... wearing a patch on his eye while Simon proved the point through experiment rather than book learning.

Sooner than argue with Victoricus Patrick followed his teacher's method. Taking a pebble from the ground he called out, "Catch!" and threw. Victoricus put his hand up and the stone whistled right past it.

"That was a lucky shot," Victoricus snapped. "Try again."

After five more attempts he gave up, in a huff. Patrick was angry, both with himself and Victoricus. He felt he'd been pushed into a position where he had no choice but to remind a man he respected that his body was failing. Victoricus was no doubt a very strong man, particularly for his age... Patrick had ample evidence of that, but he was still not the man to descend the cliff face. It was frustrating that he refused to admit it. To lessen the sting of his criticism Patrick started trying to explain the

Greeks' theory of binocular vision, before trailing off embarrassed. For one thing, Victoricus was far more knowledgeable than Patrick when it came to the Greeks. For another thing, it didn't improve matters to explain the mechanism by which Victoricus had lost his ability to properly judge depth and distance.

"I know what you're saying," the old man complained, though obviously cooling, now that he was speaking Patrick's language again. "I was a teacher myself, remember. It's blind I am, not stupid."

"I'm sorry," Patrick was truly upset, responding in the people's Greek as a gesture of apology. "I didn't mean to hurt your feelings."

Victoricus sighed, and shrugged. "I suppose you meant no harm."

"Anyway," Patrick said, "I know you're strong enough to hold my weight, I've seen you carrying the sheep across your shoulders."

"Now you're just flattering me." Victoricus did, however resign himself to the situation, and as they organised the rescue effort he took charge again, and began to cheer up. Once they had made their mind up as to who did what the rescue attempt progressed rapidly. Patrick was secured to the strong rope, secured around a boulder that jutted up out of the earth like the protruding tusk of a pig. For a long time Patrick had resented this rope, wondering what possible reason there was for it to be taking up space in the lean-to when he had nowhere to cover his head. Now that he had a purpose for it, he didn't complain. Victoricus braced himself behind the rock, wrapped the rope around his waist, and with plenty of slack looped behind for him to feed out between his hands, he nodded his head, signalling Patrick to go.

The moment the descent began Patrick was hit by a wave of dizziness, so bad that he could feel it all over his body. It was as though his feet, chest, and belly were caught in a cold fire. He could feel the lack of earth beneath him as a tingling in the soles of his feet. He shut his eyes for a moment, convinced he was going to wet himself. The wind was pushing him flat against the cliff face, and even though his bare toes were splaying out as deftly as fingers in their search for cracks, he knew he was going to fall.

"You don't know that at all," he said aloud, though he could barely hear his voice over the thump of his heart and the crying of the wind.

"That's the devil telling me that, and he's a liar." Pressing his forehead against the rock he calmed his breath, then spoke again. "The wind is my friend. It's nothing but the palm of God, pressing me safely against the wall. It carried the lamb to a safe place, and it will keep me from falling. Victoricus has the rope. So, listen, Patrick, don't be afraid."

Slowly, very slowly, he stretched his right foot down, found a lip of rock to rest his toes on. Then he inched his right hand a little lower, finding a crack to cling onto. Sure of his balance he gently moved his left foot down, and found a hole, into which he jammed his foot as far as it would go. He stopped, breathed, and brought down his left hand. He paused, for as long as it took to thank God that he hadn't died yet, and began the whole painful process again. With the rope taut above him, like an umbilical, he continued his descent, urged on by the phantom bleating of the lost lamb, blown hither and thither by the wind.

The lamb had fallen in the mid morning, and it was noon before he finally spidered his way onto the ledge. The baby ewe turned her terrified face toward him, with a pleading expression. Patrick remembered keenly the verse, 'I am the good shepherd, Who lays down His life for his sheep.' If someone had told him a year ago that he would not only volunteer to risk his life for a lamb, but would actually argue the point and demand to do so, he would have said they were mad.

"Lord, I don't want to lay my life down for this sheep, I'd be much happier if you'd save us both together."

Gingerly he knelt on the ledge next to the lamb, his feet jutting behind him over the terrible space beneath. He was grateful that the croppy spur was such a wide piece of shelf. It almost felt as though he had reached firm land.

Almost, but not quite.

"Hello, little land gull," Patrick whispered to the frightened lamb, gently, to soothe himself as much as her. "I know what happened, you looked up at the clouds, and you thought, 'look at those sheep over there, I'll go and play with them'. You thought, 'if they can fly, why can't I?' That's it, isn't it? Come here, little lamb, let me look at you. Don't be scared." With a gentle voice Patrick crooned to her, and somehow, miraculously, she allowed him to fasten her up safely. Perhaps it was fear, he thought, making her so docile. He knew how that felt. Strapping her to his belly, he carefully bound her to him with knots that one of the fishermen had taught him the previous summer. He remembered that slow hot night on which nobody could sleep, and wondered where such slow nights had gone.

"You see, little cloud, everything will be fine. God knew I'd need to tie a good knot one day, and that's why you're safe. Now, be a clever little lamb, and don't try to fly away again."

With jagged caution he stood, found his centre of balance, prayed, and tugged on the rope three times. He started to climb.

He had expected the climb back to be harder, given the bulk of the lamb at his belly, but the rope was being pulled up far more quickly than he'd expected. In fact, the ascent was so swift that he barely had time to find finger and toe holds. He became alarmed by the thought that Victoricus might be over exerting himself.

The solution to the mystery revealed itself when he looked up, and saw over the edge of the cliff two familiar heads peering down at him. Colm and Caithail were adding their weight to that of Victoricus and the three men lost no time in heaving him back to solid land. Before he knew it he was over the lip of the cliff, lying flat on the grass, arms wrapped round his precious bundle, panting.

"Thank you," he gasped, and crawled inland. He didn't feel safe until he was well away from the edge. He looked at Victoricus, who was grinning from ear to ear.

"You must have thought I'd gained the strength of giants," he said.

"I admit, something like that did cross my mind."

Colm and Cathail joined them, and plopped on the ground.

"You, Boy," Colm said, "are without a doubt the maddest man I have ever seen."

"You think I'm mad," Patrick jerked his head at Victoricus. "I had to throw rocks at this one to stop him from going over."

The fishermen looked from one to another, incredulously.

"You're joking."

Solemnly Patrick declared, "I never joke. You know me, I have no sense of fun."

There was a moment's silence before everyone cracked up. The extremity of fear past, Patrick's dizziness had taken on another turn, and he felt expansive, light, and a little bit drunk. The world was a very beautiful place. As he untied the lamb who had caused all this trouble Victoricus went to release her mother. Nathan had been confined with her also, lest his devotion to Patrick caused him to follow him down the cliff. The moment of reunion between mother and child raised a round of noisy Irish applause from the fishermen, and Patrick joined in, enthusiastically smacking his palms together. Nathan chose this moment to alarm the fishermen by springing over their heads, and bounding all around Patrick, nipping and nuzzling him, as though to reassure himself that his friend was alright.

"Are you his mother?" Cathail asked, incredulously, as Patrick kissed the questing nose of his favourite charge.

"He thinks I am," Patrick replied. "Poor Nathan."

"Oh by the heavens and the deep blue sea," the fisherman exclaimed. "He's only gone and *named* them."

"Well, how else can I have a conversation with them?" Patrick looked at the man. "They all speak British, you know."

Victor interjected, in his poor Irish. "They do not. They speak Greek. Any fool knows that."

Colm shook his head. "It must be the height," he said, "you're both as mad as each other. I've never seen anything like it – what were you thinking climbing all over the cliff's face for a lamb?"

"She's called Scammall," Patrick said. "She used to have a dull name, but she's earned this one, chasing clouds."

The men laughed, then Colm said, "I suppose you weren't afraid because of your god?"

"I was petrified."

"Well, you're not utterly crazy then. You know that if the wind had been different we would have been out on the ocean, and wouldn't have been able to come and help?"

"I'd have managed," Victoricus huffed.

"Probably, you look like you have roots for arms. But even so... you were lucky we saw you, Holy Boy. If we'd been on the boats you'd have been strung up on that cliff for the rest of the day."

"If the wind had been different Scammall would have blown out to sea, and I wouldn't have had to go after her."

"Well," Cathail said. "You're not his favourite slave, but I think the master will have to admit you did a good job today."

"Never mind the master, he's down in the valley, and we are on the top, under a sunny sky on a broad blue day... and we have food for you mad heroes." Colm opening a sack spread out bread, cheese, fish and boiled eggs on the grass.

Patrick realised how hungry he was.

"God is good," he said, and lay on the grass to eat.

"God is good," chorused the fishermen.

Victoricus caught Patrick's gaze, and winked with his good eye.

At first he was far away, a pale dot in the far distance, so far and so small she hardly knew it was him. Then with a dizzying rush he was standing in front of her, at the altar in Potitus' little church, his face illuminated with the golden lamplight, an unreadable expression in his eyes.

"Patrick," she called, and he turned toward her with a smile. He held out his hand to her, but as she moved to touch him she woke.

This time when she started to cry she let her husband hold her. Finally, her sobs gentling, she fell asleep in his arms.

Calpornius lay awake for some time, his face covered in her hair. When he slept he dreamt of her warmth and comfort, and he woke to her kiss in the morning.

Perhaps God loved them after all.

Chapter Eighteen

Ewing was followed by shearing. For weeks Patrick had been too busy to descend into the valley, but there was more commerce up and down the crag than there had been in winter. Most days the master would send a couple of slaves up to fetch fleeces, or to take a lamb for the slaughter. Patrick always made sure that Scammall and Nathan were well out of sight when the men came.

Shearing had none of the charms of the birthing season, and was simply hard, thankless, sweaty work. The sheep who had so trusted Patrick through the long winter, and who had been glad of his ministrations while they laboured, took fright at his first, timid attempts to relieve them of their fleece. Victoricus did the bulk of the work, pinning the sheep firmly between his thighs, and slicing with the blade smoothly, and with a speed that made Patrick fear he would cut the sheep's throat by accident. Yet it was Patrick who caused the most injuries, his fumbling attempts often interrupted by nicking the skin, and causing a little bleed, which he would have to tend immediately before starting again. He felt all thumbs, and foolish, and was sure that the sheep thought so too. He wondered how on earth he was supposed to take charge of this operation the following year, when he would be up on the top alone.

He didn't want to think about that. Already he was missing Victoricus, and his complete failure to shear even one sheep without assistance was beginning to worry him. It appeared also to have been noticed in the valley below. After several fleeces had gone down in less than perfect condition the master sent up Gill with two men that Patrick had never seen before. Victoricus, despite his poor eye, spotted them first. Squinting down the slope he said, "Patrick, here comes trouble."

"What?"

"That's the Keeper of the Slaves, isn't it?"

"It is," Patrick remembered the beating he had received in the winter, when the old ewe Mara died. "I think I'm in trouble."

"He's got a couple of others with him, I recognise them... freemen from my master's household. Relatives of your master, doing him a favour I suppose. They must be back up if you decide to fight. This doesn't look good."

"It's because I made a mess of the fleeces, isn't it?"

"Everyone makes a mess of the fleeces when they start. You did better than some. You just need to be very careful and calm when you're doing it, and trust yourself. That's all."

Patrick couldn't imagine how his master thought that beating him would calm his nerves. He stood uncertainly, watching the men ascend.

"He's done this before," Victoricus said, scornfully. "When he's in a bad mood he'll take it out on a slave's back. The poor little boy before you... I only met him one time, your master hired me to sheer the sheep. Well, that little boy's back told the story. Maybe you should hide in the woods."

Patrick shook his head. "That wouldn't help; he'd send him back again, this time with an army. Or he might strike you instead."

"He can't, I'm another man's slave. They might be 'Dirb Fine' as they say, sharing the same great grandfather, but if he hits me it could break their friendship. He'd not risk that."

"If I hide, they might say I've run away, and then they could kill me."

Victoricus sighed. "You're right, of course. You'll have to bear it."

For whatever reason Gill had been absent from the valley when Patrick descended, briefly, in the spring. Perhaps the man had been sent back to market. Whatever the reason, since then Patrick had been so busy with the ewing and sheering that he simply hadn't had time to make the descent again. The last time he had seen Gill had been the previous winter, after the death of the black ewe. On that occasion he had been so ground down by the weather, and the loss of the sheep, and the long despairing nights that the beating had hardly registered. Gill himself had not bent to the task with any relish, and rushed the job, perhaps not wanting to be up on the top for too long.

This time was going to be different. It was obvious from the moment Patrick could see his face that Gill was in a far more buoyant mood than he had been on that wintery day. There was a spring in his step, and he was smiling, everything about him speaking of his anticipation for the task ahead.

Patrick gnawed his thumb. He was beginning to think he should have run.

"I can pretend it was me," Victoricus said suddenly. "They don't know it was you, after all, and if I say it was me they can't beat me."

"They'll never believe you," Patrick said, "you've been a sheep slave for years now. They know your work." He looked grimly at his friend. "I'll not give them the satisfaction of trying to wriggle out of it. They'll beat me anyway." Gritting his teeth he shrugged himself out of his tunic and handed it to Victoricus. Commending himself to God, he made his way to Gill and the strange men.

"Get on with it then," he challenged, and turned his back.

When he came to he was lying flat on his stomach, and his whole body felt on fire. Someone was touching him, and he screamed.

"Oh. *Now* you cry out." Victoricus's voice was shaking. Patrick tried to think, to figure out what was happening, but nothing made sense. He felt again a hand on his back, reaching inside him, playing his pain like a harp. He bucked, and heard a noise coming out of him, like a dead tree groaning in a storm. He tried to scramble away from the ugly noise he was making, but his limbs were out of his control. He flailed instead like an injured crab. Something cold and smooth was stealing across his skin, where the hand was working. Fear rose up in him, with a swift dark intensity, like the night rising up from the sea in the West, swallowing the world. He started to weep. He was going to die.

Then, at the most terrible moment, the world snapped, and there was silence. The pain continued but no longer as part of him. He was somewhere else. Patrick hung suspended above the scene, watching

Victoricus kneeling beside him, applying liniment. Now he understood. God had allowed him see that Victoricus was helping him. The hand that hurt was the hand that healed. In the moment of understanding he was plunged back into himself, burning. He tried not to scream again, and bit the fleece. At some point, mercifully, he passed out, and Victoricus completed his ministrations in peace.

For the next week he lay on his front, while Victoricus cared for his injuries. He wasn't the only person who attended Patrick at this time. It seemed the story of the savage beating had descended to the valley below. There was a division in the very master's household, since one of the men who attended the beating was a cousin of the family. He had, as Victoricus suggested, gone as a favour to his kinsman. He spread the story abroad that Gill was wasteful of the master's resources, and had attempted to beat the sheep slave to death. Patrick learned at some point in his recovery that this man, who had originally been sent to hold him down, had finally let go of him, and been forced to pull Gill off.

He could only remember the start of it, the two freemen taking his arms and Gill walking backward to take a run up. He had bitten his tongue so hard with the first blow that it bled, but he didn't cry out. Victoricus had been praying; he remembered that. And he remembered hearing Greek, and British, and a voice saying urgently over and over again, "Patrick, Patrick, cry out or he'll kill you."

A steady stream of visitors came up from the valley. On days when the boats couldn't put out to sea the fishermen sat up top, declaring vociferously that Patrick was a lunatic, and any sane man would have cried out instead of taking the beating like a stone. "You know that's what Gill hates most? He was spitting about it when he came down... he'd have stopped if you'd only screamed a bit."

"I didn't want him to enjoy himself," Patrick said, dourly, and the men laughed their appreciation at this peculiar form of triumph. The sheep slave might be mad, but you had to admire him for his madness.

Fionula increased her visits from once a week to daily. The Lady sent up honey and mead, which went straight to Patrick's head, since he had not touched any drink other than water or milk in over a year. He was glad of it, since it seemed to take the pain away.

"Tell her I'm eating," he said, woozily. "I don't want her to think I'm fasting against her."

"I will," Fionula said. "She's very upset. She thinks you will stop praying for her child."

Patrick realised that he'd not prayed for days, he'd been too busy drifting in and out of sleep. He still could not move, but he could at least pray, he chastised himself.

"Tell her that if she will pray for me then I will pray for her."

"She'll pray to Brigid or Oghma."

"Tell her to pray to the Living God," he said. "Brigid and Oghma are no friends of mine."

"I'll tell her. Patrick, she has a secret, that she didn't want me to tell you…"

"What's that?"

"She's pregnant. She hasn't told the master yet."

Patrick, lying on his front, suddenly smiled. "Didn't I tell you God looks after us," he said, completely oblivious to how incongruous his statement sounded, coming from a man with a flayed back.

"You did," Fionula pulled a face. "I'm going to have a bit of a word with Him though," she said in a surprisingly disrespectful manner. "I wish He'd hurry up and look after you."

Eventually, Patrick was well enough to walk. The guests slowed down to a trickle, then stopped, apart from Fionula's visits, which continued once or twice a week. Before long the summer was rolling toward autumn.

Patrick and Victoricus spoke less. They were aware that their time together was running out, and that once they were parted they might never see each other again. Patrick was trained, and from now on he would have to manage the sheep by himself. If he was ill someone might be sent to help occasionally, but apart from extreme emergencies, he would be on his own.

Finally the dreaded day arrived. Word came up from the valley with Finn that Victoricus was to return to his master. The two men sat down, wordlessly, and stared at the ground. Finn, catching their mood, hunkered down between them, then, with an impulsive gesture of sympathy, caught a hand each, and held them.

"I'm sorry," he said. "You'll miss each other."

"We will," Patrick said.

"You have me. I can come up sometimes. You can teach me your way of catching words again."

Patrick tried to smile at the boy's eagerness to study, so unlike his own attitude at that age. "Thank you."

The boy smiled, then got to his feet. "Christos be with you both," he said formally. Then he grinned, the impish grin of the young, and waved to them. "I have to go," he said, and bounced off, running down to the valley. He looked to Patrick like a lamb, springing easily over the grassy steep.

Victoricus's one bright eye glistened, and his ugly face was suffused with regret. He stood, slowly, and looked at Patrick. His lips worked as he struggled to speak.

"I have to go." His voice was choked with grief.

"Father," Patrick said, urgently, and stood. He towered over the old man, and realising that this was his last goodbye corrected himself by kneeling. He put his arms round Victoricus' waist and hugged him. "We will at least meet in heaven," he said.

"I'll see you before then, my Son," the old man replied, and kissed Patrick's head.

Patrick would see Victoricus again, once, for just a moment. It would have brought him no comfort to know it. That late summer day, as his companion departed, he learned a strange truth. He knew now that he was finally a man, with all the bitterness and sorrow that came with it. It would be many years and a world away before he glimpsed his friend again.

Perhaps he already knew it, for he felt his heart fly out of him as he watched the old saint go.

Potitus could feel it now, his own age. He knew it in his bones, as though frost were settling in for winter. He wouldn't survive this siege. His lungs were beginning to rattle and all his joints were sore.

One morning, he found it, his death. It was a solid lump between the skin and muscle of his abdomen. He prodded it, and it shifted slightly. He found it not painful, but uncomfortable, feeling somehow unclean. He nodded his head silently, a little grim. He had seen this kind of thing before, when visiting the sick. It was the seed of his own death. It might grow rapidly, and take him in less than a year, it might grow slowly, but now that it was in his flesh his end was sure.

Was it any surer than it had been a year ago, though? All men would die, unless the Lord came first. Potitus sighed, and glanced East, automatically, the habit was so engrained. It could not be long now till the Lord came, the world had grown so ill. When He came all His children would be changed, in a moment, in the twinkling of an eye, and receive heavenly bodies, like unto His own. Until He came Potitus, like the rest of the world, would have to deal with corruption and death.

What bothered him most though was not this canker in his flesh. When he did come to die, or be snatched up with the Lord, whichever came first, the question which haunted him was... would he find Patrick there? Potitus knew that he should trust God, and accept His justice, whatever finally happened. But the idea of gaining heaven while losing his grandchild struck him as a painful victory. He bent his head, and asked God to forgive him his family pride, but asked again that, if possible, Patrick be made safe against that great and terrible day.

When it came down to it, he was resigned to his own death. He had always known that he was going to die after all – there was nothing new in that. But the eternal death of that young boy was more than he could bear. "Lord God," he prayed, "You can do anything You desire, all things are possible for You. Please, if it is Your will, let me see Patrick one more time before I die. Glorify Yourself in this as in all things, and let me have the impossible, for your Son, but also, oh God..." he was weeping now, "for Conchessa, for my own son. For me."

CHAPTER NINETEEN

Summer rolled into autumn, and autumn to a merciless winter. The ground was once again iron, and every morning Patrick would trudge to the stream, and break the water, until the frost deepened near even to the bottom of the pool. He and the sheep drank snow.

First Niamh, then the Bhean Uasail were brought to childbed. Both were delivered of boys. Early one morning, in the teeth of a chill wind, Finn struggled up the icy slope to give Patrick the news that an heir had been born to the 'big people', in answer to Patrick's prayers.

Finn had taken to bringing his writing tablet with him when he climbed up, and no matter how cold, would huddle next to the fire for a lesson. Patrick taught him first the alphabet, then, as best he could figure a spelling, some words in Irish... sheep, mountain, sea, snow, cloud. The boy marvelled at the mystery of being able to catch a word out of the air, and pin it down. Eagerly he scratched out his lessons with a sharpened stone on the wax, sometimes holding it near the fire to soften it enough for writing. By midwinter he was able to inscribe in Gaelic, 'God so loved the world that He gave His only begotten Son,' or 'Do not worry what to eat, what to wear or put on your feet.' With a flat stone Patrick would smooth the wax between inscriptions, and the boy would eagerly start again. His love and respect for Patrick grew, though his teacher insisted that he was not in the least bit learned. Deep down Patrick wondered why he was filling the boy's head with a love of learning, when there was no hope it would ever do him any good. And yet the boy continued coming up the hill on any pretext for a lesson. His hunger for the word of God grew.

One bitingly cold morning Finn arrived with a gift of food, a leather jacket, and mittens. Patrick shared his meat with the messenger, and together they huddled over the fire and the lesson until the boy seemed able to begin the descent again.

"You need to get going, or it will be too late. Better to get in the warm."

Finn suddenly blurted out. "I want to stay up here."

Patrick looked at him, astonished. "Why would you want to stay up here?"

"I hate it down there. I hate, I hate..." the boy burst into tears. "I hate Gill."

Patrick's jaw dropped, and a dreadful suspicion came over him. "What, has he hurt you?"

The boy rubbed the snothers from his nose, and sniffed. Quietly he whispered, "he says it's because I'm his favourite."

Patrick exploded to his feet. "I'm going to kill him," he shouted. "By the Wolf, I'm going to kill him." His jaw worked convulsively. "I'm sorry," he said, "I shouldn't have shouted." He blinked hard against the snow. His eyes were as hard and grey as flint. "I'm coming down with you."

Finn jumped up and took a step back. "You can't, the master will be angry."

"The master can choke on his anger," Patrick declared. "If he lets that Man... if he lets that Man..." he stopped talking, paled, and puked. Finn was shaking. The Holy Boy looked so fierce. Patrick abruptly snatched his crook, and grasping the boy by the shoulder started marching. The boy was forced to run to keep up with him. He was scared. Patrick was talking to himself, whispering rapidly in British. What was he doing? Praying to Christos? He didn't hear the Holy words. Who was the man talking to?

"Please," Finn cried out with fear, "please, who will look after the sheep?" Looking down at the boy Patrick replied tersely, "God can look after the sheep."

By the time they had arrived in the valley Finn was as scared as he'd ever been. Patrick was grasping the boy's hand now, tugging him toward the huts. The snow had turned to rain, and the boy skidded in the slush as Patrick cast his eyes about, hunting down his prey. Whether the master or Gill the boy didn't know. The few slaves who were working outside in the bad weather paused in their labours and stared. They'd never seen anything like this before.

Patrick came to the big stone house, and stood outside it. It had a wooden door, not a flap. The boy had never been in it, or even this close to it. He bit his lip, not sure whether Patrick was going to knock on the door, march through it, or kick it down.

Instead the man stood, planted his crook in front of him, and raised his voice.

"Man of the House," he cried. "Come out now."

A scattered group of people were beginning to gather, drawn by the unexpected ruckus like crows to a carcass. Patrick barely noticed them. He called out again.

"Come out now, I have a message for you, and the Keeper of the Slaves."

The door opened, and Fionula put her head out, her eyes wide with fright.

"Patrick, Patrick," she stammered in astonishment. "What are you doing, you mustn't..."

"Tell the master that I have a message for him, from the God of heaven, and that the message will be heard."

Fionula stepped backward into the interior. There was panicky whispering, and suddenly the Lady was in the doorway, clutching her baby.

"Please, Holy Boy," she said, "don't let your god be angry with me. I couldn't bear it if he took my child away."

"The message isn't about your child, but this one." Patrick put his arm around the terrified Finn, and hugged him to his side.

"The little slave?"

"Not just your slave, but God's slave, as we all are. Your 'Man'," his lip curled on the word contemptuously, "is guilty of misusing the slave of a great Lord, the God of heaven, and he will answer for it."

Suddenly the Lady disappeared from the doorway, as though she had been pulled back, and the master stood in her place. His face was working with fury.

"How dare you come down here, on this day of all days, the day my son is to be named, and try to instruct me on how to keep a slave! The women might think you're something, with your prayers, and strange ways, but no freeman would listen to you. Why, you're nothing but a sheep boy. I'll have you flogged to death for this."

By now it seemed every slave in the place had gathered to listen, but Patrick was beyond seeing them, and maintained his burning gaze on the master.

"You can't kill me, unless God allows you to, and God Himself sent me down here with a message for you, and your 'Man.' This boy, Finn, he might be your slave, but he isn't Gill's slave. And if Gill does not get down on his face and beg the boy's forgiveness, I swear by heaven..." he lifted his crook, like a staff, "I swear by heaven, God will strike him dead."

In the dreadful silence which followed this pronouncement everyone could hear Finn weeping. Patrick looked down at him, and in a flash saw himself as the boy did, as they all must do... some wild haired, crazy, foreign creature, a Gaill, who had lost his mind on the mountain, and forgotten all the rules of man.

"Oh, Jesus," he prayed, suddenly afraid for himself and for Finn. He was going to get himself killed and do the boy more harm than good. The only prayer he could think of was the name of the Lord. "Jesus," he said, "Jesus Christ..."

The master became pale, at the sound of his praying, and stepped outside.

"Sheep boy," he said, then looked to his wife who was peering through the door. "What's his name?"

"Pudrig, I think..."

"Pudrig," the master said. "If as you say the man Gill has overstepped his boundaries in the discipline of this boy..."

"It is not discipline to use a child as he used him," Patrick found his voice again. "He used that child as no child should ever be used, and the whole household winked at it. But God does not wink. He sees sin, and this child was sinned against. Is this place a farm," he demanded, "or a brothel?"

The master said nothing, white with a combination of anger and dawning fear. He looked at the gathered slaves. They all knew, as he did, what Patrick was talking about.

Finally the master conceded defeat; looking over his shoulder he called to the house.

"Gill," his voice was sharp. "Get out here."

The Keeper of the Slaves came out, resentment and trepidation written across his face.

The master, keen to reassert control, folded his arms and looked at Gill. "You've heard the accusation," he said. "Is this thing true?"

Gill said nothing, furtively examining the ground.

"I'm speaking to you," the master said, voice cold.

Gill looked up, and seeing no sympathy there, looked away again. He blurted out, "I've not done anything wrong, there's no law against it."

"There is now," the master said. "I have a son born this day, and I would kill a man who used him so. You are lucky that you only touched a slave."

Gill made a shuffling gesture, and bent his head. "I will not do it again."

The master turned to Patrick, with a look on his face which said that he considered the business concluded. Patrick shook his head.

"Master of the Slaves," he addressed Gill, "that is not enough."

Gill sneered at him, trying to cover his fear. "What do you expect? A boy slave needs no restitution." This was not strictly correct, but the honour price for a slave was low, and the master was unlikely to enforce it.

"This boy is not only a slave of man," Patrick said, "but a bond slave of the Living God. You have wronged the God of Heaven, and He demands that you get down on your knees and beg His forgiveness."

Gill blanched, remembering his superstitious dread on the road, when Fionula had told her tall tales, of headless druids, and strange powers. Those tales, and the boy's strange long gaze had driven the taraigeacht away. The sheep slave stood before him, now a man, with the same dreadful eyes, and it suddenly dawned on Gill that perhaps he did have some power... why else would he have come down here? The man had stood against the Slua Dubh and won, if even a fraction of the slaves' gossip was true.

But still... to beg? To beg the boy's forgiveness? For what should he beg to be forgiven? Slaves were there to be used.

Despite his fear Gill shook his head. "I will not beg," he hissed against the sudden pain in his chest.

Patrick looked at him, and calmly replied: "You will kneel at this boy's feet, and beg his forgiveness, or God will strike you down."

"I will not kneel. I will not beg." Gill gritted his teeth at the increasing pain, and told his last lie: "I'm not afraid of your invisible god."

"Well then," Patrick's face took on a peculiar aspect of pity. "You will be dead."

Gill thrust his finger forward, pointing, and tried to speak, but no sound came out. Astonishment came over his face, and he took a staggering step sideways, as though someone had hit him. There was a moment's expectant hush, then Gill clutched his chest, and went down like a felled tree.

Those watching cried out in alarm, and started to push and shove, as some of them moved closer to see what was happening, while others backed away. Gill was lying on his back, opening and shutting his mouth like a suffocating fish.

Patrick dropped to his knees and took the man's hand. "It's not too late," he said urgently. "You have to repent of your sins, and call on Jesus, you don't *have* to go to hell."

Gill's eyes were bulging from their sockets, and he was making a noise, part speech, part choking, but nobody could understand him.

"Oh, Jesus, Jesus, Jesus," Patrick whispered.

The wet noise stopped. Patrick let go of Gill's hand, and looked up.

Nobody was moving, and all eyes were on him.

"I'm sorry," he said, into the stunned silence. "I did... I did try to warn him."

The master stepped backward, putting distance between himself and the sheep slave. His voice shook as he asked, "Am I safe from your terrible God?"

Bewildered, Patrick tried to think of something to say. All he could think was that Gill had died, and if he hadn't repented in his last moments, he was now in hell.

He swallowed convulsively, and hardly knowing he spoke said, "Nobody's safe from God."

One of the women knelt beside him, touching his arm. It took him a moment to realise it was Fionula. "Patrick," she whispered, "are you alright?"

He shook his head. He couldn't speak. He was bewildered at himself. He couldn't understand why he'd done what he'd done, how he'd had the courage to come flying down the mountain in such a rage, how he'd stood his ground when every law of the land was against him. The 'red mist', these Irish called it, when someone was in a holy temper. It had come over him like a storm, but now that it was gone he knew himself a slave again.

Wretchedness surged up in him. He was sick of everything. From the depths of his being he longed never to have to speak again. He wanted nothing more to do with the sons of Adam. He got to his feet, and staggered. The people around him shifted nervously, whispering. Patrick shook his head, and abruptly turned his face back to the mountain. It would be dark by the time he had returned to his sheep.

That winter he lost three old ewes to the weather. The snow heaped up on their carcasses, and they froze like stones to the landscape. When the bodies were taken down, and his failure discovered, there was no consequence. The master never sent for him to be beaten again. Even if he had wanted to, he could not have found a man who dared.

The Bhean Uasail continued to send up gifts of good food, which he accepted graciously, though he maintained his secret fasts. He was given permission to construct a hut immediately outside the sheep gate. When Finn came up a month later, shin deep in the snow, he brought news. The baby had been named.

His mother called him Pudrig.

Potitus was noticeably frailer. Toward the end of a long day his son often had to lend his shoulder to the old man, to support him on the walk home. So far he hadn't slacked off in any of his duties, working to the full extent of his strength as always, but Calpornius could see the day coming when the fight would go out of his father. He dreaded that day.

The old man muttered to himself out loud sometimes, not realising that he could be overheard. One expected a priest to talk aloud, after all, they were always praying, but these prayers were strange, as though Potitus had an argument with God. It made Calpornius uncomfortable.

One day, as they were tidying up the little church at the end of the prayers, Potitus asked a surprising question.

"If you could pray, Son, what would you pray for?"

This was the first time the old priest openly acknowledged his son's lack of faith, and the question, though innocently intended, twisted like fright in Calpornius' heart. He wanted to be able to answer it, but was struck dumb.

The old man looked at his son, the question still in his eyes. "I'll pray it for you," he explained, gently.

Calpornius blinked, and swallowed. Put point blank like that he knew the answer to the question, but he couldn't tell his father. He knew he should pray for faith, or trust in God.

But all he wanted to pray for was that his son was alive somewhere in the world, that there might be some children born who would call *him* grandfather.

That was one of Conchessa's impossible prayers though. Calpornius shook his head, smiled, and put his hand on his father's shoulder.

"It's alright, I can pray," he lied, and turned his head away from the disappointed expression on his father's face.

CHAPTER TWENTY

Patrick's hair and beard lengthened, though it did not become wild and woollen, as it had in his first winter. The old woman sent up a comb, carved from bone, and every time he used it he thought of her, and prayed. His body continued to strengthen. The soles of his feet were broad, splay-toed and hard as leather. Other than in the coldest heart of winter, he never wore shoes.

Only once did he go back down into the valley, the following spring. Fionula came up to him, accompanied by Finn, and told him that he was needed to come below.

"Finn can look after the sheep," she said, "the old mother's asked for you."

She was sitting in the hut, propped up in the same corner as that in which he had first seen her. The fire was blazing, and she was wrapped thickly in fleeces. The blaze threw dark shadows on her face, and he remembered again how terrified he had been of her when they first met. Now he wanted only to hold her, and take her fear away. It was written on her face.

"Patrick", she said, "you came."

"I ran all the way." He sat next to her, putting his arms around her fragile form. She rested her head wearily on his chest. She was egg shell frail, and he was afraid that she might break.

"Patrick, I've heard a lot about your god," she said, haltingly, "even when I didn't want to. Fionula talks of him..." she paused and coughed, and caught her breath before starting again. "She says that he is a god of love, but..." she gasped, "he's become a terror to me." She looked up at

Patrick, and he could see the fear in her eyes. "He punishes the wicked, does he not?"

"He does," Patrick said.

"Oh, Patrick," her eyes were heavy with unspilled tears. "I've been a very wicked woman."

"Mother, we've all been wicked, everyone has committed crimes against God."

"Not like mine."

"Everyone thinks that their sin is the worst, that God can't forgive it. But God does forgive."

"I don't understand," she said, "in the same moment your god is an angry god, and he punishes sin. He struck Gill dead. But then he is a great god, and loves his child. He protected Fionula, and has blessed her here. But you he has punished, again and again. Did you commit some sin?"

"I committed a terrible sin before I loved the Living God," Patrick admitted, "before I was taken. And as great as that sin was, I was in death and bondage long before I got here. I was raised in a household with the knowledge of God... and despite everything I was taught, and everything I heard, I refused to believe. I raised my fist at Him, I mocked Him."

"And so you must suffer," the old woman whispered, her voice like leaves. "Is that how it works? He makes you suffer until you have suffered enough, and he can forgive you?"

"That isn't it at all." Patrick squeezed her gently, and kissed the top of her head. "Oh, Mother... If I could only explain it to you..." He closed his eyes for a moment as words failed. How could he explain this to her?

"He loves me," he assured her, looking deeply into her eyes. "I'm already forgiven. I wish I could tell you. He's a good, gracious Master, and a loving Father. No matter what happens, He is with me. I suffer because man is evil, not because God is..." he struggled to find the word "capricious" in Irish, and gave up. "What I mean to say is... God is good. He allows me to suffer as a slave, but He does not cause it. And He gives His children strength to bear it."

"Ah... you don't understand. Patrick, may I tell you the story of my crime?"

"It says in the Book of God that if we confess our sin, He is gracious and will forgive us our sin."

"I've done many wicked things in my life," she said, "more than I could name if I lived another life time. But one of them crowns all." Her voice cracked. "Once, a long time ago," she turned her face away from him, "after all my children had been taken from me, sold to all corners of Ireland, perhaps even beyond... once, when I thought myself past the bearing of children, a man took me. And nine months later I bore a son."

She closed her eyes.

"I bore a son. And he was beautiful, and he was perfect, and I loved him with all my heart."

Patrick held her, gently, and stroked her hair, guessing what was to come.

"I loved him with all my heart. And I could not bear to have him sold away from me. I loved him with all my heart, so I took him to the river, and I held him under the water. And when he was dead, I took him back in my arms, and told everyone that he had been born dead. And then I buried him... outside the door here, by the beech tree where the snowbells grow in spring." Her whole body began to shake, and her tears were lost in the wrinkles on her face. "I loved him with all my heart, and he never had a name."

Patrick kissed the top of her head.

"God knows his name."

"How can he? I never gave him one."

"It says in Scripture," Patrick closed his eyes to remember, "it says in Scripture that God will give all the saints a white stone, with a name written on it that only He and they shall know. It says that we will be gathered into His kingdom, and stand unshakeable and strong, like columns in a temple..." he realised that he had slipped into the wrong language, and that she would not know what he meant. He tried again, "like trees in a forest. We will be like a tree, quiet and peaceful by the side of a river, and there will be no more crying, or pain or grief. He will wipe every tear away from your eyes."

"Why would he wipe away my tears? What I did was such a terrible thing."

"God has a Son too. Did Fionula tell you?"

"I tried not to listen."

"God has a Son, and His name is Jesus. He was taken by wicked men, and wrongly arrested, and was beaten, and they nailed Him to a cross. And God's Son died, and God's Son went to hell."

"What did god do to the ones who killed his son?"

"He forgave them."

"How could anyone forgive such a thing?"

"God is not just the Father, He's also the Son, and the Spirit of Life... And as the Son He rose from the grave. He was in the ground three days, and He burst up out of it, alive, and there were many dead in Jerusalem who were raised. And then the Son rose into heaven, and sent the Holy Spirit. The Holy Spirit lives in those who love God, and He will show you that you are forgiven, He will heal your broken heart."

"Oh, I wish I could believe this thing. I am so afraid to die."

"Well then," Patrick stroked the tears from her face. "Don't die. Look at Jesus, on the cross, dying for you. God does hate sin, you're right. He does punish sinners. But Jesus took your sin for you, and God punished His Son, instead of you. That's why Jesus died, so you don't have to. Believe in Him. Believe in Him, and be forgiven, and the day you slip your skin you will be with Him in paradise."

The old woman was breathing rapidly, her tears had made her tired. Patrick cast about desperately to find some comfort for her, then suddenly said, "Jesus had a mother too. A human woman, just like you. And just like you, she didn't want anyone to take her child from her. She stood at the foot of that cross, and she watched her dear Son die, and it broke her heart."

"Poor mother," the old woman whispered.

"But she saw Him again, when He rose from the grave. He rose, and took all her pain away." He looked down at her, and tears filled his eyes. He realised that he had named every sheep on the hill, but this woman had never had a name.

"Mother," he said, "can I give you a name?"

She opened her eyes, and looked at him, in something like wonder.

"A name?"

"The name of another mother, who loved and lost her Son. She was the mother of our Lord, and an angel said to her, 'all generations will call you blessed.'"

"You mean the mother of Jesus? I cannot have her name."

"But He forgives you... Mary."

The old woman groaned, then started to openly sob.

"Oh God," she said, "Oh Jesus, thank You for forgiving me."

Two days later, Mary died, with Fionula on one side and Patrick on the other. She was burned on a pyre at some distance from the huts. When the fire was finished Fionula gathered the ashes and bones, and Patrick dug a hole beneath the beech tree, next to where the snowbells bloomed in spring.

After that he no longer went down into the valley. Several autumns after Mary's death he was given unprecedented permission to gather wood and stones for a wall. For several days Finn minded the sheep while Patrick wandered deep into the forest in search of timber. The woods felt like a different country from the open spaces he had become so accustomed to, claustrophobic, and haunted by a different spirit. There were people living in the woods, escaped slaves, or criminals who had been banished from their tribes for some crime or other. They flitted like ghosts between the trees, striving to remain always out of sight. Victoricus had told him that the Irish had no death penalty, and no prisons. It seemed to Patrick, when he glimpsed these souls, that to the Irish this banishment was a living death. To have one's honour and place at the communal fire stripped away was to be utterly undone. It was like a glimpse of hell. He marvelled at how far a man could fall, become fugitive, hunted, eludach, lower than a slave, and still be prepared to suffer, just to scratch through another day. Without God, he thought, he couldn't have born his *own* exile. How much worse for those who knew not God?

He worked hard and fast on his wall, driving sharpened stakes into the earth at regular intervals, weaving them together with long thin strips. He was careful to leave narrow gaps in the woven panels, since he knew that the sharp wind would fill them like a sail otherwise, and his efforts would be wasted. With the help of whatever men were free from the valley he then built an extra layer of protection, on the near side of the fence. Together they lined rocks, for extra strength, carefully placing them so that even the most persistent of sheep would recognise a barrier. The men knew how to build a solid wall with only rough rocks, and Patrick learned fast. *So God fences us in,* he thought, *with His law, and His punishment and His love. Not because He wants to confine us, or trap us, or trick us, but just to stop us from falling, to keep us from death. Because He loves us. Because He loves me.*

The whole barrier was completed in late autumn, just as the first sleet came in from the sea, and the extra hands were called back down.

Apart from Fionula he had little company, and most of those who were sent up the mountain stood in awe of him. The exceptions were Colm and Cathail, who despite their early distrust of him had grown fond of him. In the winter, they would deposit the animal feed, then weather permitting, would stand and chat to him for a while, as though he was any other slave sitting in the hut by the fire. Their banter would cause him to smile in spite of himself, and they burst out laughing at the wry expression on his face, clapping his back and wishing him well before trooping down into the valley below. Patrick wasn't aware of how he appeared to the valley dwellers these days, a far cry from the naked sickened child who had first arrived. He had grown solemn eyed and stately as silence sank into his bones. Finn in particular worshipped him as a hero. Yet despite his seeming aloofness he would courteously listen when his guests described their problems and asked for prayer. He would always assure them that he prayed for them, and would urge them to seek the Living God themselves.

Little snippets of gossip made their way up from the valley, seeming to him to belong to another world. Little Pudrig had started to crawl, or talk, or walk. The weather was bad for the crops, too wet, or too dry. The master had hurt his leg hunting, or someone had broken a plate. All these things unfolded within his sight. He could watch the distant people as they went about their business; sometimes even the ringing of the blacksmith's hammer might echo up the slopes. Patrick knew that somehow, even on his high hill, he was linked into their adventure.

One dreadful day Cathail came up the mountain alone, and brought the news that Colm had been lost at sea. Patrick had watched the storm that overtook the fishermen's ship, with his heart in his mouth, and prayed for them both to be saved. Cathail wept as he sat with his back to the wall. Patrick sat silent beside him, and could not weep. Colm and Cathail had become the nearest things he had to male friends since Victoricus had left. Finn was more like a son. Thinking of the loss of Colm he was numb. Finally he told Cathail that he trusted Colm had looked to Jesus in the end, and that he had washed up on heaven's shore. Cathail reported Patrick's hope as a certainty to Niamh, and six weeks later Patrick was given a woollen knitted jumper in appreciation of his hope from Colm's young widow. All the following winter it reminded him to pray for her, and her child, as he blessed her for keeping him warm.

Despite Patrick's continued commerce with the valley below, the passage of time was working on him like a spell. He felt divorced from them all, separate from everything. It seemed at times, when the gossip came up, as though these lives of bustling, and friendship, and community, with all those loves and losses, was nothing but a story he was being told at the fireside. *Or perhaps,* he thought, *I am the story, the one being told.* He felt increasingly unreal, as though the wind could blow right through him.

A day came when Fionula arrived unexpectedly. He could see immediately that she'd been weeping. He put his arms around her, and let her rest on his chest for a moment. She alone of all his visitors understood and respected his silences.

When she'd stopped crying, he placed his hands on her shoulders, and stepped back, examining her face.

"What's wrong, á Shiun, sister?"

"It's good news, but bad."

He waited for her to explain.

"The master's tribe have made a new treaty, with a people to the North."

He raised an eyebrow, still not understanding.

"I'm from the North," she said.

"Ah," he replied, flatly. "I see."

"One of the guests recognised me, he says he's my mother's brother." Fionula sniffed. "I didn't know him, but he says I look just like my mother. And I remember his name, and the names of all my family, so it's certain that they're right."

"And so you have your freedom."

"And so I have my freedom. They have already redeemed me, paying my honour price to the master." She dropped her head, covering her face with her hair. "I never thought I would be so sad to be free."

"Don't be sad," he smiled, to cover his own sorrow. "To be free will be a good thing. You can marry if you like, you could still have children. You could be happy, in your own home."

"I will not marry," she said fiercely. "God called me to be a virgin for His sake."

She said 'virgin' unselfconsciously, because although she had been bought, and sold, and bought again, and although she had borne four children to as many men, until she was bought as a wet-nurse to Patrick's mother, she knew that she was a fresh creation, that God saw her whole, and healed, and clean.

Patrick gazed at her silently, acknowledging her choice. When he had been a boy, long before slavery, long before he had any sense, he had always laughed at those who chose chastity for Christ. It wasn't just him: all the boys had thought it was terribly funny. Priests were allowed to marry, and it was generally thought that anyone who chose abstinence was touched in the head. Patrick understood now. Especially for a woman, he realised, it made good sense. All he knew of sex was violence and pain, and even though it could be different in a marriage – Scripture said, the marriage bed was undefiled – for all that, the getting and raising of children was heartbreak, and many women died of it. As a virgin Fionula belonged to herself. She could dedicate herself, body as well as soul to her heavenly Master.

"I wish I could bring you with me," she said, wringing her hands. "For my sake, my kinsman would have bought you, but the master refused. He says you are a talisman, that you guard the high places, and bring luck. He thinks if he sold you, something terrible would happen. I'm sorry."

"It's not your fault the master believes nonsense," Patrick said. He tried to smile, though his face hurt. "Fionula," he said, and took her hands. He stroked her work worn fingers, then lifted them to his lips and kissed them. "Oh, God forgive me," he cried out abruptly. "I will miss you."

"There, there," she said, and petted his face, as though he were still a child. "Don't cry, sweet Patrick, I won't go..."

He pulled himself together. "You *must* go. You go with my blessing, because God freed you."

"Perhaps He will free you too."

Patrick said nothing. He had long given up hope.

"When you go," he said, "remember that God goes with you, and the same God that you pray to is the God I pray to. He holds us together in his hand. We'll always be together in Him."

"I know, I know," her face was streaked with tears.

"Tell your people," he said, "tell them about Jesus."

"I will."

He smiled at her again, and blinked. "Go now," he said, "go quickly, before I shame us both by crying."

She stood on tiptoe, and he bent his head to the kiss.

"I love you, Patrick."

"I love you too, Fionula." His voice caught. "I love you too."

Winter took hold, and the frost bit deep into his lungs. First he shivered, then he burned. With Fionula gone his food rations diminished, and he grew weaker every day. The snow was so bad that no provision came up for the sheep in over a week. He struggled for the first few days to keep warm, and did everything he could think of to make the food last. Even with careful rationing, their store was empty for two days. One morning he pulled himself up with his staff, planning to let the sheep out to quest for their own food, but his head span, and his legs gave way. He lay down in the snow and did not get up. When Cathail and Finn finally made it up the slope, later that day, they found the animals distressed, and Patrick dull eyed and sweating, talking to the air.

Finn stayed.

By the return of spring Patrick was still weak, and so Finn was introduced to the mysteries of lambing and sheering. Patrick felt a pang of memory as Finn knelt at the back end of Scammall, his eyes squeezed tightly shut, saying, "can't I watch you do it instead?"

Wryly Patrick smiled, and quoted Victoricus. "It helps if you open your eyes."

The seasons turned, and Finn was required again for fishing, so Patrick was alone once more. He was given permission to build in stone again, and this time worked alone, pulling rocks from the earth like reluctant teeth, lugging them from all over the mountain top, to the sheep pen. The wall grew stronger every day. *If this keeps up,* he thought, standing back to admire the finished work, *I may be allowed to build a stone shelter for myself this winter.* He was fully resigned to finishing his life on this top.

One whole month went by, without him speaking a single word to another human being. He prayed, constantly, as the days heaped up like leaves. Rain swept the top, and sleet, and the wolves in the wood grew ever bolder. For the first time he found himself confronted with one, a silver grey animal, slavering over an injured ewe. Patrick had never used the spear, and did not have it with him. But recognising the injured sheep, he threw himself, furiously, at the wolf, screaming in his face. As the creature backed off snarling Patrick started to beat him with the staff, and when he turned and ran Patrick pursued him, throwing stones, his cries of anger bouncing off the rocks.

When he returned to his injured sheep, she turned her head trustfully to him, and cried in the same plaintive voice that she had done, a lifetime ago, on the ledge. Patrick lay down on the ground next to her, and put his arm her over torn body. He whispered to her, nonsense, about sheep that flew, and woolly gulls. Scammall closed her eyes and died.

After that Patrick took the spear with him wherever he went. The wolves did not return.

Toward the beginning of spring, Patrick had the strangest dream.

In his dream he was sleeping, his body stretched in front of the sheep gate, with his spear and his staff by his side. He was surprised to see his face, how thin it seemed, and how long his beard was, burned from red to blond by the weather.

As he slept, he heard a Voice.

"You have fasted well. You are going home."

Patrick woke with a start. All was just as he had seen it in his dream. Beside him his staff and spear lay where he had left them. The sun was rising in the East, and away to the left was the ghost sunrise, the reflection that swelled up from those vast waters in reply to the coming of the sun.

The Voice had sounded so real. He couldn't imagine that this was just a dream.

As he turned to his task, letting the sheep out for the day, the words kept echoing in his mind. What could it mean? Fionula had been freed, and he had known then that God was in it. What of this? Could he truly be freed?

Perhaps, he thought, *the people in the valley are right. Perhaps the loneliness up here has driven me mad. Why would God speak to me? Hope is a killer,* he told himself. *That's why it was in the bottom of the box. It's a wolf, it comes to tear you.*

But then, as he was turning to watch the flock, he heard the Voice again.

"Behold, your ship is ready."

Patrick felt the staff slip from his fingers. The world stood still.

The Voice was real. He could not ignore it.

Woodenly he started to walk. He didn't stop to get food, he didn't think to take his small bundle of spare clothes. He simply put one foot in front of another, and began the long descent.

'Who will look after the sheep?' a whining voice in the wind asked.

"God will look after the sheep," Patrick replied.

'You can't leave your Master,' the voice said. 'Scripture says you should obey your Master.'

"I *am* obeying my Master," Patrick said, "He tells me there is a ship prepared, and so I go."

'When they find you've run away you will be nothing but an eludach, a fugitive slave. They will kill you, and where will you be then?'

"If I die I go to heaven, but God tells me that I'm going home. Nobody will touch me if God is with me."

The voice was blown away on the shreds of the wind, and Patrick carried on walking. Down the steep, rocky path, past the stunted trees, by the running spring, one foot in front of another, down and down and down.

Nobody looked up, nobody turned their head, nobody saw as he left. Patrick passed, invisible, from the place of his captivity, and nobody watched him go.

CHAPTER TWENTY-ONE

The journey took a long time. It had been six years since Patrick had crossed Ireland, and most of that journey he could barely remember. Even so, scraps of memory floated up, assuring him that he was walking in the right direction. Not knowing the countryside he didn't consider the other roads he could have travelled. Gill had chosen an open route, avoiding wooded places, in order to evade war gangs. This did make Patrick's journey safer in some respects, but the great problem he foresaw was that it would be hard to hide when other users of the wooden highway passed him on the floating road.

In the end Patrick decided it was easier to hide in plain sight. He no longer looked like a Roman, and his colouring and stance were as Irish as that of any local. If he kept his mouth shut nobody would notice his treacherous accent. He remembered Victoricus saying that the Irish and the British had sprung from the same Grandson of Noah, that they were distant 'Fine'. When he got home he was going to find copies of the Scriptures, he was going to read it; he was going to study every word. He would find the names of Noah's sons, read about his ancestors in the days before the Flood. God had ordered all things so well, all the peoples of the world had a common blood. Patrick thanked God that his people were such close kin to these Irish, and that he looked so similar. When he first arrived in Ireland he had feared and hated this people, half believing as he'd been told that they were part demon, not entirely human. Now, despite everything that had happened, he saw them as brethren, sons and daughters of Adam and Eve. They were not the terrible people of legend, for all the savagery of their worst customs.

He could pray for this people now, wherever he was in the world. And soon he would be home.

The thought of home buoyed him up. Perhaps that too made him invisible to others. Nobody would have looked at the tall, confident ragged young man striding purposefully along the road and thought him anything other than a poor farmer going to market. Escaped slaves hid, and looked fearful. Patrick shone with joy. Some of the other travellers took him for a peasant farmer going to meet his bride. Nobody looked at him twice. He was safe, and he knew it. God had spoken to him. He was going home.

He didn't know any fear until he finally arrived at the port. This, he realised, was the very same harbour onto which he had first stumbled six years ago. Walking through the market he saw other slaves, standing shackled, waiting to be sold. He tried not to stare at them, fearful that his expression would give him away, frightened that someone would take one look at him and know him for a slave through some invisible sign. *Cain had a mark,* he remembered with a slither of anxiety. He feared he also was marked out, a runaway, eludach, that the stain of slavery was so indelible it would take a blind man not to see.

Then, of course, he realised that he really *did* have marks, white scars on his neck and wrists and ankles, where he had been bitten by the irons during the long weeks of the forced march. They shone silvery and stark against the tan of his skin. Anxiously he tried to arrange his clothes and hair to hide them, and prayed that nobody would see. No matter how he tried, he couldn't help but look at the slaves. Haunted faces, some of them intact, others battered and bruised. Some crying, some stone faced, all of them betrayed.

Patrick felt his heart might break within him, and he carried on walking, back down the churned mud path that he had first taken for a giant snake.

Then he saw it. The moment his eyes fell on it, he recognised it, amongst all the other vessels. His ship, not yet in harbour. The ship that God had chosen for him.

Patrick felt his knees weaken, and his heart was in his throat. For almost thirty days he had walked, sleeping in the open air, soaked by the rain, swallowed by mists, thirsting in the sun. He had been hungry, eating scraps of food that other travellers left on the road, digging up roots, and devouring leaves and worms, sometimes feasting on raw fish snatched thrashing from plashy streams. With no salt to soak them in the worms were gritty, and with no fire or butter to cook them in snails were all but inedible. But he was hungry enough that he ate them anyway. He had no money, in fact, had *seen* no money since the day he was sold. Even if he'd had money he wouldn't have known the currency, and his traitor tongue would have betrayed him as an eludach fugitive the moment he opened his mouth. Yet for all this hardship and hunger, he had not been afraid.

Now he was afraid. Now he knew he would have to speak. He would have to wait for the ship to come in, not be recognised as a slave by some pirate or trader, and finally ask the Captain for work. If he was recognised as a slave, by his accent, or his scars, he could be captured, sent back to his master, flogged – even killed in the market place as an example to other slaves.

"Oh God," he whispered. "Hide me."

He turned, and there before him was a hut with the roof broken in. He went in and sat against the wall. *It must be God,* he thought, *protecting me as He has all this long journey.* Nobody had questioned him, or even looked at him... who but God could have kept him so safe? This place had been set aside for him. It had obviously been abandoned long ago. He lay down, and closed his eyes. His ship had not yet arrived in harbour, and there was nothing he could do. Whispering so that he would not be heard, he fell asleep, praying. His weariness was so immense that despite his fear he could not keep his eyes open. In his dreams he saw the promised ship growing larger and larger as it neared the land. When he finally awoke his chosen ship had docked.

Seeing her ready, he closed his eyes, thanked God for His mercy, asked Him for courage, and with his heart beating in his throat like a trapped bird, made his way to the waterfront.

It was immediately obvious which man was the Captain. Patrick did not know much about sailing, or sailors, what their garb was, or how they organised themselves. But this man was standing astride the dock, arms folded across his chest, bristly black beard jutting out aggressively, shouting at men who ran up and down the gang plank, scuttling like ants. The cargo included large wolfhounds in cages that were being loaded with a speed that Patrick found unnerving. Many of the dogs howled, and Patrick, though not fond of them for their wolfishness, felt pity. However, he squared his shoulders, and approached the Captain.

"Sir," he said with a boldness he did not feel, "I would like to sail with the ship. I'll work."

The man ignored him, and carried on shouting instructions. Patrick thought that perhaps he had not understood his Irish, and addressed him again in the people's Greek.

"Sir, I would like to work for my passage."

The man stopped what he was doing, and looked at him contemptuously. Patrick shrank under the Captain's glare. He felt all too keenly what the man must be thinking. Here was a ragged urchin, possibly a runaway, no experience, no references, no credentials. If he was a runaway why should the Captain risk offending the locals by giving him passage? On the other hand, Patrick tried to reassure himself, he was strong, or had been. But after so many weeks of hunger on the road, already thin from fasting, he didn't look like much. Patrick flushed with shame at the sorry figure he cut, but held his ground.

The Captain laughed. "Forget about it," he said, curtly. "There's no way you're going with us."

Patrick blinked. God had told him that he was to travel on this ship. So... what had happened?

He didn't argue with the man. He turned, and whispering began to pray. He was not even sure what the words were that he was praying or in what language. His thoughts were in turmoil. God could not lie to him. Was it possible that Patrick had been wrong? That in his loneliness he had imagined it? Or if God had spoken, could it simply be that Patrick had misunderstood?

As he began to walk back to the hut, he heard footsteps running up behind him.

He stopped and looked, heart in his mouth, but it wasn't a slaver. "Stop," the man said in Greek. "Come back… we want to talk to you."

Silently Patrick turned, and followed the man back to the dock.

The sailors looked him up and down, and the Captain shrugged. "He'll do."

The man who had followed Patrick grinned, and clapped him on the shoulder. "We'll be glad to have you aboard," he said. "You look like a man who knows how to work. So, take the oath of allegiance, and things will be fine."

"I swear allegiance and that I will work faithfully, by the Living God," Patrick said.

The man lifted his tunic. "That's very good, but you need to suckle."

Ah, Patrick thought. He remembered this custom, a means of showing loyalty between men. It was a common enough thing, but he realised as a Christian he couldn't do it.

"I'm sorry," he said, "my word is my oath before God. I can't suckle."

The sailor looked surprised. "Well, your word will have to do then. But your god is a strange one. You don't look like a Jew."

"I'm a Christian."

"Oh, one of those." The man laughed. "Welcome aboard."

One morning Conchessa woke, and was happy. It had been such a long time since she had felt such simple contentment that it took her by surprise, and only lasted a moment. What did she have to be happy about, after all? Oh, certainly, she had the love of her husband, and her health, and a home. These were all things for which to be thankful. But to be happy was surely unnatural in her. What mother could be happy? She felt as though she had betrayed Patrick by waking with a smile.

Yet, despite it all, the smile kept returning. It felt as though, finally, everything was going to be alright. Perhaps it was nothing but the weather, she thought. Or perhaps she was going to die soon, and all the suffering would be gone.

But whatever it was, it seemed like her joy was a good omen. An omen of what she could not imagine; what she dreamt for was hopeless. Even *she* had given up wishing for it.

Yet here it was, that joy.

She sang as she went about her work, startling the slave girls. Her happiness started a contagion, and soon all the women of the house were smiling too.

Her joy only lasted a day, but was remembered, and later was recognised as a sign.

CHAPTER TWENTY-TWO

It was a strange feeling to look back and see Ireland fading into the sea. The long green strip of land sank beyond the horizon, almost like the mythical country under wave, or Atlantis, the great city that had drowned in the flood. Patrick knew he should be glad that he had left the land of his slavery, and he was very relieved to see it go... and yet he thought of Fionula, a free woman now with her own people in the North, Niamh with her little child Colm, named for his father, and the Bhean Uasail who's boy Pudrig he had only seen once, on his naming day, both children now walking, and talking. Would the boy Pudrig grow up as Patrick had done, oblivious to his slaves? Would he ever come to know the Living God? And Colm... would he be sold away from his mother? As for Finn... Patrick's throat clenched with sorrow and guilt. Finn must by now be the sheep boy, living alone on the mountain top. Patrick knew that he had no choice but to obey the Living God, yet he felt guilt and sorrow for Finn.

He closed his eyes, and pictured them, the old woman, Mary, absent in the body, now present with the Lord, and thought of her ashes, lying beneath the beech tree, waiting with her baby for the Last Day. Mostly he thought of his good friend Victoricus... whether living or dead, he did not know. It was strange, but Patrick found that his face was wet with more than sea spray as the green was swallowed by the blue.

The work was not onerous to him, used as he was to hardship. He was an inexperienced sailor however, and was asked mainly to stay out of the way, his only task above decks being sweeping. As soon as the sailors knew that he had worked with animals he was given the job of feeding the wolf hounds, and making sure that they did not sicken in their own faeces. Patrick had never cared for dogs before and found them unnerving. Nothing like sheep, they snarled wolfishly at him, through the bars of their cages. Sometimes in their eyes he would see terror, and in the back of his mind, always, as he tended to the dogs, was the picture of human beings, chained neck to neck, so crowded together that nobody could lie down. Amongst the broken pieces of his memory he gathered no fragment that anyone had fed them on that voyage, or cleaned their living space. He remembered someone throwing water on them from above, and the stink of urine, blood and faeces. It seemed that these dogs, destined for the Coliseum were worth more than a man. Thinking of Scammall, her body macerated by a wolf, he imagined the final outcome for these hounds. Raised and bred to fight in the arena. Despite his fear of wolves he found himself pitying the terrible creatures. Surely this was not part of God's design.

The journey took three days, a little longer than expected, and on the third day the Captain cursed the wind. They had been blown off course, and when they landed nobody was sure as to where they had put down.

"*You're* British, where do you think we are?"

Patrick shrugged helplessly. They were on a wide white shore, with barren flats stretching in all directions. The ship was stranded on a sandy spur, and they had been forced to wade with as much cargo as they could carry, hip deep in the sea. The dog's crates had been impossible to move, and so they had led the hounds out on chains, those men who were used to dogs leading them alongside, and all of the men, even the Captain, carrying bundles of non perishable items on their backs. The grain could not be removed from the hold, the jars were too heavy for transport, and if they carried them in sacks, it would have been quickly spoiled by the sea.

Everybody was tired, hungry, angry and wet. Mostly they seemed to be angry with Patrick. Their dislike of this British coastline had bled over into a dislike of the British, and this runaway slave (for such they now knew him to be, from glimpses of his old scars) seemed a perfect target for their irritation.

"I don't know where we are," Patrick admitted, apologetically. "I've never been here in my life."

"Well, it's a crowded country," the Captain said. "You people breed like rabbits. You'll be all over the Empire if we're not careful. I suppose it can't be too long before we come among people."

Within days they were starving. The Captain's supposition was wrong, and the more time passed without them coming across food, the more he began to blame Patrick. The escaped slave had a curse on him perhaps. That was why the ship had been blown off course, and that must be the reason why they'd landed in a wilderness. It was this runaway slave's fault that the crew, like the dogs, were starving.

"Well, Christian, what are you going to do," the Captain snapped. The men were getting hungry enough that they were considering eating the dogs, but the Captain stubbornly refused, still clinging to the hope that he'd be able to sell them and not make a total loss on this dismal adventure.

They had stopped for a brief respite at the start of a wooded country while the crew tried to regain their strength. One of the men muttered angrily, "the Briton will have us eating worms and twigs along with him before we're finished."

There was a murmur of angry assent; the men glared at Patrick as though it was his fault that they were hungry. The Captain sneered, and continued his diatribe. "You say this god of yours is so great and powerful – why don't you pray to him for us? We're dying of starvation here!" He spat, contemptuously. "I don't think we'll ever see another living soul again."

Patrick was leaning, wearily, his bundle on the ground and his back against a tree. The truth was that he was as hungry as any of them, and just as weak... perhaps even more so, since he had known hunger for longer than they had. It seemed years since he had last had a good meal. Even so, he smiled. The lightness in his head and body felt good, and the earth beneath his feet was that of home. He closed his eyes, and heard himself saying, "just turn with your whole heart to the Lord my God, because nothing is impossible to Him. Today He's going to send food right into your path, plenty to fill your bellies, because His abundance is everywhere."

The men started laughing, and Patrick smiled. He'd gone way beyond tired, and could not be afraid. It felt like he was drifting rather than walking on this long road home.

The shadows had lengthened by a hand span when Patrick's prophecy was fulfilled. They were traipsing through the forest when a herd of pigs came blundering toward them. The sailors were armed, and ready in a flash. Patrick stood back, bewildered, watching the carnage, as the hungry men hacked and stabbed at swarm of pigs. The Captain, desperate, took a risk, and let slip his dog; the men, following his lead, let their own hounds loose. The desperate animals flew after the escaping pigs, and in the shadow of the trees brought down several more.

Patrick sat with a thump on the ground. As the sudden flurry of activity settled down, and the dogs returned triumphantly, he was aware of the sailors looking at him. It dawned on him that their expression had changed from one of mockery to something new. Respect.

That night they all feasted, men and dogs, on pork. Patrick gave thanks to God for it, and to his joy everyone joined in with his praise... even the Captain acknowledged that Patrick had been right. He knew that their thanking God did not mean that they truly knew Him yet, but it was a start.

The good, warm food on top of so much travel and weariness was too much for Patrick, and after eating he simply lay down and slept, while the sailors talked into the night. In the morning, there was still plenty of food, and the party decided to remain where they were for another day, and regain their strength. For two days they feasted. When it was finally time to move on every man carried ample portions.

Several days later, as they were sitting eating cold pork, one of the sailors came proudly presenting wild honey to the crew. There were jubilant cries as the comb was offered around, and Patrick remembered again how much joy the honey had brought to the Irish slaves. Just as he was raising it to his lips one of the men said, "it's not only your god who can find things."

"What do you mean?"

"I kept my eyes open, I knew it wasn't just your god who could find us food. And this turned up, so I dedicated it to the gods of this place."

Regretfully Patrick put the honey comb down. "Thank you for telling me," he said, wiping his sticky fingers against his tunic. "I can't eat food that's been dedicated to a false god." He knew that dedicating food to a false idol didn't change the food, but he also knew that if he ate it as a Christian, these unbelievers would be confused, and think he was acknowledging their gods.

The crew looked at him dubiously. It was a strange thing for anyone to turn down honey.

"More for us then," the Captain said.

Patrick smiled and let them eat.

That night, for some reason, he woke early – long before the dawn. There were noises in the woods, and some of the sailors were talking in their sleep. Patrick lay in a glade surrounded by trees, watching the stars above, and those that flickered through the gaps in distant moving branches. He listened to the night breathe. All was calm and peace, and yet... an old fear scrabbled in his chest. He didn't know what had brought this on. Perhaps it was the proximity of the men, reminding him of his first days in the slave quarters, before he had returned to his right mind. Yet it hadn't bothered him before. He closed his eyes, trying to ignore their noises, trying to ignore the memories of his delirium. He wished for the quiet of a mountainside, wished for the safe shuffle and muttering of the sheep. Whatever he was feeling, it was wrong. God had answered him so far; he was back on British soil, going home.

He should be glad, not fearful. So why was he afraid? He was being ungrateful. Not trusting God's promises. Something could still go wrong. Some terrible thing might still befall him. He covered his face with his arm, and tried to pray. In spite of all God's goodness, an old panic was welling up. He hadn't felt like this since he was – since he was a boy, first taken slave to Ireland. Since he was...

Terror rose inside him, a pressure in his chest – from nowhere it seemed. He tried again to pray, but no words came.

Horribly, a weight fell on him. A terrible something; a great dark presence, like a rock, bore down upon him. Desperate he tried to move, but his arms, legs, head... his whole body was pinned down by the weight, and he knew with despair that he lay under the thrall of a sickening someone.

He struggled, frantically trying to escape, but could not move an inch – he tried to cry for help, but could barely even breathe. His mouth was dumb, and full of dirt. The blackness filled his lungs, and he was drowning, or being buried alive. A thin whistling noise was coming from his lungs, every breath an agony, and the weight crushed down and through and in. He couldn't even scream. He knew with horrible clarity what it was, the weight, the pressure, the blackness. He remembered this. This was satan. Time stopped between one heart beat and the next, and he despaired. The terror was so great that he thought he would die of it.

Then, with a burst of hope, he saw the first rays of the sun stealing up in the Eastern sky. God's good sun, and God behind it. He remembered Elijah, who had been snatched up out of the world, and escaped death in a fiery chariot. Patrick lifted his voice and cried out to him, "Elijah, Elijah!"

In later years he would wonder why he called out to Elijah, but at the time, he knew only that it worked. As suddenly as the Weight had fallen upon him, it was gone, and God's good sun was cleansing him with gold. He rolled over into a ball, and covered his head. The world was still there. The sun was still rising. He knelt and looked up to heaven. Exhausted, his chest heaved as he filled his lungs with air and light. *Thank you, Lord Jesus,* he prayed. *Thank you for my rescue.* He had not been able to cry out, or even moan, until Christ gave him his voice back. He had been frozen and dumb, dead and helpless as a stone. It barely seemed credible, but satan himself had attacked him. If not for Christ, he would surely have died.

Palm to palm and wrist to wrist, cuffed in prayer, he closed his eyes. He was the captive of Christ, Christ's slave, and no man could touch him, except his Master. "Thank you, Christ Jesus, thank you," he spoke aloud. He shivered at the horror of what he had endured at the hand of his accuser, and remembered the coming judgement. "Oh Lord, please speak out for me on the day of my judgement, as you spoke for me just now. Don't let the accuser destroy me. I cannot speak for myself, oh Lord, keep me safe. Don't let me walk alone."

At long last, twenty eight days after they had landed on the barren beach, they came amongst other people again. They saw the smoke first, then heard the voices. The crew began to laugh and clap each other's backs, then hug each other. Even Patrick was embraced. The men had long forgotten their distrust of him in their gratitude. After the pigs they had regularly found food of one sort or another. Fish, eggs, and berries had supplemented their pork rations, and in the end the food lasted right up until the very day that they walked through the walls of a Roman town.

Patrick was overwhelmed.

He was not yet home, but he was back amongst his own people. More clearly than ever now, he knew that his homecoming was just a matter of time. A very brief conversation with the locals told him where he was, and which roads he should take to get home. The ship had fetched up in Cornwall, hence the vast distances they had travelled in barren lands. The Captain was glad of it. These people were rich in tin, and he began immediately to talk business with them, arranging transport. First on his agenda was organising a return party to see if his ship had survived, stranded along the flats, and if it was possible to rescue the rest of the cargo. It seemed, that after the grinding difficulties of the previous month things were looking up for him and his crew. The men were jubilant to find themselves able to do a little business and recoup their losses.

Patrick turned to the Captain, and grasped his hand, like an Irish man, two handed, squeezing it in friendship. "Thank you for giving me passage," he said, "even though you must have known I was a slave. I pray that God will bless the rest of your journey, and also that you will come to know Him and fear Him as the Living God."

The man looked at Patrick, wryly. "You're a strange man," he said, "I don't know if you are mad, or touched by your god, but I thank you for your prayers nevertheless. May your god go with you, and bring you back to the family you left behind."

"Thank you," Patrick said, then turned, smiling, to the rest of the crew. "God go with you," he told them, and began the last stage of his long road home.

This final leg of the journey was in some ways the hardest. The stone flags felt alien beneath his feet. He missed the bend and sway of the Irish floating roads. The unrelenting straightness of his path gave him a bizarre sense of dizziness. He had become used to more natural contours; curves, and steeps, and heights. The dwellings he passed on the road were hard lined and straight, too well defined, the walls too smooth. He found that he couldn't judge distance, and the road seemed to be moving by itself, gliding under his feet, rather than he over the top of it. At other times it felt like he wasn't moving at all, and that he would be stuck on this stone road forever.

The land was not so green as he had become used to. When he had first arrived in Ireland it had struck him like poison on his eyes, too vivid, an assault on his senses. He found now that he missed it.

After a while he ran out of the food that the sailors had insisted on plying him with as he left them. He felt it had done him more harm than good... for weeks he had been eating, so when hunger came back it hurt more. For several days after the food ran out, he felt his stomach clenching, as though famine was an animal inside him, trying to chew its way out.

Then the hunger starved itself to death, and he was simply dizzy, and light, and far away, watching himself walk along a straight Roman road. He never spoke to anyone he met on the path. He was so used to silence now that it simply didn't dawn on him that he could have told another traveller who he was, and where he was going. He never even considered asking for help. He simply kept on, putting one foot in front of the other, walking in a dream.

Finally, when he was so weak that he felt he might just lie down and not get up again, he saw in the distance the walls of the town in which he had grown up. Despite his exhaustion he felt new strength in his bones, and he pushed himself to walk faster, as though after six years he couldn't bear to wait another minute. When night fell he continued walking, weaving slightly in the darkness, like a man drunk. He was afraid to stop walking, in case he could never start again. All the while he walked he talked to God, asking Him to forgive him for his cowardice and weakness, thanking Him for bringing him out of the house of bondage, and pleading with him that he would be allowed to see his parents' faces again, and that of his grandfather, so that he could drop to his knees and beg their forgiveness, for all the hurts he had done them, and all the grief that they had suffered these six long years.

Dawn came as he finally reached the walls. Banna Venta Berniae. At last – the place where he'd been born.

It was a small town, only a few thousand lived inside. But there was always a guard at the gate. He blinked, and recognised the young man standing, armed, but sleepy, at the end of his night watch. A school friend, someone with whom he had once run to the river in order to swim, or fish, or bother the slaves doing the laundry.

"Tertius," he said, and the young man looked at him.

"Who are you?" he asked, puzzled. "Do I know you?"

"You did, a long time ago."

"You look like..." the man blanched. "We thought you were dead."

"Not dead, taken into slavery."

"But, they were Irish pirates," Tertius said, "nobody comes back from their raids."

"God brought me back again."

Tertius looked at him, apprehensively. Like Patrick, in the days before the raid, he had never believed in God, and mocked Him. To hear this skeletal creature, dressed as an Irish barbarian, cite the name of God struck him with a chill. It was as though God had brought Patrick back from the grave.

"Are my parents within?"

"They are."

"And my Grandfather?"

"Potitus is ill... I don't know whether he still lives. He did when I started my watch." Looking at Patrick warily, he added, "I'm sorry."

"Can I go in?" Patrick asked, "I would like to see my family again."

Tertius gestured his assent and stood aside. He watched Patrick enter the town with fearful eyes. Patrick was recognisable as the friend of his school days, but only just. He was tall, and savage looking, and very thin. Tertius had not known that a man could be so thin and yet live.

Patrick had no sense of how foreign he appeared. He was so close to the end of his journey, and so weary, that he walked through the little streets in a daze, without taking anything in. He was fixed upon walking to his parents' villa. To pass through those doors, and see his family, again, to kneel before them, to beg their forgiveness, to hold them, to let them hold him – that was everything.

He was at the villa. He was at the door.

He stood, and leaned his head against the wood. He had run, finally, to a stop; now that the moment had come, he didn't know what to do. He was already weeping, silently.

He raised his hand, and struck the wood with his knuckles. The knocks rang out more sharply than he'd expected. He waited, then knocked again.

There was movement in the courtyard. A voice.

"Who is it?"

He was speechless. *That's my mother.*

"Who's knocking?" she repeated, alarm in her voice. The town was walled, and very safe, but still, early morning knocking often meant bad news. Patrick realised that she had probably heard of his capture in such a way as this.

He managed to pull himself together. He managed to stand upright. He managed to break his silence.

"Mother," he said, "it's Patrick. I've come home."

CHAPTER TWENTY-THREE

For years Conchessa had been praying. For years she had seen Patrick's ghost in every strange face, or heard his voice whisper in the bustle of the streets. For years, everyone had known she was a mad woman. Everyone had known of her stubborn unwillingness to admit the truth – that her son was dead.

And here he was alive again. Here he was, finally home.

The whole history of their loss crushed her with the sudden impact of its reversal. She was dazed, she could barely even remember what happened after she gathered her son into her arms.

And, oh, Calpornius. Her poor husband. He had come to the sudden knocking at the door, just behind her, thinking that perhaps it was the expected news that his father had died. When he saw Patrick he stood frozen like Lot's wife, staring at his son as though – well, as though he'd risen from the dead.

Conchessa could never quite remember the hours which followed. Just that Calpornius finally wept.

Conchessa had worn her knees out with praying. She had never been able to give up on her only son. She had prayed eight long years for a child, and she could not believe that God could snatch him from her. God gives, and God takes away, her husband told her, bookishly correct in his theology, and she knew that this was true. Yet, despite all evidence to the contrary, in spite of the reports of those who had survived the raid, in spite of the hopelessness of the situation, despite the fact that no captive had ever come back from Ireland, she, like her father-in-law, clung relentlessly to her hopeless hope. She knew that the slave women pitied her, and thought that she was mad. But still she prayed.

And now... that voice...

"Mother, it's Patrick. I've come home."

The voice was not the boy's voice of her memory, it was her husband's voice, slightly altered, hoarser in the throat, an accent perhaps... but still, the moment she heard it, she knew, she just knew that it spoke the truth.

She ran to the door and began to unfasten the locks. Behind her one of the man slaves stood, uncertainly. "My Lady?" he asked, but she said nothing. The bolt stuck for a moment, but she drew it, and pulled the door back.

There he was. Tall, so skinny he swayed where he stood, and dressed in barbarian rags. But despite the change in his appearance, the long hair that descended past his shoulders, the wild beard, she knew her Patrick. He looked at her from his dear grey eyes, and tears were running down his face.

She threw her arms open, and he fell into them, weeping.

"Oh Patrick," she cried out, "Oh, my Son, my Son."

The home coming was everything he could have hoped for, and more. He tried to beg his parents' forgiveness for all the mockery they had endured at his hands in the years of his rebellion, but those days were forgotten in the joy of his return. His mother hung on his neck like an amulet, and Calpornius sat stunned, shaking his head, and shaking his head. He had truly believed that his son was dead, and ever the realist, had mourned him, and tried to move on.

Potitus was carried from his sick bed, and his litter brought into the courtyard, where the whole household was gathering. Patrick looked at the old man, and was again overwhelmed with joy at his return, and grief that he had been the cause of so much pain. He remembered again the last time he had seen Potitus. He had been then an arrogant boy, jeering at the old priest, mocking him for his faith. Potitus had not wept then, they had parted in anger. And later that night, in an act of pure spite, Patrick had crept back to his grandfather's church, and committed the sacrilege that had haunted him all these years, the sacrilege which drove Simon,

Potitus' best friend, to run after the prodigal. He told his grandfather now of how Simon had fought and died to try and save him, and how he regretted being the unwitting instrument of his death.

Having confessed all, in whispered tones, Patrick knelt next to his Grandfather, and bent his head for a blessing. He couldn't keep the tears from flowing. It seemed that all the grief of six years was pouring out of him, and he might never stop.

Potitus spoke.

"God has brought you home again," he said.

"God has brought me home," Patrick replied. "I ran from Him, and He pursued me across Ireland, all the way to the farthest sea, but He never let me go, and He protected me, and He brought me home to you."

"I am glad that He allowed me to live to see this day."

The old man put his hand on his grandson's head, and closed his eyes and prayed.

The days passed in a flurry of well wishers, and astonished guests, coming to see the returned prodigal. On the day of Patrick's return Potitus rallied, and insisted on being carried to his little stone church, where he was seated on a chair at the front. In front of a hushed congregation, crowding through the door, he delivered one final sermon, about the goodness of God, and His infinite care. Without Patrick having yet described his life to him, the old man spoke of the good shepherd, who leaving the whole flock went to seek after one sheep. After the service, Patrick told his grandfather of Scamall, his little Cloud, and how he had remembered this very parable, on a cliff face, with a lost lamb in his arms, at the very edge of the world. Potitus took his grandson's hand, and smiled. "The Lord has let me see His salvation," he said, "in front of all the people. Now I can depart in peace."

A few days later the old man died in his sleep. Although Patrick knew that he had reconciled with his grandfather, and that Potitus was finally with the Lord, he couldn't help but cry.

Meanwhile, all the visitors were overwhelming to him. He was overcome by fits of emotion, anxiety that struck him dumb, waves of irrational jollity, or sudden grief that broke him down in tears. He was ashamed of himself, and didn't want anyone to see him like this. At times he wished he could run up a high hill, and sleep again beneath the sky, with only sheep for companions. But there was no choice, he had to endure it. He told no one of these feelings. If his mother were to hear of his desire to flee, it would break her heart all over again. He sat surrounded by his well wishers, smiling, and nodding, and attempting to answer the multitude of questions as best he could. Did the Irish really eat human flesh? If they did, he said, he had never seen it. (His mind flinched from a memory of the raid, and what happened to the children afterward, and the smell of charring flesh.) Did they put people in wicker cages and set them on fire? Again, he said, if they did he had never seen it. Could they really turn themselves into wolves or horses? Not as far as he knew, why, could anyone? Did their druids really turn people into trees? Patrick paused, trying not to antagonise his questioners by laughing hysterically. He responded, with a straight face, "It seems highly unlikely."

At times he thought that people didn't so much want to talk to him as simply to see him. He had become a celebrity, and people came from miles around to ask him of life in the land of the barbarians, and how he had finally escaped.

The most painful questions were those of his parents.

From the first day Calpornius took charge of Patrick's rehabilitation into normal society. Putting his arm around his son, and looking up at him (Patrick was now taller than his father) the man tried to rally his spirits by suggesting he go to the baths, for a much needed wash and a shave.

Patrick blanched. The baths were public. He was already notorious. He didn't relish the idea of being a public spectacle... he could imagine the baths filling up with spectators of one sort or another, since everyone had now heard the news.

"I'm sorry, Father," he stuttered, "I don't think I can go to the baths yet."

"Well, you need to do something with yourself," the man said, in a jocular tone of voice. "You look quite the red barbarian. It took me a few moments to recognise you."

Patrick said nothing, looking at the floor. Calpornius clicked his fingers. "Ah, I understand it, you're ashamed to be seen in public looking like this. Well, never mind, we'll have you bathed and shaved here. Then when you do step out, you'll look quite the civilised man again."

Patrick smiled his assent, though his father hadn't entirely understood. He knew how much appearances meant to the man... they always had done. And besides, Calpornius did have a point. He knew that if he was ever going to pick his life up again, he had to become civilised.

The bathing was excruciating.

His mother insisted on coming in to wash him, something that a mother might do for a grown man, if he was sick or injured. Patrick insisted that he was neither, but the look of pained disappointment on her face was so great that in the end he conceded defeat, and let her have her way. He realised that he couldn't hide from her forever. The metal bath was brought into the courtyard, and was filled with heated water by slaves, most of whom Conchessa then sent away. The one who remained was a Greek, a physician who would act as the barber, whom Patrick had never met before. He realised that his parents must have bought in quite a few new slaves, since the raid, to replace those who had been stolen from them.

It struck him with a horrible irony that he was being served by slaves. He smiled apologetically at the Greek, who stared back at him with a cool lack of expression. Ashamed, Patrick turned his head, not sure where to look.

The moment came that he had been dreading. He closed his eyes, and got it over with, stripping quickly before climbing into the bath. Behind him he heard the inevitable gasp.

"Patrick," his mother was standing with her hands to her mouth. "What have they done to your back?"

"I was flogged, Mother."

"For what?"

"I don't remember all the reasons," he said. "Sometimes when a sheep died. When I was first taken, and I refused to walk." He kept his mouth shut about the other time he was flogged, for Fionula's sake. He didn't know how to tell that story.

His mother was weeping, and he covered his face.

"What is this on your back? It looks like they burned you."

"The sun burned me."

"You had no shirt?"

"For the first month I was naked. I think they meant to break me, like a man might break a horse."

"How could such savage people live on the earth!" she was angry. "I'll not have them under my roof, tomorrow we'll gather all the Irish slaves and sell them."

"Mother, you can't do that," Patrick turned and looked at her. "They could end up with someone cruel as a master, and it was not the slaves who did this to me, after all." Technically it had been a slave, Gill, but Patrick kept that fact to himself. "You remember Fionula?"

Conchessa's face softened as she remembered his wet-nurse. "I do remember her, Patrick. Did she survive?"

"We were sold together, to the same master. She kept me alive, when anyone else would have given up on me. She tended my wounds, nursed me through fevers, and saved my life, on more than one occasion, even at peril of her own." He had eventually heard the full story of her quick thinking on the road, but realised he couldn't tell it here. The Irish slaves would understand, but his own family simply wouldn't comprehend the background, and would find the whole thing foreign, ugly and strange. Patrick sighed. "I know that their ways are different from ours, but they are not all savages. They can be good people."

"If you say so," she asked. "But I pray that those who did this to you are punished."

Patrick thought of Gill, lying choking on the ground, turning blue, and his face twisted with pain at the memory.

"The man is dead."

His Mother gently washed his back. "Good," she said. "I couldn't bear to think of him walking the earth."

After he had been cleaned, his hair cut, and his beard shaved, he felt peculiar; a stranger to himself. His mother stood him in front of a polished mirror, and smoothed his purple edged toga as she encouraged him to inspect himself. In the dim brass he couldn't see himself clearly, but she could, and her hands kept anxiously fluttering around the scars on his neck and his wrists.

"You look so much better, Patrick", she said, as if to reassure herself. "Now all we need to do is feed you, and make sure you rest, and then we'll think of something we can do to get your life back together again. You missed a lot of schooling, we could get a private tutor for you, so you could catch up. How's your Latin? You haven't forgotten it all?

"I have not, Mother," Patrick said, in Latin, and smiled at her. He turned from the mirror, uncomfortable. He did not want to see his own face, staring at him bald cheeked from the mirror. He realised that he had become accustomed to Irish manners in hair and dress, and it made him uncomfortable to see a Roman looking back at him. Even the toga made him nervous. His family was entitled to wear the purple, but it felt somehow – *wrong* on him. He did not feel like an aristocrat, but simply a sheep slave, mutinously dressed up in his master's clothes.

He could never tell his parents this. He might deny it all he wanted, but he was a Roman, and he would have to study to catch up with his peers. He carried on reassuring his mother, talking to her in his halting Latin. "I was fortunate," he said, "there was a slave, older than me, who had been studying to be a priest when he was captured. My first two years, I spent a lot of time with him, and he was good to me. We talked of the things of God, and he kept my Latin alive."

Patrick knew that his Latin was imperfect, but what ability he still had he felt he owed to Victoricus. With study he might yet catch up.

His mother hugged him. "My good sweet boy," she said. "You see, God was looking out for you. There are all sorts of things you can do in the Empire with Latin."

Patrick smiled again, though with a sinking feeling. He had never thought beyond getting home again, and now that he was here, he found himself increasingly lost. What was there for him to do in the Empire? Tax collector? Soldier? Official? He didn't know. None of them sat right with him. At least when he had been a sheep boy he had known every day what was expected of him. He had learned to work, to be busy. Having been home for a few days he found himself at a loss. Apart from trying to avoid his visitors, there seemed to be nothing that he could do. He had lost the art of indolence.

The presence of the slaves bothered him. The meals bothered him. A table spread out before him, he and his parents reclining on the dining couches, and each one of them with a slave standing by them... it bothered him. His grandfather's absence hurt even more, although he knew Potitus was in heaven. He saw his father's grief in particular, unspoken though it was, and he found it hard to eat. At the end of the day, when the slave went ahead of him to prepare his bed chamber, it unnerved him. He took his sheets off the bed, and slept on the floor.

After a week of tension the dining table was making him ill. He would come in for the meal, his stomach churning, knowing that his parents would expect him to eat more than he could comfortably fit in his stomach. He was constantly aware of the slave at his shoulder, and the weight of his parents' gaze... they examined his reactions with a bird like intensity. He felt like a worm, ripe for the plucking.

The tenth day after his return was the funeral of his grandfather. Scores of guests filled the household, ostensibly offering their condolences to the family, while using the visit to examine the prodigal. Before he had any chance to escape they began again to ask questions about the Irish savages, and their druids. More than anything, they seemed to have an unholy fascination with the religion of the pagans, to which they attributed all sorts of absurdities and horrors. *How do they think of these things,* Patrick wondered, sickened. The questions didn't amuse him anymore. He answered, curtly, that he had never seen a druid, though as far as he could tell they were as much like lawyers as priests, and that the Irish, their soldiers excepted, were not so savage as people had been led to believe. Despite his attempts to correct them the noble guests persisted in their questions.

Casting about desperately for some means of escape Patrick glimpsed a young slave girl, standing in an archway, a jug of wine in her hands, waiting to be asked to pour. She was not a regular slave of the household, and had probably been brought in from the farm for the day, to cover the extra work generated by the funeral. At his first glimpse Patrick knew that she was Irish. Her colouring, her stance, and her wooden expression gave her away. She had obviously heard what these guests were saying about her people, and it was just as obvious to anyone with eyes that she was hurt.

The room was closing in, and he felt like he was at the bottom of a stream. The light was sluggish around him, and his knees were weak. For a moment he remembered swimming in the furthest ocean, beneath the green waters, fish breaking around him like scattered glass.

This whole thing was unreal. The only real things in it were himself, and the slave girl.

"I'm sorry," he blurted out, in Irish. She turned her gaze on him, startled. "I'm sorry that we're such fools. Forgive us."

She said nothing, her lips parted in shock. He shook his head, and pushed his way through the flock of noble and semi noble guests who surrounded him. He couldn't stand this comedy anymore, these people, allegedly here out of respect for Potitus, but simply seeking amusement, diversion. His grandfather deserved a better memorial than this.

Behind him he heard his mother, soothing the ruffled feathers. "He's been very tired... he's not himself..."

He ran up the stairs to his private room, and slammed the door. Some slave had been there ahead of him, and tidied up. Whoever she was, she had lifted his bedding from the floor, turned the sheets. Prepared the room for the master, as though a Roman lived there, and not another slave.

Patrick turned his back on the bed, and groaned, clenching his body. His mother came in, just in time to find him striking himself on the forehead.

"Patrick," she said, grasping his wrist, "what are you thinking? You just broke out in gibberish in front of all our guests... what were you doing, talking that barbarian tongue?"

"Don't, Mother... please, don't."

"You need to talk to me, Patrick, what are you thinking?"

"I'm not thinking, there's nothing to tell."

"Patrick," she shouted at him, exasperated. "You've been sleeping on the floor. You won't let the slaves do anything for you... Talk to me."

"I can't," he shouted, "I can't." Pulling away from her he felt trapped. She was standing in the doorway, he couldn't push past her. Even if he did there was nowhere to go. With a yell he rushed at the wall, and struck his head against it. White exploded into red, and she screamed, throwing her arms around him, as he staggered back, dazed. He struggled and tried to pull away.

"Stop it, Patrick, Son, stop it."

He dropped to the floor, realising with a sickening thud what he had done, and how he was hurting her. He scrabbled backward, pulling his legs up to cover himself. He remembered being naked on the road, and felt it now. Hunching his head over his knees he wrapped his arms around his legs and rocked.

She sat beside him silently, until he had sobbed himself dry.

When he was finally silent she asked again.

"Patrick, what are you thinking?"

He sighed, and dropped his head on her shoulder, and let her stroke his hair. There was nothing he could say. He couldn't remember how to live like this. He had simply no idea who he was anymore, couldn't even imagine what he was to do next. And the worst of it was that there was no way he could explain it. He couldn't explain it to himself, much less think of how to express any of it to his mother. He loved her, but though he longed to unpack his whole heart, he was dumb. Why weigh her down with things she could never truly understand, just so that his own burden felt lighter? She had suffered enough. And yet, he couldn't help but hurt her, just by being his being here, just by his inability to slot back into life as before.

So he simply sat, cried out, silently defeated, while the reception for his grandfather continued underneath.

After a long time his mother kissed his forehead, rose to her feet, and rejoined the party. He stretched out, the whole length of his body, with his back to the wall, and waited for night to fall.

Calpornius cried without shame for the first time in six years.

After the departure of the last guests the man paced. Normally when he had a problem, he would talk to his father about it. Often they would disagree, but until now Calpornius had never realised how much he had depended on their conversations, their disagreements, their awkward, lopsided friendship. Potitus had been the real priest in the family, and taken it all so seriously. Calpornius had followed in his father's footsteps, but only as far as a deacon. He suspected that his father had known all along that his motives were not entirely godly. Although Calpornius believed, granting intellectual assent to the doctrines of the Church, the tax benefits of being a clergy man had been the major attraction. He and his father had been very different men.

And yet, despite their differences, Potitus was probably the only person Calpornius had ever shared his inner life with. Even his wife was kept outside. When Patrick was taken it was Potitus who, mastering his own grief, comforted his son, while Conchessa took refuge in God, and lost her sense of reality. Potitus grieved deeply, but he didn't wail like a woman, didn't make a show of his grief. For that Calpornius was thankful. For all his stern unyielding faith, it was Potitus who sat quietly while his son wept. It was not that he said anything, or did anything unique. He didn't offer words of wisdom, nor take advantage of the tragedy to impose his views of scripture... It was much simpler than that. His father was simply there.

Right now Calpornius wanted nothing more than to talk to his father. It seemed to him that all along he had underestimated the man, always thinking that his staunch faith was childish, foolish. How the old priest could keep serving the God Who had taken Patrick was a mystery. Calpornius had struggled to understand, and arrived at the grim knowledge that God's ways were unknowable, and He could do whatever He willed. It was just the way things were, no better or worse for his family than for anyone else's. And yet it was Potitus and Conchessa's unreasonable faith in the love of God that had been vindicated, the moment Patrick walked in the door.

That was the worst of it. Calpornius' heart was full of joy at the return of his son, grief at the loss of his father, shame that he hadn't believed God could or would perform miracles. He resented the fact that his father's death was overshadowed by Patrick's return, and equally resented the fact that Patrick's return was overshadowed by the death of his father.

On top of all this, God Himself had grown, terribly. He was no longer a backdrop, the focus of mere ritual… He filled everything, He demanded a response. Potitus had been right… God was all in all. Calpornius didn't know what to think or feel, or how to react… and there was nobody to talk to about it. Prayer had been answered, but not *his* prayer. Calpornius had been too realistic to pray for the impossible. Instead the impossible had jumped out and seized him, shook him like a dog shaking a rat. Patrick was back from the dead. It wasn't so much a return, as a resurrection. 'Resurrection changes everything,' his father had told him, long years ago, before he was ever a husband or a father. For the first time Calpornius believed it. Resurrection changes everything.

It had certainly changed Patrick. This was his boy, his dear, his only, the one they'd all had such high hopes for, the one who had died. Calpornius was not able to express his feelings, didn't even know if it was obvious that he loved his son. Everything he tried to do to help him was coming out wrong… When he talked to Patrick about his future, he heard himself nagging. When he tried to persuade him to go to the baths he unwittingly shamed him… How could he have known about those dreadful scars? No wonder the boy wanted to hide. When he tried to correct his manners, which had become awkward, and uncivilised, he saw himself as being unreasonable. *Give the boy time,* he thought. Yet he couldn't allow Patrick to sink all his chances, he couldn't allow him to behave in public like a barbarian. What would people think? How could Patrick better himself if he alienated everyone who mattered?

And so, here was Patrick, still obstinately himself, still obstinately failing to fulfil his father's hopes. Before he was kidnapped the boy had been arrogant, witty, sarcastic, determined to disappoint. And now that he was back he was just as obstinately obedient. So why was it that his very obedience smelled like rebellion?

Calpornius knew that his own heart was broken, had been for a long time, but he didn't let that touch him. He had always been a pragmatist, never cared much for his heart. Conchessa had worn her brokenness like a badge of pride, and it had shamed him. He had allowed the distance to grow between them, so that he would not be stained by her loss of realism, her loss of reason. Even when they reconciled, he kept an interior space, a part of himself where she could not go. He needed distance to preserve himself from the perverse persistence of her grief.

And it was her unreasonableness which had won the day.

What sort of father did that make him? He was glad that his son was home... and yet he resented it. He resented the fact that his wife's ostentatious grief, her public prayers, her lack of sanity, had won the day. And now, on the day his father was put in the earth, he was confronted with a horrible fact about himself. He resented even the fact that his father might have loved Patrick more than he did. After all, Potitus had prayed. And Calpornius resented the fact that his boy had come back a man, that he had missed so much of his youth – and that, no matter how much they looked alike, he could see barely any of himself in his son. The boy even spoke with an Irish accent.

Not only that, the boy prayed constantly. Calpornius had realised it with a shock, when he sat from a distance watching his son's lips move. The boy didn't pray aloud, as any sane man would, as Potitus had, but his lips moved silently, like a Greek scholar overly learned, the one man in a hundred who read, and kept the word silent, in his head. It was uncanny, unnatural. What on earth had happened to the boy, to make him pray in such alien spaces?

Calpornius had left the guests at one point in the evening, to see if Patrick could be persuaded to rejoin them. He had heard the consternation as his son fled the room, and he had endured the backhanded whispers, the gossip being born. All these things would hurt later on, but for now all he wanted was to know that his son was well. He could endure mockery, public disapprobation... things that had always stung him to the quick before. Yet now, although those things still hurt, what hurt him more was to know his son was hurting, and that not one thing he had said since the boy's return had helped in anyway.

He knocked on Patrick's door, and heard no response. For a moment he waited, pressing his forehead against the wood. His father had always prayed, he would mutter to God at the oddest of times. Calpornius found himself, at this moment, wishing to pray, but didn't know what he should say. God, bless my son, perhaps... but it seemed so little, so beneath the notice of God. God, help me... For a moment he wished he could pray silently, like his son... but to do that, perhaps you needed to pray in an ordinary fashion first, out loud, so someone could hear. And even if he did, would God hear him if he asked for anything anyway? God had answered the dearest cry of his heart, for his son to be returned, and yet Calpornius had never prayed it, never even dreamt of praying for it. How could he pray now, ingrate that he was, when God had already given him everything he had ever wanted?

He knocked again, and there was no answer. Perhaps Patrick had already left, and he had missed him somehow. Calpornius turned, about to descend the stairs, when he heard a moaning sound behind the door, like a child crying in their sleep.

Silently, he pushed the door, and it eased open. Stepping into the room, his heart stopped for a beat, and he brought his knuckles to his teeth.

His son was sleeping on the floor, like a dog.

For a moment his heart twisted with sheer shock at the image. As he bit his fist he sank briefly onto the empty bed, and watched his boy sleeping. He put his hands over his face and found that he was weeping.

He had secretly observed his son that morning, eating breakfast, thinking that nobody saw. Instead of lying on his couch, and eating in a civilised fashion, like a Roman, the boy had sat back on his haunches, and ate sitting upright, the food balanced on his lap. Like a savage. When he ate an apple he consumed it even to the core.

And yet despite every misdemeanour, every indiscretion, every faux pas, Calpornius loved his son. He loved him so much it hurt, and he knew he must do something to rehabilitate him. He longed to talk to his father about this, but the old man was gone. Calpornius had lost too much, he couldn't lose his son again.

He thought of waking Patrick up, telling him to sleep on the bed like a man, but couldn't face humiliating his boy like that. Instead he stood, took a blanket from the bed and covered him. The boy moved beneath the weight of the sheet, and murmured in Irish, some word of thanks, perhaps. Calpornius heard the name, "Victoricus," a name which he had heard before. A man who had befriended him, tended him when he was sick. It hurt the father's heart that the boy thought of someone else as his protector, that he thanked a foreign slave. And yet he was glad that somewhere in his dreams Patrick knew there was a man who cared, even if that man was not yet him.

When he returned to the party below he made excuses for his son, and smiled and nodded appreciation as the guests shared their memories of his father. He felt their insincerity, and wondered if Patrick had felt it. Everyone was more interested in his son than his father... and they weren't even interested in his son. Only as a spectacle, something to while away time between engagements. The next acting troop that came along, they'd all depart.

He felt like shouting, or running, or hiding like Patrick, taking cover from the throng.

Finally all the guests were gone, and he hit silence like a wall.

It came to him in an instant that he was now all alone. Nobody now stood between him and the grave. His father had gone on before him, and he was next in line.

For the first time in years he wept openly in front of his wife, and put his head on Conchessa's shoulder. She held him, and crooned to him, like a baby. *If only,* he thought, *if only I could have her faith. If only I had ever loved God, or anyone, even a fraction as much as she does, as my father did.*

He tried to pray, and all he could say was, "God, help me."

She held him, and stroked him, and kissed his hair.

CHAPTER TWENTY-FOUR

As the weeks passed Patrick began to lose his celebrity status, and the family set about constructing a new sort of normal.

It had been decided that the most important matter at hand was that Patrick catch up on his schooling. To that end a private tutor was hired, a freed Greek, who came to the house in the mornings and sat with Patrick, instructing him in Latin grammar. Patrick worked diligently, but was constantly ashamed of his lack of fluency. He remembered teaching Finn his letters up on the roof of the world, and how the boy had looked up to him as some sort of great scholar, how the boy had eaten up every scrap of knowledge that Patrick could remember and teach.

Here he was now, flushed, and anxious, a headache always just between his temples and behind his eyes, increasingly aware of his own stupidity. His misery seemed to shut down the door of his memory, and he found himself unable to understand lessons that he had mastered as a child. It was as though his intellect had stiffened during his captivity. If his mind were a wax tablet, waiting for the imprint of knowledge, the wax had hardened, and was no longer pliable. As his lessons staggered on Patrick became convinced that he was unteachable, a lost cause.

Although he could still read the Latin Bible, and hold a conversation, he was sure that this was mainly because the stories were so familiar to him. When it came to writing his thoughts down he felt again the humiliating weight of a foreign tongue... only this time it felt as though his mind was the stammerer, not his lips. He knew that his Latin skills had not stood still... they had retreated like the tide, exposing his mental inadequacies, and he was now more than six years behind his peers. The

Greek was patient with him, but he could see in the man's silent frustration that he was a disappointment. He began to fear that his parents also would be disappointed in him. With the best will in the world, he couldn't see how he could catch up on his education. Latin was fundamental to the study of rhetoric, logic, philosophy... and here was he, Patrick, struggling with simple verbs and nouns.

His father came to him one day after having had a conversation with the Greek.

"Have you thought of management, Patrick?"

Patrick felt his shoulders sag. So his father had given up on him pursuing an academic career too. He could understand that... in fact, he should be relieved, but it still felt like an ember of hope had been extinguished. His father obviously had come to terms with the fact that his son was too cloth headed to learn.

"I don't know what a manager does," Patrick replied. "I could learn," he added, trying not to focus too much on the thought that maybe he was too much of a dolt for even that.

"A manager simply manages things. You could certainly manage the farm, you have experience with animal husbandry. You could get the most out of the land, buying and selling crops and slaves."

Patrick felt his heart go cold.

"I couldn't do that," he said.

"Why not? You've got more experience with slaves than most people gain in a life time. You understand them, you could probably get them to work harder than a normal master could hope to."

Patrick let the last comment go. He had suspected for some time that his father did not think of him as 'normal.'

"I can't manage slaves, it wouldn't feel right. I've got no authority to tell another person what to do, where to go."

"Patrick, it would be good for you. You need to get used to the way the world works. The fact is that the world needs slaves. They don't have to be used harshly, but they do have to be made to work."

Patrick shook his head. He knew his father was telling the truth, that this was what the world was like – yet at this moment he was unable to accept it. His father looked at him with an almost pleading expression on his face, and Patrick felt a pang of guilt. It was as though he had been born to disappoint his parents.

"You need to be a realist, Son. You walk around as though you don't deserve the position you were born in. You behave as though you are still a slave... you have to get over that. The fact is that some people are meant to be slaves, and some people aren't."

"How do you know which one's which?"

"Well, you obviously weren't meant to be one, which is why God freed you."

"There are so many thousands who are slaves... do you think they all deserve it?" Patrick didn't mean to be disrespectful. He honestly wanted to know.

"It's not what they deserve, Son. It's what they are meant to be. God has established an order, and we're not to break it. The fact is that you are not a slave, and you have to stop acting like one." Calpornius paused, exasperated. "You insist on bathing yourself, you won't let anyone scrape your back or wash your hair. At the end of a meal, you clear the plates, and take them to the kitchen. Son... people will talk. The slaves won't respect you for behaving like one of them."

Patrick was silent. He knew this was true. The Greek who had cut his hair, and seen the scars on his back sneered at him, and he heard some of the kitchen slaves whispering behind their hands when he came and went.

"Patrick," his father said gently, "you are not a slave."

Patrick shook his head. "I'm sorry, Father, I'm a slave now, and I always have been. I was born in chains, we all are."

"What on earth does that mean?" Calpornius threw his hands up in frustration. "You're talking nonsense!"

"We're chained to the world, Father." Patrick closed his eyes. He wished he could explain this, it was so big, but the words were hard to find. "It drags us along behind it," he tried, "like slaves behind a cart, and most of us don't even see where we're going."

"Son," Calpornius' voice was uncomprehending, and held a note of anger. "I'm not talking philosophy, or theology, or anything like it. I'm simply telling you, you have a role in the world, and it's about time you lived up to it."

"I'm sorry," Patrick was truly ashamed. "I can't manage the farm."

His father clicked his tongue angrily, and walked sharply out of the room.

Calpornius knew he had been harsh on the boy, but couldn't think what else he could do. The conversation with the Greek kept repeating in his brain, and he worried at it, like a cat with a ball of yarn, trying to tease a solution from the mess he found himself in.

"It's not that the boy is without natural ability," the man had said, "He reads well enough, and understands what he's reading. He can speak well about what concerns him, and obviously thinks very deeply... but..." The Greek paused, with a pained expression on his face.

"But what?" Calpornius was curt with the man. He was paying him after all, he deserved a straight answer, not some Greek sophist dancing around the problem. Because it was obvious there was a problem.

"Well, to be honest, I think the student thinks too much." The Greek put his hand up in a 'stop' gesture as Calpornius opened his mouth. "I know this may sound peculiar, but the fact is that what would be a virtue in a trained mind has become a positive nuisance in your son."

"Explain yourself."

"Well, for years he had nothing to do but watch sheep, and think. And he's thought so deeply that, to be candid, he has erected barriers and hurdles that are keeping him back. He seems to feel acutely that he's not good enough, that there's something amiss in his mental makeup, that he's simply not able to learn."

"Well, he needs to be persuaded otherwise."

"I'm afraid it's not so simple. These thoughts are not merely unwanted intrusions, they are very much a part of who he is now."

Calpornius strode the length of the room, hiding the misery on his face by turning his back. Mastering his expression he inclined his gaze again upon the Greek.

"So you are telling me that my son sees himself as broken or defective, and that this is holding him back in his attempts to learn?"

"Only in certain areas... the mathematics, grammar. When we discuss matters of philosophy or politics your son is second to none."

"What's the use of that, if he can't sign his name?"

"Oh, sir... he is not an illiterate, that is not what I'm implying at all."

"But he does not enjoy his studies, and he will not excel at them?"

"No, sir. I think it would be best if he was to apply himself to some practical skills. Things of which he has experience."

"So I should send him to the farm as a sheep boy?" Calpornius could not hide the bitterness in his voice.

"Oh no, sir, not at all! His experience has given him a great insight into the way men work. He could perhaps be a soldier, or he could manage business operations, work as a merchant... There are plenty of options."

Calpornius pursed his lips, and restrained himself from berating the man. After all, he reasoned, at least the Greek was honest. He had given him a fair assessment of Patrick's abilities. A dishonest teacher could have drawn a wage for years by holding out false hope.

"Thank you," Calpornius nodded curtly to the Greek. "I'll bear your advice in mind, and consider my next move. You've been very helpful."

The Greek had bowed, and dismissed himself. Calpornius had sat on a window seat and wrung his hands.

Looking back on the conversation again, Calpornius was no nearer a solution than before. Even further, perhaps. He had broached the subject of management with the boy, and got a response which totally threw him. Patrick's clear cut rejection of his plan seemed to leave no realistic options for his son. The idea of his going to be a soldier was utterly wrong, demonstrating only the Greek's lack of appreciation for his employer's social status. Quite beside which, if Patrick refused to manage the farm out of concern for the slaves, how would he ever be persuaded to take up an employment that could, at least in theory, lead him to taking a human life? The political situation had become unstable, the Empire was no longer as respected as it had been, and so standing armies had to be prepared to fight. He knew already that Patrick would not fight. He could just hear him now, quoting Christ, "He who lives by the sword dies by the sword." No, Patrick could not be a soldier. A merchant was just as unsuitable a profession, since inevitably he would be involved in the buying and selling of slaves.

What else *was* there?

Calpornius then did something he had never considered before. He got down on his knees, and pressed his head against the wall. Unlike his son, he prayed aloud.

"God, if You're listening, I know you care for my son. I can't provide for him. He tells me that you were Father and protector to him in all his years of wandering. God, be a Father to him now, show him a straight path, and make it clear to us what it is you want him to do with his life. I cannot choose for him, I don't know what to do. Please, protect him, and show him the way."

Unspoken in Calpornius' prayer was a deeper need, a need to see God as a Father, to be guided by Him, to trust Him. But Calpornius had never paid attention to himself before, and would have thought such a prayer self indulgent, weak. Nevertheless, when he had prayed for his son he continued to kneel, thinking of Fathers and thinking of Sons. How much a father missed a lost son, how much a son missed a lost father. He longed to be a son again, longed to be a loving father. But he had no words for any of it. He leant his head on the stone wall till his forehead grew numb with cold, and wordlessly unpacked his grief with a groan.

That night Victoricus came, as he had promised, to see Patrick one last time.

Patrick seemed to wake, and looking up he saw that the furthest wall of his room had vanished, opening out, instead, to the windy roof of the world. He saw, under the moonlight, Foclut – the mountain top, the forest that sprawled up the northern slope, and behind both forest and mountain, the dark of the furthest sea. If he had wanted to, he could have got up and walked straight from his room to the craggy height, as easily as he might walk to the door, falling through space to the earth beneath. The sheep were in their pen, and a small figure was sleeping across the entrance to the fold. *Finn*, thought Patrick, *all alone, at my station. I condemned him to this.* There was a smell of salt and ocean in the room, and the wind was cold on his face as he sat up, and leant his back against the wall.

There were voices in the wood.

A slow horror crept up Patrick's back, and he longed not to hear those voices. They whispered through the haunted trees, and rustled across the floor of his room like dry leaves blown on an autumn wind.

As he watched he saw a man coming toward him, emerging from the forest. Patrick's heart expanded and contracted, in an instant, stumbling between joy and grief. Victoricus... the sudden delight of seeing the familiar figure was instantly swallowed up in anguish at his loss. Patrick knew that this was the occasion Victoricus had spoken of, the one meeting they would have before heaven.

Victoricus now stood, with one foot in Patrick's room, the other in the world beyond, and looked at him. He seemed to strengthen, and straighten, and he captured Patrick's gaze with two bright eyes. His arms were filled with scrolls. He walked right into Patrick's room, and stood directly in front of Patrick. He opened his arms, and a vast number of scrolls fell at his feet. Patrick stared at him, unable to move. Victoricus smiled, sadly it appeared, and opening the first of the letters, handed it to Patrick.

Trembling Patrick unrolled the scroll and read the first lines: "The Voice of the Irish," it said.

Suddenly he understood the voices in the forest, all of them calling out in one accord, "We beg you, Holy Boy, come and walk among us."

Patrick dropped the letter, full of tears, unable to read any more. His heart was breaking. He tried to touch Victoricus, but in a blink the man was gone. Dazed, Patrick found himself kneeling in an empty room, all four walls intact, and his friend departed.

He groaned, and hugged himself. He was filled with a terrible sorrow. There were so many, many thousands in that land of slavery, so many in bondage to the evil one. How could he have left them, without the knowledge of God?

Patrick knew, absolutely, that his friend had gone to be with the Lord. And he knew, absolutely, that God had commanded him to go back to the land of his slavery, to again cross that sea, to answer the voice of the Irish.

The following morning, he told his parents of his night visions. As he had expected, his mother wept. His father, however, surprised him.

The man stood, staring into space, as if he heard a voice himself. Then, abruptly, Calpornius smiled; a twisted thing, that looked as though it hurt.

"Go, Son, with my blessing. I know that God is with you."

Patrick felt a lump in his throat, and stepped forward into his father's awkward embrace. He had met with no resistance. Calpornius was in agreement with him.

And although it would be many years before he did go, that moment of reconciliation and understanding stood in his memory forever as a testament... the day and hour that his father believed.

Author's Afterword

I've always loved St Patrick; so much so in fact that my son is named for him. Being Irish it was impossible to grow up without hearing stories about St Patrick, and as a child my view of him was simple. Bishop of Ireland, battling druids, driving out snakes! Go Patrick! He was like a superhero taking on the forces of evil – natural, human or supernatural, it didn't matter. Kings, evil wizards, demons – he turned bad guys into trees, he made food appear from nowhere to feed the starving. No matter what, he stood up for the underdog and always came out on top.

Of course, children grow up, and I discovered that most of those stories were heavily mythologised, or even outright untruths. To cite a well known example – there weren't any snakes in Ireland for Patrick to 'banish.' There hadn't been snakes in Ireland since they were wiped out in the Ice Age. Patrick did not in fact write my favourite hymn, 'Be Thou My Vision' – though he may be responsible for the tune – nor is it likely that he wrote the 'Breastplate of St Patrick' – though it is of ancient provenance, he may have heavily influenced one verse, and he would surely agree with the sentiments. The famous story wherein he explained the doctrine of the Trinity with a shamrock proved to be yet another fable. And it turned out that shamrocks do not grow only in Ireland, as I had been taught – it is just that everyone else calls them clovers. Imagine my disappointment as a child to discover shamrocks growing alongside Lancaster canal.

The more I studied history the further away Patrick felt. From superhero he faded to someone I couldn't recognise; a mysterious figure in the past, who had left an indelible mark on Ireland, but about whom little could be known. I felt like I'd lost a childhood friend – who was the man behind all those legends? I assumed I'd never know, that he was swallowed up by myth and history.

A turning point came when I went to Oxford. My very supportive Dad had schooled me in Latin, and I was able (painstakingly and with dictionary to hand) to finally read Patrick's writings in the original. (I was supposed to be studying something completely different, but then I never have done what I'm told.) I was so excited – Patrick had left documentation; there really was a way of knowing the man.

Something about Patrick's written record – quite beside the contents of it – was terribly poignant. Here was an old man struggling to defend himself and a group of Irish slaves from those in authority, someone writing in a language clearly not his own, yet still determined to get his story told. Someone who wasn't afraid to tell a powerful Christian king that he was going to go to hell if he didn't release the prisoners he had taken, someone who spoke out about slavery and sexual violence, someone who had forgiven a terrible past and fought for those he could have been justified in hating. Someone who perhaps wasn't quite mentally stable. (Goodness knows what a modern psychiatrist would make of his self-reported aural hallucinations and physical struggle with the devil.) Here was someone who went back to Ireland, on pain of capture and death, to try to save the souls of the family who had enslaved him. Who pleaded with the Bishops who threatened his excommunication to at least 'let him die in Ireland.' The words jumped off the page. They were so authentic that the scribes hadn't even bothered to correct Patrick's spelling or grammatical mistakes.

Patrick was real – not a myth, not a superhero. A man. Not a modern day Catholic nor a Protestant, very much of his time, with pagan sensibilities that seem odd to us now. But undeniably Patrick, after all these centuries. I remember vividly sitting in the library crying when I realised my childhood friend was back. That was twenty-four years ago, but my love of Patrick continues.

For those who want to study more about him, read his letters and other academic resources, the website http://www.confessio.ie/# is invaluable.

My favourite book on the subject is 'Patrick of Ireland' by PhilipFreeman. It is rare to find an academically well researched a book that reads like a thriller. There are many good books on Patrick – this is the best. It can be found at http://philipfreemanbooks.com/stpatrickofireland.html

Please also visit my blog. www.leahmacmoire.co.uk It shall be kept up to date with links to other sites, a full bibliography, discussion, and updates on the rest of my series on Patrick.

Glossary of Terms

Bhean Uasail: an honorific for an aristocratic or high born lady. *(Gaelic.)*

Breid: the mother goddess in the Celtic pantheon. Later her roles were subsumed by St Bridgit and Mary the mother of Jesus. *(Gaelic.)*

Bouachalin: diminutive of 'bouchal', boy. Often used affectionately, as by a mother. 'Little boy.' *(Gaelic.)*

Cailleach: interpreted in modern times as 'witch,' this word also carried the connotation of wisdom in an elderly lady. *(Gaelic.)*

Christos: Christ. *(Latin.)*

Coracle: a small open-topped boat used by fishermen. *(Gaelic.)*

Curragh: a large coracle. *(Gaelic.)*

Dirb Fine: kinsmen, tribe, related by oath or blood. *(Gaelic)*

Dryad: Greek spirit of the trees and forests. *(Greek.)*

Eludach: outcast, a rebel slave. *(Gaelic.)*

Gaese: Taboo, oath. To break your gaese to a god was to call down damnation and punishment on yourself. For example, the Irish hero Cuchulain had taken an oath never to eat dog-flesh. On being tricked into eating it, he was cursed. *(Gaelic.)*

Gaill: alien, foreigner. *(Gaelic.)*

Gill: Slave. *(Gaelic.)*

Hagar: the Egyptian slave who bore Abraham his first son. *(Hebrew)*

Inion Dia: Daughter of God. *(Gaelic.)*

League: unit of measurement. Romans measured distances in space – miles and so on. The Irish divided distances into units of time. A league was what a healthy man could be expected to walk in a day. (English.)

Lugh: Celtic sun god. *(Gaelic.)*

Medusa: character from Greek mythology, a witchlike figure with snakes for hair whose gaze turned her victims into stone. *(Greek.)*

Morrigan: Celtic goddess of battle and vengeance. Part of the female trinity, the crone. *(Gaelic.)*

Mudebroth: 'Wrath of God.' *(Ancient British, related to Welsh.)*

Oghma: the male diety (son of Breid) who was believed to have brought the healing arts and writing to Ireland. The Irish pre-Roman alphabet is named for him, 'Ogham.' *(Gaelic.)*

Ollam: a travelling story teller of the druidic class. *(Gaelic.)*

Pater Noster, qui es in caelis, sanctificetur nomen tuum. Adveniat regnum tuum. Fiat voluntas tua, sicut in caelo: 'Our Father, Who art in heaven, holy be Thy Name. Thy Kingdom come, Thy will be done, here as in heaven.' First lines of the Lord's Prayer. *(Latin.)*

Potiphar: an Egyptian official, whose wife dishonestly accused the Hebrew slave Joseph of rape. *(Hebrew.)*

Sarah: Abraham's wife, who bore him a son in her old age. *(Hebrew.)*

Shema Yisrael: 'Hear oh Israel,' the start of Judaism's greatest prayer. 'Hear, oh Israel, the Lord our God, the Lord is One.' The Shema is often spoken when faced with death, as an acknowledgement of God. *(Hebrew.)*

Slua Dubh: the Black Host. Similar to the English 'Wild Hunt.' Along the west coasts of Ireland and the outer isles and west coast of Scotland belief in the Host continued right into the twentieth century. *(Gaelic.)*

Strigil: a long, curved stick used by Romans to scratch their backs when bathing. *(Latin.)*

Scammall: Cloud *(Gaelic.)*

Selkie: A seal that sometimes sheds its skin and walks in human form. *(Gaelic.)*

á **Shiun:** Sister in the vocative. *(Gaelic.)*

Taraigheacht: a war party – land pirates. *(Gaelic.)*

Tartarus: the Greco-Roman conception of the land of the dead. Akin to Limbo. *(Greek.)*

Theseus: name of the Greek hero who descended into a maze and defeated the minotaur. *(Greek.)*

Zeus: King of the Olympic gods. *(Greek.)*